The Birds

Lindsay Woodward

ISBN: 153993957X
ISBN-13: 978-1539939573

For my mom and dad. Thank you for always supporting my writing. I love you very much.

ONE

Simon Bird pulled his Aston Martin Rapide S into his expansive driveway and turned off the engine. He and his wife, Beth, sat silently next to each other for a second, taking stock of yet another unexpected event in their lives.

Less than an hour earlier, when Beth had sent the pen sailing through the air with just her mind, she'd been in such shock, Simon had not hesitated to get in the car and bring her home. She'd spent the first half of the journey staring hard at her hands, wondering what power, if any, she really had in them. It had all been so sudden, she wasn't even sure whether it had actually happened or whether she was just a little burnt out from the recent madness in her life.

Beth's shock, though, had slowly evolved into curiosity, and from that it had manifested into pure exhilaration as she'd toyed with the idea of being magic. She could have actual magic powers! It was insane yet undeniably thrilling. It was the kind of thing she'd had many daydreams about as a little girl, but as she'd got older such fanciful ideas had dissolved away with the reality of life. But now it seemed possible - just maybe - and it was making her feel like a girl all over again; playing in a fantastical world where the limits of real life were no obstacle.

'Come on then,' she smiled, almost bursting with anticipation. She jumped out the car and raced to the front door of the mansion they now both called home. Letting herself in with her very own key, she headed straight to the living room and waited eagerly for Simon's instructions.

'Calm down for a second,' Simon said, following Beth in.

'You said as soon as we got home you'd show me how to do it. I want to see if I can do it again!'

Beth, barely able to keep still, was the complete opposite of her husband, who stood motionless on other side of the room. 'Let's just take this one step at a time,' he stated in his typical, level-headed manner; although his pensive glare betrayed his cool exterior.

'Do you think I'm a Malant?' Beth asked, fizzing with questions, feeling nothing but optimistic about it.

'I don't know how you could be. You have to be born a Malant, you don't just become one.'

'You're back, sir?' Jim interrupted, opening the door to the living room. This brought Beth to a standstill.

'Beth had a funny turn so we decided to come home,' Simon explained, not at all thrown by Jim's sudden presence.

'I'm sorry to hear that, Mrs Bird. Are you okay? Can I get you anything?' Beth didn't move. She was very wary of what she could or couldn't say in Jim's presence.

'A cup of tea for both of us, I think,' Simon replied.

'Certainly sir. Anything else?'

'No.'

'Good, I'll get the kettle on.'

Jim closed the door behind him and Beth knew that she had to find out where things stood. 'Does Jim know about the Malancy?'

'No. He knows nothing. I only use my magic when I have to, it's not something usually present in the house. After a lifetime of being different you learn to blend in wherever you can.'

'So you just use it at work?'

'I don't even do that. We have spell workers at the office who do all of that. I just make sure everything runs smoothly. Think about it. When have you seen me use my powers?'

Beth considered his question. She'd witnessed it all quite clearly when he'd defeated Damien, but before that she couldn't really think of a time when he'd used them. Except, of course, to show her that he could when he first told her about the Malancy.

'So you have all this power and you never use it?' she finally asked.

This time is was Simon's turn to momentarily consider his response. 'It's there when I need it. It's got the better of me so many times, I need to be careful. Like when I had that fight with Damien; if I don't control it, it will control me.'

'Oh. I thought it might be more fun than that.' For the first time, Beth's excitement started to dwindle.

A tiny smile edged up onto Simon's lips, cracking through his restraint. 'There's plenty of fun to be had.'

'You don't seem to enjoy it.'

'Well, things are never as much fun when you're on your own.'

'You're not any more, though, are you? We might be able to enjoy it together now.'

'Oh Beth, I'd love that so much.' Simon moved over and kissed her gently, his whole aura relaxing at the very idea of them sharing their powers. 'I don't know what to make of the idea of you having these powers. It makes no sense, but it would be incredible.'

'You think so?'

The pair fell silent as Jim brought their tea into the room. He placed the tray on the coffee table. 'Will there be anything else?' he asked.

'No, thanks Jim. We'd just like to be left alone now.'

'You're looking quite well, Mrs Bird. Whatever the ailment, it appears to have had a positive effect. You're glowing.'

'Thank you,' Beth smirked.

'Are you sure there's nothing else I can get for you?'

'That's everything Jim, thank you,' Simon asserted. Jim nodded and left them in peace once more. 'I don't know what's got into him.'

'He so thinks I'm pregnant!' Beth giggled.

'What?'

'I'm glowing? He definitely had that look in his eye, like he's in the know about something. I bet he's all excited about being uncle Jim!'

'Uncle Jim? He's my butler.'

'Don't be so snobby!'

'You're not, are you?'

'I'm not a snob.'

'No, pregnant?'

'No!'

'It would make sense. Maybe the powers could have come from you... being with my child. It would be a Malant baby, and with me as its dad who knows what powers it will have.'

'Good theory, but...' Beth's certainty went from definite to diminished in seconds. She wasn't late but they had just had a very loving honeymoon weekend, and with the prospective baby being half Malant, the effects could be strong.

'You could be pregnant?' Simon whispered, placing his hands near her stomach.

'Do you think we should do a pregnancy test?' As soon as the words left her mouth, Simon stopped and quickly backed away from her. She could see a glimmer of guilt in his eye, like he'd been caught doing something that he shouldn't. 'Are you upset?'

'How do you feel?' Simon simply responded.

'Scared.'

Simon stared deep into Beth's eyes. His usual velvet chocolate swirls seemed darker than normal. 'We'll be in it together, Beth, that's all that matters.'

Beth suddenly felt panic set in. She barely knew Simon, this was far too early. Yes, she was married now, and she had, in a ridiculously short space of time, managed to secure her dream of being a director of an international company. Thinking about it, she'd manage to fulfil two of her major lifelong goals in a matter of weeks, so maybe being pregnant this early was just following suit. It didn't change the fact, though, that she really wasn't ready for children, and it was also way too scary.

'Isn't it a bit early for a pregnancy test?' she queried, more to herself. 'I mean, don't you have to be late first? Would it really give us an accurate result at this stage?' Beth's panic was now becoming animated. She wanted to pretend that it just couldn't possibly be true.

'A pregnancy test is probably a sensible idea. That's the normal thing to do, isn't it?'

'It's too early, though.'

'There's no harm in doing one now. Let's get it first and see what it says. Then we can tackle the next step when we have to.'

'Oh God.' Beth sat down on the settee. She took a deep breath. She should be used to the rollercoaster that was life with Simon Bird by now, but, as usual, everything came storming at her and knocked her off her feet.

'Have your tea and then we'll go out,' Simon said. Beth looked to her tea, but she just felt sick. 'No, I tell you what, don't touch your tea. Instead, try this.' Simon sat down next to Beth and promptly focussed all his attention on the cup before him. A few seconds went by and he didn't move an inch. Then suddenly the cup delicately rose from its saucer and floated effortlessly towards his hand. He took a sip and smiled. 'You have a go.'

'How on earth am I supposed to do that?'

'It's all in your gut. Whereas other Malants focus

completely on the element they're drawing power from, we need to focus on our emotions. Look deep within you. Find some happiness, anger, sadness, fear, whatever it might be, and then concentrate all of it on the cup. It's a feeling, nothing more than a feeling.'

'I have no idea what you're talking about.'

'Okay, well I know you've got a lot of recent emotions to tap into, what with Damien's repeated attacks just for starters... No, let's keep this light. How did you feel when we first got home as man and wife?'

'Simon!' Beth giggled, the smile now stretching across her face. 'Delighted. Insanely happy.'

'Glad to hear it,' Simon grinned in return. Now remember all of that, channel it deep within you, and then try and focus it all on to the cup. Then imagine the power of all that emotion can actually lift the cup up.'

Beth did as she was told, despite being highly dubious. She couldn't help but smile again as she recalled the moment that they'd got home from Malancy HQ, once Paul had left for the hotel, when it had first started to sink in that she was in fact now Mrs Simon Bird. Sheer joy bubbled inside of her. She did as Simon had described and she tried to concentrate it all. Then, when she felt the intensity of her emotion peak, she imagined throwing it at the cup, willing it to move.

But nothing happened. No matter how hard she pushed, nothing at all happened.

'How did you learn to do it?' she asked, giving in.

'I'd been doing freaky things for years, never quite knowing how or why they happened. It was only when Paul told me the truth that we worked through it together. We realised that it was connected to my emotions, so we made sure my emotions controlled it. It's more natural than forced. Try again.'

Beth focussed harder this time. Instead of thinking about their love, this time she thought to the possible pregnancy and her fear steamed inside. She felt queasy at the prospect of being a mother so soon. Before she'd even told her own mother that they were married; before they'd even had their proper wedding day. She'd be all fat and pre-natal in her wedding dress, not able to drink champagne and feeling sick at the sight of the lovely food; it would ruin everything. All the worry trembled her body, but no matter how strong it was nor how hard she tried to channel it, the cup remained motionless.

'It's useless,' she said, picking up the cup with her hand. 'And now my tea's gone cold.'

'Maybe it was just a one off; a bizarre accident. I don't know, it's always been so easy for me.'

'Or maybe I am pregnant and the pen power came from baby Bird, not me. Oh God, we can't call it baby Bird.'

Beth could feel Simon's glare once again bearing down on her. She prayed that this was nothing to do with baby Bird. They were so far from ready for baby Bird, she was terrified what it would do to their relationship.

'I suppose the sooner we get this pregnancy test the sooner we'll know,' Simon uttered.

The closest pharmacy was in the local town about five miles away and they wasted no time in buying a few tests, just to be sure. The tension was almost palpable between them as they headed straight back home to delay no further.

Making a beeline for the bathroom, Beth ensured the stick was appropriately dipped, and then they both stood together in their en suite, their breath jointly held. All that was left to do was wait for the results.

TWO

'Sir!' Jim called up the stairs. 'Sorry to bother you, but your phone is ringing down here. It's Mr Bird.'

'Not now!' Simon hissed to himself.

'I'm sorry sir, it seems you have quite a few missed calls from him.'

'Oh shit! Sorry Beth, I'll have to call him back. Paul will be wondering where the hell we are.' Simon dashed downstairs, leaving Beth alone to wait for the results, his heart pounding with anticipation.

He grabbed his phone from Jim, headed into the living room and quickly re-dialled.

'Where are you?' Paul asked.

'We had to come home.'

'Is everything all right?'

Simon hated keeping stuff from his uncle, but what could he say? Was she pregnant? Did she have powers? It seemed so much was going on but he didn't have any actual facts to share, so he chose instead to keep it simple. 'Beth wasn't feeling herself, so I brought her home. It's been a crazy few weeks, I think it's all just got the better of her.'

'Is she okay now?'

'I hope so. She just needs some rest.'

'You both need rest. Take some time off. Will you just go on a honeymoon!'

'No. I keep telling you, I promised Beth that we'd wait until after the proper ceremony. We need more than just a quick exchange of vows brought on by deeply unfortunate circumstances. She's in every way my wife now, but we need to repeat the wedding to make it feel right; to make it a happy occasion. To make it one to remember.'

'You are stubborn. Well, make sure you look after her.'

'You know I will.'

'Do you need anything from me?'

'No, we'll be fine.'

'Right then, if I'm not needed, I'll head up north as planned. I'll be back in about a week, then I'll spend a couple of days with you before heading back to the States. Okay?'

'Perfect. See you then.'

'See you, Si.'

Simon threw his phone on the sofa and then slumped down himself to catch his breath. In all honesty, he was glad that Paul had called. It had given him an excuse to grab a minute to try and compose himself. He felt on the verge of something monumental.

When Beth had sent that pen flying through the air, he'd been initially quite shocked, but the trepidation had soon melted into joy. He'd met hundreds of Malants in his life, but he'd never met another person who could do what he could do. He was so afraid to get his hopes up, though, it all seemed too good to be true. As much as he loved Beth and she'd become the companion that he'd always wanted, it was only when she'd moved that pen that Simon had truly stopped feeling so alone.

If that wasn't enough, there was now the possibility that Beth might be carrying his baby. This had the potential to make him happier than he ever thought possible.

He couldn't quite believe that just a few weeks ago he'd been so lonely and sad, sitting in New York, tucked away from the world. This was a road that he'd never believed he would go down. He'd not once imagined himself to be a father; but now it was seeming likely, he realised how much he wanted it. He actually felt complete for the first time in his life.

All he could ever wish for, if not more, was quite literally on the verge of coming true.

'Simon?' Beth said, pushing the door open.

'What's the verdict?' he asked, his heart ready to burst through his chest. Her face was unreadable. He had no clue what she was about to say. Then, for a moment, he couldn't help it, he convinced himself that the test was positive. His heart suddenly doubled in hyperactivity as he revelled in the idea that he was going to be a dad.

'It's negative.' The smile dropped from his face as her words seemed to echo around the room. Although, in reality, he'd lost nothing, he suddenly felt a wave of grief. 'It doesn't mean I'm not pregnant, though, does it.' Beth moved over and sat on his lap, wrapping herself around him as if she needed protecting from the world.

'I suppose we just have to wait now,' he replied, stroking her hair.

'I can't wait!' Beth cried. 'What if I am pregnant? What if your baby is making me powerful? It could be more than a pen next time.'

Simon held her closely. He now had a dilemma. He knew that he could give her the answer. He knew that he'd be able to sense whether she was pregnant or not, he just didn't know if it was one step too far in her delicate state. He remembered how moving a pen was quite a shock when he first did it. It seemed like such immense power, but in reality the pen moving couldn't be simpler. His power went a lot further.

If he used his strength to tell her if she was pregnant or not, would she be able to cope knowing the potential of her own power? Wouldn't it be better to let her take it one step at a time?

He looked into her screwed up face. She seemed utterly terrified, almost sickened by the uncertainty of their future. He knew that he had to do it. As much as he was worried about scaring her, he couldn't leave her in such a state.

Besides, he wanted to know quite badly himself if she was, indeed, carrying his child.

'Okay... I didn't want to scare you but...'

'What?' she said, leaning back to look him in the eyes.

'I can do a little more than just move a pen around.'

'Well, obviously.'

'Do you remember how I stopped Damien's heart?'

'Vividly.'

'Well... I can manipulate anyone's body. I can sense their insides.'

'That's gross.'

'It means I can heal people, like I've done to you before.' He paused, giving himself a second to back out if he wanted to. 'It also means that I can tell if someone's pregnant.'

'What?'

'I can tell you for sure.'

'Why didn't you say that before?' Beth shrieked.

'I didn't want to freak you out. You have quite a lot going on as it is. If you do develop my powers, I thought you might cope better believing that you could just move a few bits around. At least to begin with.'

Beth stared at him for a second, taking him in. 'You really are powerful, aren't you?'

'There are always limits.'

'Do it then. Let's get this over with. Will it hurt?'

'I'd never hurt you, Beth. You know that.'

Simon kissed Beth softly on the lips and then he gently placed his hand on her stomach.

He let his emotion take hold and he absorbed her body against his skin. He could sense her heart, her veins, her stomach gurgling, almost everything going on inside; the one thing that he couldn't sense was any more life. There was nothing out of the ordinary, and he felt quite certain that there was no baby.

The dream was gone. It had been exciting while it had lasted, but now it was all gone. He moved his hand away slowly, his heart dipping as he had to tell her. 'You're not pregnant.'

Beth's eyes gleamed and a broad grin swallowed up her face. 'Thank God!!' she screamed before hugging him tightly. Simon wrapped his arms around her in return, but her happiness left him winded.

'Great news,' he lied, the disappointment palpable in his tone.

'Such a relief! Are you sure?'

'Positive. You're not pregnant.' He stared into her emerald eyes and felt so bitter about her joy.

Then he knew he had to be honest. More than that, he had to know how she really felt; where they really stood. Until that moment he hadn't known how much he'd wanted a family, and he needed to know if she didn't feel the same. 'Do you not want children?'

'What?'

'You don't have to be quite so happy that you're not carrying my child.'

'Oh Simon, don't be silly. The thought of having your babies is a wonderful one. It's just a bit early, don't you think? Aren't you relieved?'

'Too early?'

'I've known you, what, six weeks, and we've been married for three days. I'd say planning our first child at the minute might be rushing it a little, even for us.'

Logic kicked in and Simon breathed again. 'You're right. We've just never talked about it – not that we've had time – but I would like a family one day.'

'Me too. So much. You'd be an amazing dad! But I'm still just twenty-five; although very close to being twenty-six, don't forget.'

'How can I? Your not so subtle hints haven't been wasted, don't worry.' A smile curled up on Simon's lips as he realised the dream wasn't gone, just postponed.

'Good! Mrs Bird likes to celebrate!' Beth kissed Simon on the cheek and then she turned to the test in her hand. 'That's another possibility eliminated then. My power didn't come from your very unborn child.'

'Baby Bird.'

'We are not calling it that!'

Simon tucked Beth's hair behind her ears and he breathed her in. She truly was unique.

He considered how she couldn't be a Malant, so what else could had given her that brief but very real power? He needed to believe that she'd developed powers just like his, but he couldn't think of a logical reason as to why. 'The only other rational idea, I suppose,' he muttered, 'is that I've somehow rubbed off on you. Maybe I helped you along a bit. I've never been as close to anyone before, it could be a symptom of our love.'

'Aww, what a sweet thought,' Beth smiled, then her face dropped. 'So that means I don't have any of my own super powers?'

'Super powers?' Simon chuckled. 'It's magic, you were never going to be Super Girl.'

'You don't know what I could be capable of,' Beth argued with a pinch of humour.

'Never a truer word spoken,' Simon smirked. He glanced to the clock on the wall and saw it was well into the afternoon. Any hope of work that day was truly gone. He then turned his attention back to Beth, his eyes alight. 'So we've decided it's too early to start a family, but how do you feel about having a practice?'

'Now?'

'Have you got something better to do, Mrs Bird?'

'Hmm, let me think. Okay, we can practice. As long as we're extra careful. I do not want another shock like that anytime soon.'

'Agreed.' Simon then kissed Beth lovingly before carrying her up to their bedroom.

THREE

Tuesday morning soon arrived. Simon had requested that they get to the office early. He wasn't used to having a backlog of work to plough through and he wanted to try and stay on top of things as best he could.

As much as he tried to concentrate, though, he couldn't take his mind off recent events. He was thrilled with his new wife, and his new life, but the past few weeks had been fraught, and the newest drama of the pen flying incident was dominating his thoughts. Then he had other issues to contend with, again not work related.

After reading the same email five times and still not taking it in, he decided to leave work aside for the moment. He turned his attention to a very important contract that lay on his desk. Probably the most significant contract that he'd ever dealt with; certainly the most personal.

He read through it for what must have been the tenth time, thinking of how Beth had been manipulated into signing it before almost having to marry Damien. She'd been so worried about the terms of it before they themselves got married, he'd promised her that he'd find a way out of it. And he'd done just that. As was his forte for solving such problems, he'd spotted a loophole almost immediately, but he wanted to double check his facts before taking further action. He liked to be thorough and he knew how important it was to Beth that this contract be voided as soon as possible.

Convinced as to the action that he needed to take, Simon picked up the phone and called Jane, Malancy HQ's Senior Law Enforcement Director, and the only lady who could help him.

'Good morning,' a male voice answered.

'I'd like to speak to Mrs Parker, please,' Simon responded.

'I'm sorry, Mrs Parker is out of the office for a few days. Can I help?'

'Out of the office?' This was highly inconvenient. He needed to talk to her now.

'Is there anything I can help with?' the voice asked.

'No, thank you for your time.' Simon placed down the phone. He had to get in touch with her, no one else could help. Then an idea came to him. He called his uncle.

'Si! Everything okay?' Paul answered.

'Not if you can't help me. You don't happen to have Jane Parker's mobile number do you?'

'Jane Parker?'

'I need to speak to her to sort this contract out.'

'And you think I have her number?'

'You're friends with her aren't you?'

'What contract?'

'The contract that Beth had to sign.' This was becoming far harder work than Simon had hoped for. 'The one that's hanging over our marriage.'

'Jane can help?'

'Do you have her mobile number? She's out of the office, but it's imperative that I speak with her.' Simon's patience was dwindling.

'Err... You never know. Let me check.' Paul went silent for a few seconds and Simon started to drum his fingers with irritation. 'Yeah, I've got it. I'll text it to you.'

'Thank you,' Simon sighed. 'I hope you're having a good trip?'

'It's all great here, mate. You take care of that wife of yours.'

'Will do. Speak to you soon.'

As promised, just seconds after Simon hung up, Paul texted him the number. He wasted no time in trying to call her.

'Jane Parker,' she answered, much to Simon's relief.

'Hello Jane, it's Simon Bird. I hope you don't mind me calling you on your mobile?'

'Simon! How lovely to hear from you. Not at all. I'm out and about at the minute, but always happy to help out one of the Bird men. What can I do?'

'It's about the contract. The one that Beth had to sign.'

'Of course, I recall how displeased she was about having to marry you under such stifling terms. Not surprisingly.'

'Not surprising at all now that I've had chance to read it. Damien is more twisted than I gave him credit for.'

'Well, he's' been taken care of now.'

'I'm very relieved to hear it. Going back to the contract, I've found a loophole that will render it null and void once and for all, but I need your help.'

'Of course, anything.'

'It says that, when requested, Beth's husband will go willingly to Malancy HQ where, following your instructions, he, or I as it now stands, will allow my heart to be stopped for one minute so as to sever the spell that's... already been severed. I know that's not important now, but what is important is that it adds if I fail to agree to your terms then all other parts of the contract will become null and void.'

'Yes, I remember now. If you don't do as Malancy HQ requests, the contract ceases to exist. Didn't it say you had a fortnight to do it in?'

'Yes.'

'So in two weeks the contract will just be eliminated?'

'I don't think so. It clearly states that I must take action within a fortnight of both the marriage and the instructions set out by Malancy HQ. I don't want to confuse matters by just not doing anything within the timeframe, these contracts can be quite sensitive.'

'So what are you saying? You want us to stop your heart?'

'No, I just need you to send me some instructions. The crazier the better. Demand of me what I can't possibly do, just to be sure, and then when I don't do it, the contract will be eliminated and we can put this whole nasty business behind us.'

'I think I can manage that. Shooting off the top of my head... would asking you to go to the moon to perform the procedure be along the right lines?'

'That sounds perfect. Could you formally send me the details so I can formally ignore them?'

'I'll do it this morning. I too would like to see this wretched business finalised.'

'Thank you Jane, I appreciate your cooperation. Not just on this, but on everything. Without you, who knows what might have happened.'

'Just doing my job. Happy to help.'

'I'll speak to you soon no doubt.'

'One more thing, before you go.'

'Yes?'

'My keen powers of deduction lead to me surmise that you must be currently looking for a Sales Director?'

'We are. Must be Malant and have experience. Eric's on the lookout, but he's not had much success so far.'

'I might know just the man.'

'Really?'

'He's a friend of a friend, but his track record is quite impressive.'

'I'm interested. We actually have a board meeting this

afternoon, why not tell him to pop in and I'll introduce him to the team. Then we can have a chat.'

'Consider it done. I'll drop you his details before lunch.'

Simon placed the receiver down feeling a great weight lift from his shoulders. He was so pleased with the outcome of the phone call, he barely noticed how bewildered Beth looked as she suddenly staggered back to her desk.

'That was a heavy session,' she mumbled. 'Eric really knows his stuff.'

'That's why he's here. I have good news,' Simon said. He didn't mean to appear uncaring, but he couldn't help the smile that grabbed his lips. 'I've dealt with the contract. By the end of the week it will all be null and void and we'll have a normal marriage like everyone else.'

'Really? That easy?' This clearly brightened Beth's mood.

'I've built a career on sorting out issues just like this. It would have been more worrying if I couldn't do it. It was actually fairly simple in the end.'

Beth ran over to Simon and hugged him tightly. 'Thank you! You're the best! I knew there was a reason I married you!'

'For my brains? Is that the only reason?'

Beth stood back and scanned Simon in full. 'Yeah,' she giggled.

The day got heavier and heavier for Beth and, by the time the afternoon arrived, she was feeling quiet anxious. She was sitting poised with pen and paper in her first board meeting and, having arrived much earlier than her fellow directors, she had nothing else to do but dwell on how overwhelming she was finding her new role.

There were so many decisions that had to be made. She'd gone from simply entering data without question to suddenly having the burden of deciding how, why and when the data needed to be entered in the first place.

Although it was quite a terrifying prospect, and she now understood the reason why people usually progressed step by step, her trademark determined spirit was fighting through, and she reminded herself of what a massive opportunity this really was for her.

To take her mind of the situation, she'd introduced Simon to her new favourite tea shop for lunch. That had most definitely been the highlight of the day. Sandwiches bought, they'd then headed back to her flat for a short while so she could make a start on packing. She still hadn't given her landlord notice that she'd be leaving. She felt bad as she'd only been there a few weeks and her landlord had been really good to her when she moved in.

She knew it was a huge waste of money putting off the inevitable, but she couldn't bring herself to make that phone call just yet. Soon, very soon, just not quite yet.

As she had the self-made gift of time, she'd planned to pack up her stuff in her lunchtimes and take it bit by bit over to the mansion. She'd convinced herself that this was the easiest way to handle the situation, in a step by step fashion.

Her mind flicked back to reality as Simon suddenly kicked off the board meeting. Sitting at the head of the boardroom, he began in his usual commanding tone. 'I want to do something a little different in this meeting. I know you all have a lot of points to raise and the agenda's quite extensive, but I'd like to scrap that for now. If everyone can just provide a quick update on their department, then I want to have a more open discussion.' The room all stared silently at Simon. This was clearly abnormal.

'It's been brought to my attention that maybe we, as the board, might be a little out of touch with what's going on elsewhere in the company,' he continued. 'And after my own investigation, I have to agree with this assessment. Take Trisha Clock as a prime example. We all thought she was an excellent employee, but it turned out she wasn't quite who we believed her to be.'

'Trisha was fantastic-' Eric argued.

'She was not. But that's not for discussion now. I want to use this time to brainstorm how we can bridge the gap between the Executive Floor and the rest of the business, and how we can better work with our teams to further strengthen Bird Consultants' offering.'

Beth found it hard to contain her smile. Simon had been listening to her. Maybe she was cut out for a leadership role after all.

'More of that later, though. For now, let's get an update from each of you. Except Beth, of course, we'll let you sit this one out.'

'Thank you,' she whispered, relieved that she wasn't going to be expected to contribute.

'Nathan, do you want to start?' Simon requested.

Nathan stood up at the front and plugged his laptop into the projector. Within seconds a page full of figures appeared against the white wall ahead of everyone. Beth had found out that morning that he was the Finance Director.

'We need to discuss last year's figures,' he began. Beth stared at the information. It was full of acronyms she'd never heard of and she quickly became quite confused. 'If we look to actual versus forecast, you can see the trend has still not improved.'

'But we've massively grown our customer base,' another man added. He was the Spell Director Beth had come to learn.

'Alongside dropping prices for our top ten customers. Then there's the ridiculous ROI on Bill's profound CAPEX-'

'We've been over this numerous times,' Simon interrupted, trying to stop the impending argument.

Beth realised she was totally out of her depth. These were powerful people who were used to making huge business decisions and already she was lost.

The meeting continued, with each director in turn raising their vital concerns and arguing their cases, and Beth found herself drifting away. She so desired to pay attention and she wanted to learn, but they may as well have been speaking a foreign language for all that Beth understood.

Just then her daydreams were interrupted by a strange man knocking at the door. 'Mr Bird?' he said, poking his head in. He was an impeccably tidy man with a bold face and confident stance.

Simon walked over to him and shook his hand. 'Brian Wolfe?'

'Thanks for the invite.'

'Guys... and Beth... this is Brian. He's here to discuss the Sales Director role.' The team all took it in turns to shake Brian's hand. 'We're just finishing off, please take a seat. We're discussing how best to bridge the gap between ourselves and our teams. Any thoughts?'

Much to Beth's frustration, Brian sat down and dozens of ideas poured out of him like he was a walking problem solver. He had no issue speaking his mind and he had a charismatic way of bringing people around to his ideas. As much as Beth wanted her lack of involvement to be because she was new, it was blatant that her inexperience was going to be her Everest.

If she'd had doubts before, she was now deeply regretting her position and she didn't quite know how she was going to survive.

FOUR

When Beth woke up on Saturday morning she allowed herself a moment's joy. Then reality hit her. Although she'd left one of the hardest weeks of her life behind her, she now had to face her first trip home since she'd moved to London, and her first trip home as a married woman. It could potentially all get so much worse.

As she rose and began her morning routine, she became increasingly aware of a mild discomfort. An irritation inside of her, that she couldn't quite put her finger on, was leaving her jittery; like she somehow felt alien in her own skin.

She convinced herself that it had to be stress related. The past week had been overwhelming. In fact, the past few weeks had been so incredibly life-changing, it would be more worrying if she did feel all right.

Just thinking about recent events made her head hurt. She'd witnessed her boyfriend turn in to a bird, and that was just before almost being forced to marry the very man that had turned him into that bird. She'd then been set free only to find herself suddenly getting married again, only this time to the man that she did love, but had only known for a short while. Then, out of nowhere, she'd magically thrown a pen across the room on the same day that she'd been catapulted into the job of her dreams. A job, however, that was drowning her slowly. No wonder she hadn't been sleeping well.

Simon had been very supportive, insisting that she needed to give herself chance to settle. At that moment in time, though, it felt like she'd never be able to cope.

If all that wasn't enough, she now had the stress of going home to see her parents. She had to somehow find a way to introduce her new husband to them; the new husband that they didn't even know existed.

She took a deep breath and tried to stop overthinking things. Simon was probably right, she just needed to give herself a break.

Having showered and dressed, and then having played with her breakfast, Beth was relieved to hear Simon insist that he drive. The first bit of good news that day. She was then even more relieved when he suggested that he take his Jaguar F-Type Coupe, justifying that it was a little more mainstream than the Aston Martin, and might not be such a shock for his yet to meet in-laws. Beth definitely needed to keep the shocks to as few as possible that weekend.

The car was all packed up and, at around mid-morning, they headed off up to the Midlands.

After about two and a half hours of fairly easy traffic, through plenty of countryside and towards lots of fresh air, the edge of Stonheath came into view.

Beth felt a familiar warmth glow inside of her. As much as she'd hated living there in recent years, she knew Stonheath would always be home. Having had a bit of time away, she could actually see the place with a fresh perspective and she conceded that maybe it wasn't so bad.

The village of Stonheath was fairly modern and quite large. There were two schools and plenty of grassland for the kids to play on, and it had a real community spirit that Beth had always taken for granted.

Her reminiscing was interrupted as another blast of

cool air blew into the car, chilling her.

'Are you still hot?' she asked Simon, bewildered as to how the rainy, grey day around them could warm anyone.

'It's so humid,' he replied, winding up his window a little to limit the impact on Beth.

'It's so not! Are you okay?'

'I'm boiling. I felt it when we first got in the car, but it's been getting more intense the more we've travelled.'

Beth smiled, guessing what this was really about. 'Are you nervous?'

'About meeting your parents?' Simon asked as Beth nodded in reply. 'I didn't think so.'

'I've never seen you looking so flushed! Oh hang on, you want to take your next left just here,' Beth instructed.

She directed Simon down a few more roads before finally reaching the little street that she'd grown up on. It was a quiet road lined with houses all circa 1960's, and down towards the far end Beth signalled for Simon to pull up on a drive.

'Ready?' she asked, taking a deep breath as Simon turned off the engine. They both looked to the large house ahead of them.

'I'm right behind you.'

Beth slowly got out of the car. Feeling dizzy with a cocktail of emotions, she headed to the door and rang the bell. She'd told her parents that she was bringing a new friend with her, but that was all they knew. She'd practiced in her head numerous times as to how she'd tell them that she was married, but now faced with the task, her mind had gone completely blank. Once again she was in strange new territory, and once again she didn't really have a clue what to do for the best.

'Beth!' her mother beamed, opening the door and immediately wrapping her arms around her in a tight hug. 'How we've missed you! Oh, don't you look tired.'

'Hi mum! I want you to meet... Simon.'

'Very nice to meet you,' Simon said reaching out to

shake Mrs Lance's hand.

'Hello,' Mrs Lance replied. Her glance went from delighted to cautious in an instant as she placed her hand in his. 'You'd better come in. Your dad's just put the kettle on. I take it you drink tea, Simon?'

'Of course he does!' Mr Lance said coming to the hallway to greet his daughter. 'What sort of man turns down a cup of tea?'

'Tea would be great, thank you,' Simon replied, shaking Mr Lance's hand.

'Frank Lance, nice to meet you,' her father greeted. 'Beth has told us absolutely nothing about you. Sorry, we're a bit out of loop when it comes to our daughter.'

Beth shook her head and made her way to the living room. She wasted no time in flopping down on the settee as if she'd never been away. She didn't need to deal with embarrassing comments like that, they weren't helpful.

'How do you have your tea, then?' Frank asked as they all followed Beth into the living room.

'Just like me,' Beth quickly answered. 'We're exactly the same.'

'Great. Just give me two minutes.'

Alice Lance sat down on one of the armchairs, not once taking her eyes off Simon. He was standing uneasily next to the settee that Beth was slumped on. 'Make yourself at home,' Alice said. Beth glanced up at him. Although his grand stature was still highly accentuated against her more dainty parents, he didn't appear to be his usual confident self. She watched him scan the softly decorated space before slowly sitting down next to her.

'We flew up the motorway!' Beth announced, trying to temper the awkwardness. 'Got to love Saturday morning traffic.'

'That's your Jag outside then, Simon?' Frank asked as he brought four mugs of tea in on a tray and handed them out. 'What's she like to drive?'

'Simon's got three cars,' Beth suddenly blurted out.

With some misguided logic, she told herself that if they knew Simon was wealthy then they might like him more. She knew she had to tell them about the marriage soon. It was getting hard to hide her ring and she needed the worry to be over with.

'The Jag's the weekend car, then?' Frank smirked as he sat on the second armchair.

Simon considered his response for a second. 'I guess so.'

'Mum, dad, we need to tell you something,' Beth said, sitting up straight.

'What's wrong?' Alice responded.

'Nothing's wrong. Quite the opposite in fact.' Beth rubbed the mug in her hand, trying to think of the best way to broach it. The direct, honest approach had always served her well in the past, so she decided to stick with that. 'We're married.'

There was absolute silence.

'Simon and I got married last Friday. I'm sorry I've waited until now to tell you.'

'What do you mean you're married?' Alice asked, more confusion than anything present in her tone.

'Just that.'

'It's not as straight forward as it sounds,' Simon stepped in, trying to help.

'You eloped?' Frank asked.

'No! Don't be silly,' Beth corrected.

'We're very much in love, and I proposed to your daughter after just a few weeks of knowing her as I realised that there was no one else in the world for me but her. You've raised an incredible woman.'

'And I just couldn't wait!' Beth added. Okay, so this wasn't quite the truth, but as new Beth had come to learn, sometimes a white lie was definitely required.

'Some unforeseen circumstances meant that our lives would be made much easier if we got married sooner rather than later,' Simon elaborated.

'Are you pregnant?' Alice probed.

'No! Nothing like that,' Beth clarified.

'So I've just missed out on my only daughter's wedding?' Alice asked, clearly quite perturbed.

'Don't worry, mum. We want to do it right. We want to do it again and plan it properly. I'm Mrs Bird now, yes, but we haven't counted that as our official wedding. I want to plan it with you. And dad. And the rest of the family.'

'Your name's Bethany Bird?' Alice asked, her vexation growing.

'That couldn't be helped,' Simon replied quite defensively.

'I don't know what to say. Frank?' Alice glared at her husband.

'I think we need to get to know you a bit better, son. What's done is done, there's no changing it. As long as our girl's happy?'

'More happy than I could ever have dreamed of. Simon is the most wonderful man and we're so good together. You'll see when you get to know him.'

'You couldn't have waited? At least introduced him to your family first?' Alice argued.

'I'm sorry Mrs Lance, it was so rushed. I know this must be a huge shock to you. But hopefully, over time, you'll see how perfect we are together and you'll understand,' Simon explained.

'I suppose if you're now my son in law, the least you can do is call me Alice.'

'Thank you... Alice.'

Beth involuntarily sighed. The worst was over. They weren't happy, she knew that, but at least they'd accepted it. Although, Beth considered, what choice did they have?

As soon as lunch was eaten, Beth wasted no time in taking Simon around the local area. She showed him her old school, they enjoyed a pint in the pub where she used to work, and she relayed numerous stories of her youth as she executed her impromptu guided tour.

In the evening her parents treated them to a meal and they finally had the chance to get to know Simon better.

Overall, the weekend had gone as well as could be expected, but Beth couldn't wait to leave after Sunday lunch the next day. As much as she'd enjoyed her little trip home, it had been a tad awkward too.

Simon had been exceptionally polite and diplomatic, but also very quiet. Her parents had made a good effort to get to know him, but it had been rather clinical at times and it hadn't been the relaxed family atmosphere that Beth was used to with her parents.

The Sunday roast had been demolished and Beth and Alice had volunteered to tidy up whilst Simon took Frank out for a spin around the block in his Jaguar. This gave Alice the perfect opportunity to talk with her daughter. 'You are okay, aren't you?'

'What are you talking about? Of course I am,' Beth replied, opening up the dishwasher.

'Simon seems like a very nice man, but I'm worried about you. You've never been impulsive, you're a considered girl. It's not like you.'

'You said it wasn't like me to move to London as well. People can change. London has changed me. I've grown up.'

'Grown-ups realise that it takes time to get to know someone. You've been gone less than two months and you come home married. It's very worrying.'

'When you know you've met the right person.'

'Marriage isn't all happily ever after, you know. It's hard work - as you're about to find out. I don't want you to get hurt.'

'Simon would never hurt me.'

'With all due respect, Bethany, how do you know? How well can you possibly know him?'

'Probably better than you think.' Beth was annoyed by this. If only her mother knew what they'd been through!

'I've been married to your father for thirty years, Beth, and he still surprises me at times. Don't think just because you're all loved up you know him. Please tread carefully.'

'You need to trust me.' Beth was quite firm in her response but her strength of voice was more to hide the fact that her mother's words had unnerved her. She didn't want to accept any truth in what she was being told. She refused to think about it anymore. She had a bond with Simon in a way her parents could never understand, and she could never explain it to them.

Alice stopped tidying up the table and turned her attention fully to her daughter. 'I do trust you. I trust that you'll always do the right thing. And no matter what happens, we're always here for you.' Alice stroked her daughter's hair. 'Oh, don't you look tired. London must be exhausting.' Beth just smiled in return. Then Alice added, 'I suppose now that you're married you definitely won't be moving back any time soon?'

'Simon has a fantastic house, you'll love it.'

'So you said last night.'

'You'll get to love him, mum, I promise.'

'If I'm going to get to know him better then you'll have to come home more often, won't you.'

'I think I can manage that.'

Simon and Frank broke their exchange as they entered the kitchen, chuckling. 'He's a safe driver Ally, I'll give him that,' Frank said.

'Frank was desperate to see how fast the Jaguar could go.'

'You have to let a car like that open up and stretch her wheels!' Frank laughed.

'You two better get on your way, you know what Sunday traffic is like,' Alice said.

'You're right,' Beth nodded, kissing her mum on the cheek.

'Our bags are by the front door, I think we're ready,' Simon said.

They all headed to the hallway and Beth hugged her dad and then her mum.

'Before you go, love, hang on,' Alice said, running to the living room. She came back with a blanket. 'Take this with you.'

'What for?'

'I noticed you've been a bit cold.'

Beth looked to Simon. They both knew it was a fine spring day, and they both knew what she was really feeling. 'I'm all right, mum.'

'I won't forgive myself if you come down with a cold.'

'It's really fine mum, but thanks.'

'It's me,' Simon added, trying to explain the chilly presence that everyone always felt around him; Beth being the only ever exception. 'I'm always cold. Blood circulation thing.'

'No Simon, it's not you, it's Beth.'

Despite not feeling cold at all, Alice's words sent shivers through Beth. Reluctantly, she accepted the blanket and they made their way back to the car. Simon placed their bags in the boot and then they waved goodbye.

'Am I cold?' Beth asked as Simon drove them away from the house.

'Not at all. It's me, you know it is. She's just confused. If anything, you're really warm,' Simon remarked, winding down his window again.

'I'm warm?' Beth asked. The prickle of realisation suddenly swept across her skin. 'Is it like a comforting warmth? Like it's thickened the air around you and when it's gone it leaves a huge gaping hole in your world?'

Simon thought for a second. 'I wouldn't have put it so eloquently, but yes, I suppose.'

'Oh my God!' Beth gasped with horror. 'I'm turning into you!'

FIVE

It had been an anxious journey home from Stonheath, followed by a rather restless night, as the newlyweds tried to rationalise another strange occurrence. Left with no other logical explanation, Simon had come to the conclusion that Beth was somehow experiencing fragments of his power, no doubt a consequence of their closeness.

By Monday morning, an air of confusion was still lingering over them, and they both welcomed the distraction of work. Sitting in their office at Bird Consultants they were deep in concentration on their individual computers, only disturbed for the first time in an hour at the sound of Simon's mobile ringing. 'Paul,' he greeted.

Beth's ears pricked up. They still hadn't told Paul about any of this, and she knew that he was due home very soon. Maybe he could shed some light on these latest events.

'Sounds great,' Simon said, still talking to Paul. 'Of course! Do you want me to book? Great. See you then.'

Simon placed down his phone and Beth looked to him with desperation. 'What did he say?'

'He's back tomorrow. We're meeting for dinner at

Marco's. You know, near Piccadilly Circus.'

'That's the best news I've heard in days.'

'Will you stop worrying now? Paul always has answers. And when he tells you that your apparent powers are just the echo of my own ability as a result our incredible closeness, you'll believe him, won't you?'

'I believe you.'

'You have doubts.'

'I know it's the only thing that makes sense, but we don't know anything for sure. I just think it's best to keep an open mind.'

'I suppose that's very wise. I have every faith that Paul will give us much more insight tomorrow. I don't know how, but he always seems to know everything about everything.'

'Us Birds are super clever!' Beth smirked, then her eyes caught the clock in the corner of her monitor. 'Shit, I've got a meeting.'

'You better go,' Simon smiled, returning to his laptop.

Beth grabbed her notebook and pen and headed towards the door. Then she stopped and turned back to Simon. 'Gus still hasn't told Gayle about the Malancy. I really think she needs to know.'

'Gus knows what he's doing,' Simon said as he started to type. 'If he hasn't told her then it's because she doesn't need to know yet.'

'I think she does.'

'Let Gus handle it, Beth. He knows what he's doing.'

'Well, I'm his boss, I might speak to him about it.'

Simon leaned back in his chair and studied Beth for a moment. 'Do you want her to know so you can talk to someone about it? A fellow non-Malant?'

'No,' Beth insisted, immediately recognising that she was lying. She didn't know how Simon could always see right through her. She sighed. 'Okay, is that so bad?'

'I can see where you're coming from, and I completely understand, but this must be handled properly. By all means speak to Gus about it and gauge his thoughts on the matter, but listen to what he has to say. He's been here a long time and he's raised the knowledge level of many employees. He knows what he's doing. Trust him.'

Beth didn't know how to respond. Simon, of course, was right, but waiting for Gayle to find out was irritating her. She so badly wanted to confide in someone, someone who was as new to it as she was. But her selfish reasons were not enough to push it, so she had to concede.

'I suppose you're right. I'll see you later.' She walked around the desk to kiss Simon on the cheek and then headed off across the Executive Floor towards the lifts.

As she walked on, Brian, the new Sales Director, caught her attention. A flash of Damien came in to her mind and how he'd sat in that very seat only a few weeks before. So much had happened since then; so much change in such a small space of time. Life had definitely been moving in the fast lane and, just for a moment, Beth wished it could all stop. For a fleeting second, Beth wished for peace and quiet. All she wanted was the chance to catch her breath so she could properly take stock of everything that had happened, and then she'd happily get back into the mayhem that had become her life.

The lift arrived at the ninth floor and Beth turned her mind to her meeting. That small journey in the lift was about all the peace she was going to get that day and she knew it.

As she headed to Gus's office, she passed her old desk. As always, she felt compelled to smile at Diane and Michelle, although they'd barely said a word to her since her promotion. She couldn't deny it was hurtful, but she looked on and tried to concentrate on the task in hand.

Both Gus and Gayle were already waiting for her, sitting at a small table in the middle of the room. She closed the door and pulled up a chair to join them. 'Morning!' she beamed, trying to emit enthusiasm. 'How are we today?'

'Fine,' Gus flatly responded.

Gayle shivered and wrapped her cardigan around her. 'Did you knock the air con on or something, love? It's gone a bit chilly all of a sudden.'

'What?' Beth asked, her heart now pounding. She looked to Gus who was spying her suspiciously in return. 'Yes,' she thought quickly. 'I mean, the air con's playing up today, so it's likely to be hot and cold, on and off. No telling what it will do.' How on earth could she tell the truth, she didn't even know what the truth was herself?

'I hadn't heard about that,' Gus said.

'Mr Bird himself told me. If you have an issue, I'd speak to him.'

'I hope they get it fixed soon, it's very cold,' Gayle stated.

Beth's mind started fogging up. Memories of that tube journey with Simon when everyone was trying to avoid him sparked through her head. She had felt so sorry for him. She'd marvelled at his ability to deal with it with such forgiveness and understanding. She didn't know if she could go through the same. It was one thing to have magical powers - that was kind of exciting - but another to emit a chilling essence that prickled people into avoidance.

'It's your meeting,' Gus snarled, snapping Beth back to reality.

'Of course,' she said, trying to remember what she was doing. 'Right.' But it was too late, her anxiety was now in overdrive. She picked up her notebook and clumsily tried to open it to a new page. Suddenly her pen flew across the room. She hadn't touched it, she knew she hadn't.

'Whoops!' she smirked, trying to look nonchalant. She stood up to get her pen from the floor, only to turn back around to find her chair floating about an inch off the carpet.

She immediately looked to Gayle and Gus, afraid they'd noticed, but Gayle was writing the date in her notebook and Gus was looking at his watch. She quickly sat back on her chair, forcing it to the ground.

Taking a deep breath, she tried to continue. 'Right then. Err... Last week, the board had a meeting and Simon... Mr Bird asked us all to meet with our respective teams to try and find ways of increasing departmental communication. He wants us all to work closer together moving on.'

'What's wrong with the way I work with my team?' Gus challenged. Beth hadn't expected this. She'd expected them to agree with her.

'It's not personal. It's a cross company thing.'

'I know my team very well, thank you. I don't need any help in improving it.'

'With all due respect, Gus, how well did you know me before my promotion? When I was just an admin junior?'

'That's different, you reported to Trisha. Your role would now report to Gayle. It's my job to look after Gayle and everyone at her level.'

'Not anymore,' Beth argued, her heart throbbing. Then her pen suddenly flew across the room again. She looked at it lying near Gus's desk on the floor. 'Slippery fingers!' she forcefully smiled, knowing full well she hadn't touched it for the second time. She decided to leave it, worried what would happen to her chair if she stood up.

'Aren't you going to pick it up?' Gus asked.

'Not at the minute. We're mid-flow,' she justified. 'As I was saying, regardless of position, Simon... Mr Bird would like all departments to work more closely together. That means right from me straight through to-'

'The person that replaces you at the very bottom of the chain?' Gus sneered.

Beth felt a pang of nausea at Gus's jab. She had her own concerns with her new position, she didn't need other people adding to her anxiety. As her bitterness towards him raged in her stomach, a pile of paperwork flew off Gus's desk and scattered on the floor.

'What the hell was that?' Gayle asked, shocked.

'It's that bloody air con! Did you feel that gust?' Beth

explained, so desperate now for the nightmare she was finding herself in to end.

'Great!' Gus moaned as he walked around to pick up the paperwork. 'Here's your pen,' he said, smacking the pen down on the table next to Beth. She glared at it with fear, not sure what was going to happen next. Then suddenly it flew off the desk and smacked Gus across the back.

'What did you do that for?' he snapped.

'I'm sorry, I didn't mean to,' Beth flapped, jumping to her feet. 'I'm just so flustered about this air con. We can't work in these conditions. Let me go and see Simon about it again.'

'Don't you mean Mr Bird?' Gus sneered.

His jab stung in the pit of Beth's stomach and she couldn't help but send the papers fluttering about all over the place once more. She didn't even know how she was doing it. Not looking back, she quickly scurried out of the office, leaving Gus and Gayle in quite a muddle behind her.

Refusing to make eye contact with anyone, she raced to the lift, desperately seeking the safe haven of her office. Trying to control her nerves, she made it to the tenth floor. Taking a deep breath she then hurried passed the desks of her fellow directors, but as she did, paperwork flew everywhere. She was totally at the mercy of these new powers and she was getting very frightened.

'It's the air con!' she shouted out, trying not to look at anyone in particular. 'It's on the blink. But we're fixing it!' She then rushed into Simon's office and slammed the door behind her.

'What on earth is going on?' Simon asked, standing up from his desk to examine the kerfuffle outside. 'Did you say there's something wrong with the air con?'

'You've got to help me!' Beth shrieked, sending all sorts of stationery flying into the air as she did. Simon looked around with wide eyes, clearly not expecting this.

'Okay,' he said. 'Calm down. Tell me what's happened.'

'I don't know! I can't stop it!' Her mass of anxiety brought more paperwork to life.

'You have to calm down,' Simon said more sternly.

'I'm trying. Just make it stop.'

'You are the only one that can do that, Beth. It's all in your control.'

'Really? Then why can't I stop it? I want it to stop. Help me!'

'First things first, stop flapping and put your hands by your side!' Beth jolted her hands down at Simon's command. With deep breaths, she then awaited further instruction. 'Now tell me what happened,' he requested.

'I was downstairs and Gayle said she was really cold. It was as soon as I entered the room...' Beth's emotion quickly got the better of her again. It was getting so bad, she had to duck out the way of an errant stapler as it flew passed her head.

'Put your hands by your side!' Simon shouted, his tone so imposing it literally shook the room into obedience. 'Now, without moving and without getting excited, calmly tell me how this started. I'm going to help you Beth, but you have to calm down.'

Beth took a few more deep breaths and tried to relax. It helped tremendously that the, what should be inanimate objects, were once again inanimate, such was the power of Simon's voice.

Simon took his eyes off her for a moment as he glanced out the window across the Executive Floor. Beth followed his gaze to find seven pairs of eyes all staring back at them, the madness of the last few minutes having captivated absolutely everybody.

Simon slowly turned back to Beth. He then raised his hand in the air and snapped his fingers. All the windows instantly darkened, stopping anyone looking in and them looking out.

Beth was in awe. How could Simon do that so easily

and so simply? He reached for her cheek and gently kissed her lips, truly helping to calm her nerves.

'Come on,' he said, leading her to her desk. 'Take a seat and tell me everything.'

Beth sat down in her chair and tried to compose herself. 'Gayle felt cold around me. It's not you, it's not my imagination, it's me. I'm turning into you. I've got what you've got.'

'It's not a disease,' Simon corrected.

'It got the better of me, things starting flying everywhere. And Gus didn't help matters. He's so horrible to me.'

'He's put out because you're now a director and he's stuck where he is. You deserve your position, though. Paul and I - the two owners of the company - could not be happier to have you as a fellow director, and that's all that matters. Gus will have to get used to it. Just ignore him.'

'Don't you think I'm a bit out of my depth, though?'

Simon curled Beth's hair behind her ears so he could probably address her. 'You're facing new challenges, probably being stretched more than ever before; but do I think you're capable? Absolutely. More than capable. I think you were made for this job. You just have to give yourself a break and ease in gently. Stop worrying.'

'Thank you,' Beth whispered, a renewed sense of calm relaxing her body.

'Now, to these powers. It's apparent that you've developed powers just like mine. I have no clue how, it doesn't make any sense. We'll speak to Paul about it tomorrow, he'll no doubt have all the answers. For now, though, just enjoy it.'

'Enjoy it? How can I enjoy it? I sent the whole office into chaos!'

'That's where I come in. I'm going to show you how. Watch.' Simon picked up a pen that had found its way to the floor and placed in on Beth's desk. He stared at it firmly and it slowly lifted into the air. He then carefully spun it around a few times before gently letting it drift back down to the desk where it began. 'That's how you do it.'

'It's not that easy.'

'It really is. Not for other Malants, but for us it is.'

'I'm not a Malant, Simon,' Beth pointed out. Simon was clearly a little wounded by this reminder of the truth, but he quickly regained his composure.

'Maybe not. But until we know more, we're calling you the first official honorary Malant. How does that sound?'

Beth couldn't help but smile. At least it gave her some sort of belonging. 'I'll accept that. So show me how to do it. How can I use my powers for fun rather than just utter madness.'

'You need to concentrate it all. Take all that fear and worry that's been niggling at you and...' Simon paused for thought. 'Turn it into a ball inside of you. Concentrate all that emotion, whatever emotion it might be, and compress it. Like I said to you at the house, it's all just a feeling, a power deep within you. But imagine it's a ball of emotion and that's the source of it all. Then just... like a fireball, sort of throw it at the thing you want to move or control. It will just happen.'

Beth took a deep breath and turned to the pen. She did as Simon had explained and scraped together all of her emotions. She took all of her doubts about her new position, all of the fear of her new coldness and all the shock of her uncontrollable power and imagined it was a fireball deep inside of her. When she felt it tight and contracted within, she then did as Simon described and threw it all at the pen.

Suddenly the pen lifted off the desk. She concentrated hard and took it high into the air and then, without even really knowing how, she sent it spinning around like a waltzer; a nicely controlled waltzer. She then gently focussed it all the way back to the desk and it rested peacefully once more.

A smile stretched across her face, ear to ear. 'Did you see that?'

'I told you.'

'I want to do it again!' she giggled, a thrill now racing through her. She stood up and looked around the office for inspiration. She then settled her gaze on her monitor. She had to up the ante.

She repeated the process of channelling her emotions, this time tapping into her new found excitement as well. Slowly, although a little wobbly, the monitor rose from her desk. But Beth hadn't quite thought this through.

'Watch out!' Simon warned, but it was too late. The monitor, having been plugged into a socket near the floor, proved too fierce a match for Beth. Reaching its full stretch, the screen hurtled to the carpet and smashed.

'Oh no, I'm so sorry!' Beth gasped, running around her desk to assess the damage.

'It doesn't matter,' Simon assured her. 'Before you stretched it too far, you were doing a brilliant job,' he smiled.

Simon leaned down and placed his hand softly on the object. It glowed a soft tinge of red before miraculously mending itself. The crack disappeared and it looked brand new. Simon then stood back and, without touching it, he lifted the monitor carefully back to its place safely on the desk.

'Oh my God,' Beth swallowed. 'That was amazing. Could I do that?'

'I would guess so. Your power seems to mirror mine.'

'So we have, what, like ultimate power?'

'No. Not at all. We have great power. More power than any other Malant. More power than has ever been known. But you must be careful, Beth. You must know your limits.' Simon addressed her more seriously. 'I want you to enjoy this. I want you to explore the possibilities and indulge a little in what you can do, but you have to understand the consequences too. You have to appreciate the curse that comes along with something like this. Beth, from this moment on, your life will never be the same again.'

SIX

The next twenty-four hours had been good for the Birds. Beth had heeded Simon's advice and he'd admired her conservative approach to her new found powers. She'd rolled her pen about a bit, but generally she'd remained calm and controlled, and he couldn't have been prouder.

Sitting in Marco's restaurant, they were now eagerly awaiting Paul's input. They had high hopes that he'd have some answers, or at the very least that he'd be able to point them in the right direction.

Simon was buzzing with elation. After feeling alone for so long, he'd now not only met his perfect companion, but she was adopting his once unique abilities too. The world suddenly felt like a much better place to be in.

'Hello!' A cheerful cockney accent appeared from behind them.

'Evening,' Simon smiled, standing up to greet Paul. Paul patted him firmly on the back, the perfect mix of macho and tender all in one. Then he kissed Beth on the cheek and took a seat at the table.

'I don't know about you, but I'm starving,' Paul said, looking around for the waiter. Leonardo, the maître d', suddenly materialised.

'So lovely to see the Birds together. Is it a special occasion?' he asked, handing out the menus.

'No, Leonardo,' Paul explained, 'just a family get together.'

'Excellent. No champagne tonight then?'

'Not just yet,' Paul laughed. 'But the night is still young.'

'That it is. I'll give you a few minutes.' He then disappeared as quickly as he came.

'How come you're staying in the city tonight?' Simon asked. 'You're more than welcome back at the house. You're not avoiding us, are you?'

'Of course not! No, I'm heading off after this as I'm meeting the guys in the casino and then... wherever the night takes us.'

'Do you have to dash off?' Beth asked.

'Not a chance! Don't worry, you'll be flagging long before the casino shuts, no fear.'

'Are you still going back Saturday?' Simon queried.

'Yeah, flight's all booked. I thought I could stay with you Thursday Friday, if that's okay? Spend a bit of time with you before I go. I'm guessing now this little lady is in your life, the US isn't so appealing anymore?' Paul chuckled.

'I haven't even thought about going back to the States,' Simon admitted.

'If you're happy, I'm happy. Just don't be a stranger.'

'I've never been to New York,' Beth said, 'so it won't be long before I'm begging Simon to take me.'

'You'll love it!' Paul enthused. 'Now tell me, what's going on with you lovebirds? And how's business?'

'We have news,' Simon stated.

'News?' Paul asked, his eyes widening with fascination.

'Something new has happened.'

Paul paused for a second, clearly not expecting this. 'Something new?'

The restaurant was far from busy, but nevertheless

Simon lowered his voice as he began. 'Beth's got powers.'

Paul paused again, now even more confused. 'What are you talking about?'

'Malant like powers,' Beth replied.

'But just like me,' Simon finished.

Paul stared across at the two of them. 'I don't know what you're talking about.'

'Beth's developed powers just like me. She can perform magic autonomously, just like me. It all started last week.'

'But you're not a Malant,' Paul stated to Beth, almost threateningly.

'I know,' Beth responded, a little defensively.

'This isn't good,' Paul declared. 'You can't.'

'It's not like I wanted this.'

'What is it, Paul?' Simon asked. 'I thought you'd be happy.'

'This isn't good, Si. No good can come from this. Who else knows? Please tell me you've kept this quiet.'

Simon's elation tumbled into trepidation. This was far from the reaction he'd expected. 'We've told no one. We were hoping you'd help shed some light on it all.'

Paul looked around nervously, checking no one was listening, but in a highly paranoid fashion. 'We need to get out of here. We need to talk, but not here.'

'We've just got here,' Simon reasoned, but it was too late, Paul had already stood up and was calling for Leonardo's attention.

'I'm sorry, we have to leave. Family emergency. Please forgive us.'

'Of course, I do hope everything's okay?' Leonardo responded, clear concern across his face.

'As do we,' Paul muttered.

Simon picked up his phone and called for Jim to collect them. He was utterly confused and a little worried as to what Paul was going to say next. He'd only seen Beth's powers as good news until now; he'd never considered it to be a bad thing. How could it be bad?

By the time they reached the pleasant evening air, Jim was waiting for them. They all got in the car and headed back out of London, and back towards the Buckinghamshire countryside. Paul made a quick call to arrange for his bags to be moved to the house, and then they all fell silent.

The journey home was tense. Everyone was unwilling to speak in Jim's company, despite the fact that they were all filled to the brim with questions.

They finally arrived home and, excusing Jim for the night, they headed straight into the living room to talk.

'What's going on, Paul?' Simon demanded to know, standing in the middle of the room.

'I don't know,' Paul replied sincerely, taking a seat on the edge of the sofa.

'You clearly know something.'

'I can't give you the answers you want.'

'Paul, you need to tell us.'

'What is it you think I know?'

'Stop it!' It was rare that Simon got angry with his uncle, but he wasn't in the mood for games. 'I have no clue what you know, but you certainly know more than you're telling us. Now spit it out.'

Paul looked up to Simon in deep thought. Then he gave in. 'I don't know why Beth has powers. I can't tell you that. All I know is that Malancy HQ has been very interested in you for as long as I can remember. It's been far from overlooked that you're different, Simon. It's been an issue. It can't be good that Beth's becoming the same.'

'That's so true,' Beth added from the back of the room. 'I remember Jane was very keen to know all about you when you turned into a bird. And she was willing to let Damien off all his crimes just to get you back.'

'I'm sure there was more to it,' Simon argued, brushing off their concerns.

'No,' Paul corrected, now standing up to look Simon directly in the eye. 'It's all about you. It's like they've been biding their time, watching you carefully, waiting for something to happen. I knew there was something up when I asked for permission to start Bird Consultants. They didn't care about the company at all, all they wanted to know was how involved you'd be and how much interaction they could have with you. They're fascinated with you.'

'I'm just different.'

'It's more than that. I know it. And now you've got these powers, Beth. You're not a Malant, it's not possible. We can't let them find out.'

'How could they?' Beth asked.

'I don't know, but we need to keep this on a strict need to know basis, just to be sure.'

'Isn't this a bit dramatic?' Simon stated, shaking his head in disbelief.

'What would they do if they found out?' Beth asked.

'Precisely. They're not going to do anything. So they've taken an interest in me, it's not such a big deal. People always fear what they don't understand.' Simon reasoned.

Paul took a deep breath. 'It's been a bit more than just taking an interest.' He paused for a second considering his next move. 'For starters, somebody's been erasing you off the internet.'

'Don't be stupid. Not everyone appears online.'

'You're one of the most powerful men in the world, Simon. Like it or not, you don't just go by unnoticed. People have spoken about you, I've seen it. And then I've seen it vanish, just like that. As if by magic.'

'Who would do that?' Beth asked, getting increasingly flustered.

'The same person who's ensuring that everyone is scared shitless of him. Granted, your aura isn't the most welcoming, but this is more. People fear you, Simon. As in fear for their lives.'

'That's just a reaction to how people feel in my presence, because they don't understand it.'

'Cut the bullshit!' Paul snapped. 'Your every move is watched and someone has been going out of their way for a long time to ensure you're kept at a distance from the world.'

Paul's change in tone forced Simon to listen; he could no longer brush it off. Paul's story wasn't a pleasant notion, but what suddenly bothered Simon was the deceit he now felt. 'If this is all true, then why have you never told me about it before?'

Paul sighed. 'Until now it never really seemed to matter. You've been more than content with being away from the world, I actually thought someone was doing you a favour. For a while I even thought you might be doing it all in secret yourself. I didn't see how telling you would help anyone.'

'Are my powers at all related to this?' Beth asked.

'I don't know,' Paul declared. 'We just have to keep our wits about us. And we absolutely have to keep this secret, just between us three. Do you understand?'

'Who else would we tell?' Beth reasoned.

'Swear you won't tell a soul,' Paul insisted.

'I swear. I won't tell a soul.'

The three of them all stared at each other silently for a few moments as they processed another blast of new information.

Simon didn't know what to make of Paul's revelation. He'd always trusted his uncle implicitly, but this deceit had left him troubled. He knew he had to give Paul the benefit of the doubt, though. Simon had to believe that his uncle had acted in his best interests; he was all that he had.

His thoughts were cut short by a sudden outburst from Beth. 'If I'm becoming like you in every way, does that mean I could turn into a bird, just like you did?'

'No,' Paul immediately answered. 'That was a special magic. Only bicantomene or some other dark magic could do that. Not only is it completely illegal, now it's fallen under the radar, the controls have been tightened even more. No one could get away with it.'

Simon saw the terror in Beth's eyes. Becoming that bird creature had been the most painful experience of his life, both physically and emotionally. It had been such immense torture, like his skin had been on fire; the cruelty so intense at times, that he could barely look back on it without feeling sick. He wouldn't wish such horror on anyone, and he would never allow Beth to go through that.

'I promise, Beth, that's never going to happen. I've been this way for over thirty years and that was a one-off; a grotesque incident caused by a very disturbed man. Please don't worry about that.' Simon moved over to her so he could hold her in his arms. He felt a sudden urge to protect her, so vulnerable was the look in her eye.

'This is all getting a bit overwhelming,' Beth admitted, backing away from him. 'As usual, you weren't kidding when you said being with you would be a rollercoaster ride. It's exhausting.' Beth headed towards the door, not letting Simon come near her. 'I'm going to get my pyjamas on. I just need a few minutes.'

'Sure,' Simon nodded. He knew he needed to give her time to process everything, he needed some time himself, but he couldn't help but worry that she'd backed away so quickly. Beth headed out of the room, shutting the door behind her.

Simon remained still, staring at the door. It was a very rare occasion that he didn't know what to do next, but he still couldn't piece together everything that was happening, and it was leaving him quite bemused.

'Can I ask you a question mate?' Paul asked, breaking the tension.

'Yes,' Simon muttered, not moving.

'What do you feel around Beth?'

'I don't know. Love.'

'Not like that. I mean, what do you literally feel when you're in her presence. And did it change when she left the room?'

This grabbed Simon's attention. 'You mean her new essence? Can you feel it?'

'Can you?'

'I know how I make people feel, Paul. I know you've always tried to soften the blow, but I can see how people react; I can see the goosebumps I cause. And now I see it around Beth too.'

'You feel the cold?'

'No, I feel warm and safe around her. And then when she leaves, it's like a vacuum. The warmth gets sucked away, leaving nothing behind.'

'That's how she feels around you, isn't it.'

'So she's told me.'

'This is weird. Very weird. I don't even know where to start thinking about this. We just have to make sure that we're the only ones thinking about it.'

'So you said. Who have I got to tell anyway?'

'Sorry. You're my only family, I worry about you. I worry about you both. I'm going to look after you, I promise. Just let me have some thinking time.'

'Think all you want, Paul, just don't keep your findings to yourself. I'm a grown man, I can take it.'

'Sorry mate. It's a habit. Like it or not, you're my boy.'

Simon moved over and squeezed his uncle on the shoulder. He knew Paul had his best interests at heart, he felt silly for doubting it. 'I think we need a whiskey.'

'Now you're talking.'

Simon poured them their whiskies then they both sat down and, for the first time since they'd got home, they started to relax.

As they sipped away, they shared their theories of Beth's new found powers and Simon updated his uncle on all his work woes; neither of them at all noticing the minutes ticking by.

It was nearly eleven o'clock when Simon eventually glanced at his watch. Beth had been gone for over an hour.

'I better go and check on Beth,' Simon said, feeling a

little guilty that he'd left her alone for so long. Although he had believed that she'd be coming back down.

He crept upstairs, so as not to disturb her if she'd fallen asleep. Then an image of her crying on the bed flashed into his mind and he knew he needed to be with her. He saw the light was on from under the bedroom door and he slowly pushed down the handle. He opened it just a crack, expecting to see Beth on the bed. But the bed was still made, completely untouched.

He pushed the door open wider, but she was nowhere to be seen. He looked in the en suite, now quite confused, but it was empty. His concern soared as he headed out of the bedroom and checked the entire first floor of the house. With still no sign of her, he then moved downstairs. He searched every nook and cranny, scanned every inch of the house, he even poked his head into Jim's room, to find him fast asleep and completely alone. Beth was nowhere.

'Beth!' he suddenly yelled, standing in the hallway, as if his voice would somehow magic her back. 'Beth!' he shouted again, hoping that in his panic he'd somehow missed a room and she'd appear as if nothing had happened. 'Beth!'

'What is it?' Paul asked, poking his head around the living room door.

'It's Beth.'

'What about her?'

'She's gone.'

SEVEN

'What do you mean she's gone?' Paul queried.

'I've checked everywhere.'

'I wondered what you were doing. Well she has to be somewhere.'

'Be my guest, please take a look.'

'What's going on?' Jim asked, coming to join them from his bedroom towards the back of the house.

'It's okay, Jim. Beth's disappeared, but it's fine,' Paul explained.

'How can it be fine? What if something's happened to her?'

'Like what? Think logically, Si. Come on, sit down.' Paul led Simon back into the living room.

'Can I help with anything, sir?' Jim asked.

'It's fine, Jim. We're fine,' Paul replied.

'Do you know where she could have gone?' Jim queried, trying to be of help.

'It's fine, Jim. We have it all in hand,' Paul insisted.

'Just let me know if I can be of assistance,' Jim finished, before hesitantly heading back to his room.

'Something's wrong, I know it is,' Simon said.

'Think rationally. So much has happened to you both

lately. Beth said it herself before she left, she needed some time on her own. She's probably staying with a friend.'

'What friend? She doesn't know anyone down here. And why didn't we hear her leave?'

'If Beth didn't want us to hear her, then we wouldn't have heard her. She's a clever girl.'

'Where could she have gone?'

'Maybe she went to a hotel.'

Simon headed to the windows and looked out through the curtains. 'The cars are still here.'

'She could have got a taxi.'

'And we didn't hear it?'

'Simon, stop it!' Paul warned. 'The hows, whats and whens don't matter. Beth clearly needed some space and she's taken some time to get her head around everything. What else could have happened? Nothing else makes sense.'

'I'm going to give her a call,' Simon said, walking across the room to the landline.

'Don't! You have to give her some space, Si. You need to respect her decision on this. It's not personal. Anyone can see that she loves you. But remember how you felt when I first told you about being a Malant? It's a lot to deal with.'

Simon stopped in his tracks and thought. 'She does get on very well with that Gayle at work. Maybe she's staying with her.'

'There you go. Give her some time, it will be so much better for you both in the long run.'

'We've only been married a week. What sort of omen is that? She can't even bear to be around me.'

'That's not it and you know it,' Paul argued. 'Not many marriages start off in such eventful circumstances. You can't blame the poor girl. I'd almost judge her if she didn't run away.'

Simon looked to his uncle sincerely. 'She will be back, won't she?'

'Of course she will, Si. She loves you so much. She lights up when she's around you. I can't imagine anything is going to keep you apart for long. Now come on, let's get some sleep. You never know, by the time you wake up, Beth could be sitting in the kitchen shovelling one of Jim's breakfasts down her neck.'

'Do you think?' Simon asked with hope.

'Definitely.'

Even though Simon had spent most of his adult life sleeping alone, the bed suddenly seemed so empty. Beth's unexplained disappearance had left him with such deep heartache, he could barely breathe. He tried to sleep, but his brain just wouldn't switch off. The worry of where she was and why she'd left kept playing over and over.

It all seemed far too dramatic to be Beth. They'd been through so much together in the short time that they'd known each other, but she had never run away from him. She'd told him to leave, granted, but at least he knew where he stood. This was so cold and nasty.

Eventually sleep got the better of him, and he drifted off. It was far from a restful night, though. Strange, vivid dreams filled his mind. He and Beth had ultimate power, more than anything they could ever have imagined, and it coursed through their veins like lava. They had absolute control over everything; they were supreme beings with a distinct purpose.

They had a purpose. If only they could see what it was. If only it made sense.

Simon quickly woke up. The daylight around him brought a moment's relief before a sickening sadness gripped him again as he realised Beth had not returned.

It was just after six thirty and, remembering what Paul had said the night before, Simon wrapped his dressing gown around him and quickly raced to the kitchen, clinging to the desperate hope that Beth had returned. But the kitchen was silent, and it was clear no one had been there for a while.

Simon slumped his arms on the breakfast bar and sighed. Where on earth was she? And when would she be back?

* * *

The first thing Beth realised was that her head really hurt. She struggled for breath as she prised open her eyes. She recognised nothing. She sat up straight and scanned her surroundings. Where the hell was she?

It was a very grand bedroom and she was sitting in the middle of a huge bed. The room was dark, despite the bright sunlight that seeped through the gaps in the curtains. Beth struggled off the bed and pulled the dusty curtains back. The large windows revealed nothing but countryside for miles. It was stunning scenery: dark green hills for as far as the eye could see, and on another occasion she might have looked at it in wonder, but now was not the time. She was easily on the second floor, if not the third. Wherever she was, it was apparent that she was in the middle of nowhere.

She turned around to take in the room better. There was very little furniture, just mainly the bed and a bedside table, and then an en suite bathroom to her right. That was it.

She headed to the door, a little scared of what was on the other side, and tried to open it. But it was locked.

She turned back around to the windows and tried to open them, desperate to find a means of escape, but they too were locked.

Now utterly terrified, Beth tried to think straight. She tried to remember how she'd got there. Her head was so fuzzy, though. She'd clearly been drugged and she was struggling to gain any clarity of thought.

All she could remember was being with Simon and Paul. They'd got home from Marco's and had been talking.

Then it all went blank.

They were talking about her powers. Of course, she had magic powers. She was powerful! These windows weren't going to stop her!

She did just as Simon had taught her and she bundled all her fear into a tightly wound ball in her chest. Then she focussed all that emotion at the window and willed it to open. But nothing happened.

Deciding the windows were probably soldered shut - and by the decoration of the room around her, it was likely that they hadn't been opened for at least eighty years - she moved her attention to the door. She'd got into this room somehow, the door had to open.

She concentrated hard again, and with all her might she tried to open it. Nothing happened again, though.

Now not sure if it was her skills or the strength of the door, Beth looked around for inspiration. She raced into the mildly clean bathroom and found a small bar of soap.

Once again she focussed all of her emotion on to the one tiny item, just as she had done many times recently, channelling all the fear that was building up inside of her; but still nothing happened. It just didn't work. She'd lost her skill. She was completely trapped and completely powerless.

'Help!' she screamed, the terror now shaking her whole body. 'Help!!' Then she stopped. She had no clue as to why she was there nor who had brought her, and looking out the window she feared that the only two people around were her and her assailant. Then she fell very silent.

She crept back to the bed and curled herself up in a ball. She felt very afraid and very alone and she dreaded to think what was going to happen.

EIGHT

Everything reminded Simon of Beth. He was sitting in his office, unable to take his eyes off her unoccupied desk on the other side of the room, missing so much her infectious smile and positive energy.

He desperately needed to concentrate. He was still catching up on the backlog from recent events and he couldn't afford any more distractions. People needed his help.

The truth was, though, he just didn't care. None of it mattered, not anymore. Not compared to Beth. He really wanted to go home, but he had to work. He had no choice.

'Are you going to acknowledge me at any point?' a voice said from the doorway. Simon snapped out of his trance and looked over. It was Paul. 'I've been here for ages.'

'Sorry, I never saw you.'

'You have to stop worrying.'

'How can I? My wife's vanished with no word and it's because I've driven her away with my complicated life. I just wish we could be normal.'

'And I bet these so called normal people would kill for

a life like yours. Stop blaming yourself, Simon. The grass is always greener, we just have to deal with our lot. Beth's trying hard to do just that, I'm sure of it. And when she returns, you'll be so much stronger for it.'

'I hope you're right.'

'Come on, I'm taking you out for lunch. My treat.'

'I'm not hungry.'

'It wasn't a suggestion. Finish what you're doing and I'll meet you downstairs in five.'

'Fine.'

Paul headed off back to the lifts and Simon stared aimlessly at his laptop. He was halfway through an email, and had been for the last twenty minutes. It was no good.

He really wanted to listen to Paul, he normally did know best, but this situation was making Simon so unhappy. He had to at least know Beth was all right. If she needed space, that's fine, he could live with that; he just had to know that she was all right. He had to know that she wasn't mad with him.

He picked up his mobile and dialled Beth's number. He waited for it to connect, his heart now thudding loudly. He waited for what felt like an eon, praying for the ringtone, and then Beth's sweet voice appeared. It was her voicemail. It had gone straight through to her voicemail.

He hung up. What could he possibly say to her in a voicemail?

Sighing, he looked back to his laptop and quickly finished his email, knowing it couldn't wait any longer. Then he picked up his mobile again and decided to try one more time.

Suddenly the text symbol flashed at the top of the screen and Simon's heart stopped. It was Beth, he knew it. It was over. He quickly opened the message and his relief was stunted. It was Paul.

I'm waiting.

Simon caught his breath and then grabbed his suit jacket from the back of his chair. He knew Paul wasn't a patient man.

Simon's mood hadn't lifted at all by that evening. Paul was desperately trying to act normally. There was nothing more he could say, and Simon knew that Paul was right. He just wanted this nightmare to be over with; he wanted his wife back.

They'd just finished one of Jim's delicious pasta dishes in the dining room and Jim was coming in to collect the plates.

'I'm glad you have some appetite sir,' he said, trying not to acknowledge how little Simon had eaten.

'Sorry Jim. It wasn't the food, you know that.'

'No news on Mrs Bird then?'

'She just needs some space, Jim,' Paul responded. 'I'm sure she's fine. Everything will be back to normal before we know it.'

'Of course it will,' Jim agreed as he picked up the plates and left.

'What can I do to cheer you up, mate?' Paul asked.

'Bring Beth home.'

'I wish I could.'

Just then the landline rang from the living room. Simon's heart stopped. This could be news. Simon paced to answer it, but Jim had already taken the call.

'It's for Mr Bird,' Jim said shaking his head.

'For me?' Paul asked, joining them in the living room.

'Yes sir.'

'Who is it?'

'One of your friends from the States, I believe.'

'Thanks Jim.'

Simon headed back to the dining room and Jim followed him. 'More wine sir?' Jim asked.

'Why not?' Simon responded, slumping back in his seat.

'I'm sorry Mrs Bird has had to leave for a few days. You appear to be missing her greatly.'

'I most certainly am.'

'If only there was some way to locate her,' Jim shrugged. 'I mean there's nothing worse than not knowing where someone is, but at least if you know they're safe then you have that peace of mind. We can all take time away from our partners, but it's knowing where they are and that they're safe that makes the real difference. Knowing that exact location. If only there was some way. I feel for you sir, I really do.'

Simon stared at Jim thoughtfully. It was so obvious. He didn't know why he hadn't considered it before. It was the one thing that could help bring him peace of mind and it was all at the tip of his fingers.

'Save that second glass of wine, Jim. I've just remembered I have somewhere to be. Could you tell Paul I'll be back shortly?'

'Of course, sir. Drive safely.'

Wasting not a second more, Simon raced straight to the hallway. He grabbed the keys to his Jaguar from the hook near the door, then darted out into the driveway and jumped in his car. He willed the gates to open quickly and then drove off, away from the direction of the city, and deep into the countryside.

He soon came across a very quiet road where he knew there was a little layby halfway down. It was late evening, although not yet dark, but he felt safe enough away from prying eyes.

He parked the car and stepped straight out, leaving his lights on for extra illumination. He scanned the ground around him, searching for the perfect item. Then he saw it, just by the back wheels. He grabbed the stone and jumped straight back into his car.

As he had done many times before, he got comfortable in his seat and then focussed hard on the stone that sat squarely in his hands before him.

He closed his eyes and summoned his strength from within. He drew just enough force from the stone to aid his power as he turned his mind to Beth. His beautiful, talented, life affirming Beth. He pictured her with such passion, his love only fuelling the magic even more, speeding up the process of this location spell.

As the images of Beth increased in intensity, the stone started to flush. A golden glow erupted around it signalling that the spell was truly working. The orange hue slowly transitioned into a fiery red as its vibrancy escalated with each passing second. The scarlet blaze then swallowed up Simon's arms, his chest and, within a few moments, his entire body; red flashes burning wildly throughout his car.

Finally, and silently, dazzling beams lit up the whole area and Simon waited for the image of Beth's location to hit him. But all he saw was blankness.

The radiation instantly vanished, as if the spell had worked, but Simon had seen nothing. Not even a clue. It hadn't even been darkness or blackness, it had just been nothing.

Having never experienced anything like it, Simon tried the spell again, positive that he must have done it wrong. His mixed up emotions must have interfered with the magic somehow. He had to do it again.

He concentrated even harder this time. He utilised every emotion within him, feeling the vibrancy of the stone burning so hot it almost singed his fingers. But when the light had vanished for the second time, he was still left with nothing. Just pure blankness.

He tried a third time. The power that he was having to use was now making him quite weary, and it was only his desperate determination that was still spurring him on. He thought so hard of Beth, summoning every tiny detail of her to the forefront of his mind. He yielded the stone of all its power; every last drop that he could drain of it. He'd never worked so hard to make a spell work, ever in his life. It had to work this time, there was nothing more left.

No matter how hard he'd tried, though, when the beams had gone, he was still left with nothing. Just

emptiness.
    Beth was nowhere.

NINE

Beth finished her millionth lap of the room and sat back down on the bed. She had no clue as to how long she'd been there; it felt like forever. Her fear had started to subside as boredom and confusion took over. It seemed as if nothing was ever going to happen.

She'd tackled the door several times in the past few hours, more fiercely with each go, but it wouldn't even budge a little. And she was absolutely convinced that the windows were in fact soldered shut. She wished she could think more clearly as she was sure there must be a way out of this prison, but she just couldn't get a grasp on her thoughts. Everything was really taking its toll on her and she really was starting to feel utterly beaten.

Her eyes were getting heavy, and as much as she wanted to stay awake, to be alert should something happen, she knew that sleep would soon be upon her and she had to give in.

She curled up tightly in the middle of the bed and rested her head on the firm pillow. She closed her eyes and tried to think of Simon. She needed to think of something happy. Surely he'd be looking for her; surely he'd find her soon. Surely he would rescue her again, like he'd done so many times before.

Literally just as her mind drifted off into a slumber, the door to the room clicked open.

Beth sat up straight, her heart now throbbing as she waited to meet her captor. She swallowed hard as she watched the door open.

A man entered. He was smartly dressed in a classy suit and he brought with him a chair. He placed it neatly in the middle of the room and sat down. He must have been in his late forties, with slightly greying hair and inquisitive eyes, and he relaxed into the chair as if he felt properly at home.

'Good evening Bethany Bird,' the man said in a very proper English accent. Beth refused to respond. He clearly knew her and that immediately put her at a disadvantage. She wasn't going to give him anything that he didn't already know. 'I hope you've been comfortable? You must be very hungry. Don't worry about that, we'll get straight to food after we've had a little chat.'

Beth had been feeling hungry, it was true, but her need for food had quickly vanished with this new threat in the room. She remained very still in the centre of the bed.

'I'm sure you have a million questions. You'll be pleased to know I'm about to give you a million answers,' the man continued. 'I seriously doubt that you're going to like what I have to tell you, but it's the truth. Everything I'm about to tell you is the absolute truth. You'd do well to remember that.'

Beth's breathing was gaining weight. She'd spent the last, who knows how long, praying for a way to escape, but just for now she decided it was best to stay still, very still, just for a while longer. No matter how much she desired to be home, and to be back with Simon, something about this man interested her. She was clearly here for a reason, and she was about to find out why.

'Let me introduce myself. My name is Mr Taylor. And I'm not a Malant.' Beth's interest spiked at this. Her adrenaline soared as she felt herself once again on the brink of being sucked in to the dark world that was the Malancy. 'Now let's talk about you. You've had an interesting few days, haven't you? How are you finding your new found powers?'

'How do you know about that?' Beth couldn't help but blurt out the question.

'I know a lot, Bethany. I don't mean you any harm, though, be sure of that. I'm not a danger to you; not at all. I'm sorry that we had to take you from your home and I'm sorry that we had to lock you up in here. I'm also very sorry that we had to block all your magic from working. You still have your skills, don't worry, but not in this building.'

'You're not alone?'

'Far from it. I have quite a group surrounding me. We're all driven by one common goal. It's been a long time coming and it's the way it has to be. I'll cut right to it. Bethany, we've brought you here because it's time for us to end to the Malancy. And you, my dear, are the key.'

Beth just stared at Mr Taylor in disbelief. What was he talking about? How could she end the Malancy, she wasn't even a Malant? And how could it end anyway?

'I can see you're confused. Let's start at the very beginning, shall we? I'm sure by now you would have been told a fictional story about a couple who, many hundreds of years ago, had hit rock bottom and had decided to go on a journey. Then, when they out of blue returned, they had magical powers. Does that ring a bell?'

'That's how the Malancy began.'

'No. Here's what really happened. The two original Malants were born with their powers. Samuel Malant was born five hundred and twenty-three years ago. Not really being able to understand his unique ability, he hid it from everyone he knew. Back then, of course, he could have been executed for showing such witchcraft. Elizabeth Wilson was born just one year later only a couple of miles away. They were drawn to each other. It was inevitable that they were to meet, and they knew it. Because when they did meet, their powers grew. Together they were invincible. They had ultimate power and nothing was stronger than them. Although they were still very wise to keep it a secret.

'This may sound like a gift, and they believed it was at first, but it was not. It was too much for them. With no guidance and no limits, the pair let their magic engulf them, and it was the same for their children. It hit a dark peak when one of their two sons unintentionally burnt down their house. They lost both their children in the blaze. That part was true.'

Beth's stomach was in knots as she listened. She didn't like where it was going.

'They wanted more children, they wanted a family again, but they realised that any more new offspring would too carry this unlimited power. So they had no choice but to find a way to constrain it.

'Before they conceived a new child, they cast a spell. The spell changed everything. It determined that all Malants from that day forward would have their ability limited. Yes, they would be able to cast spells and perform magic, but only through the use of a third party item. Never just through their own hands. So when their next child was born, he had just that, a limited magic. And when he had his children, they too were gifted with this more controllable power. And it's boded well, relatively speaking, for five hundred years.'

'How do you know all this?' Beth asked. This to her was more important than any of this supposed history lesson.

'Because the original family documented it. The first of their new offspring could see that his power differed greatly to that of his parents, so they told him everything and he kept a log.'

Mr Taylor sat more upright in his chair, as if the

pinnacle of the story was just in sight. 'They were clever people, the original Malants. They had made this decision hoping that it would bring peace to the future of the Malancy, but they realised they knew not what the future would hold. Much can happen in five hundred years, as well all know. So they included a clause in their spell. They allowed it so, centuries after their death, the future of the Malancy could be further decided by two more worthy people.'

'Is that you?'

'Don't be silly. I've told you, I'm not a Malant. The clause set out that in five hundred years' time, two people would be born bearing the gifts of the original Malants, and the powers would be theirs to decide the future.'

Beth's breathing quickened again.

'The clause laid out two very clear options. Five hundred years to the day that the original spell was cast, these chosen powerful beings could either cast a new spell together to continue the future of the Malancy as it is, or they could let the date pass by and the very notion of Malancy would vanish. At that very second, all powers would cease.'

'Why can't these powerful beings give everyone absolute, unlimited power?' Beth asked, expecting this to be a logical option number three.

'Because that power killed the original Malants' sons. That's why.' This was the first time that Mr Taylor had raised his voice.

'How do you have this documentation? Especially if you're not a Malant.'

'I may not be a Malant, Bethany. To be quite honest, I'm sick of them. The power Malants have is too strong and it's caused too many problems in this world. Companies like Bird Consultants have devalued a sacred gift and our society is too greedy for such a wonder. The Malancy has to end. Maybe in another five hundred years' time it could be re-introduced, who knows, but we're just not worthy enough today. And it's not just me who thinks it. The reason I have all this knowledge - the reason I'm here today with you - is because I'm working with a Malant directly. And I don't mean I'm working with a person who has Malant abilities, I mean I'm working with George Malant himself, a direct descendant from the original Malant family, the man ultimately in charge and the only person who can truly make this decision.'

Beth gasped. She'd had no clue that Malant was a surname and that it wielded such a rich history.

There was just one question now that was burning in her head, one thing that he was still yet to tell her. 'Where do I fit into this?' she muttered, despite being quite sure that she already knew the answer.

Mr Taylor smiled and sat back in his chair. 'We knew about Simon from birth. It was obvious that he was a chosen one. He couldn't be alone, though, two people are needed for the spell. We grew curious of you when you appeared to be able to tolerate Simon's unhospitable aura, but you'd shown no signs of power. Then just a few days ago all our questions were answered.'

'How did you know?'

'We know everything.'

'Well, if Simon and I are the chosen ones and we have the unique ability to cast this spell, surely the decision is ours.'

'Don't be so naïve. The world has got far more complex than Samuel or Elizabeth could ever have imagined. Their spell was too simple and their present family recognises that. It's their decision, not yours. It's nothing to do with you.'

'That's not true. By your very definition, we've been chosen.'

'It's irrelevant anyway. You're here and there's nothing you can do about it.'

'Simon will find me.'

'I'm sorry to say, but that's highly unlikely. As strong as

he is, it will take him a long time to realise that we've blocked all magic, and then even when he does, his power can't match ours. We have so many Malants working together, he's a useless contender.'

'So your plan is to keep me here forever?'

'Don't be silly. Of course not. As I said before, this spell has to be cast by a fixed date. And that date is fast approaching.' Mr Taylor leaned forward in his chair again. 'By this time next week, my dear, Malancy will be gone forever.'

TEN

Simon had reached his driveway, but he hadn't left his car. He was staring at his steering wheel, desperately trying to find a logical answer as to why his location spell hadn't worked. A logical answer that didn't make him feel sick.

He hadn't cast a location spell too often in his life, that was true, but he'd done it often enough to know that he'd done it right. And often enough to know that seeing absolutely nothing was not a good sign.

He toyed with the idea of telling Paul but he was worried what Paul would say. Paul had warned him from meddling, but he'd done it anyway.

He stepped out his car and edged to the front door. He sighed as he clicked the lock open, knowing that he had no real choice but to tell his uncle. This had moved swiftly from a little mystery to a complete horror, and Simon had to admit that he needed help. Even if Paul just brushed it off again as Beth somehow getting her space, he had to try and get Paul to see why he was so concerned.

The noise of the television was seeping through the gap in the living room door, and Simon headed straight in to find Paul sitting with a cup of coffee watching an episode of CSI.

'Everything okay mate?' Paul asked, hearing Simon enter the room.

Simon didn't know what to say. He felt like he'd been naughty sneaking off, but it had needed to be done. He walked over and sat down next to Paul, still jangling the car keys in his hand.

'Something's really wrong,' he finally said.

'I thought we'd been over this.'

'There's been a development.' This got Paul's attention. He flicked the TV off with the remote and turned to face Simon. 'I couldn't resist. I had to know that Beth was all right. I just did a location spell.'

'Simon!' Paul tutted disapprovingly. 'You should have let her be. Where is she, then? Feeling sorry for herself somewhere, no doubt.'

'I don't know.'

'You should have respected her need for space.'

'I mean, I don't know where she is.'

'What are you talking about? Didn't you do the spell?'

'I did it three times. I know I did it right. I know it worked. But when it got to the point where I should have seen her location, I saw nothing.'

'You can't see nothing. Be logical Simon, maybe she's in the dark somewhere. It is night time.'

'No, I don't mean I saw blackness, I mean I saw nothing. Complete emptiness. It's as if she doesn't exist.'

Paul sat up straight and placed down his coffee. 'That can't happen.'

'Could she be dead?' Simon asked, his voice cracking at the very idea.

Paul was momentarily lost for words as he searched his mind for a rational response. 'I've never heard of anyone trying to locate a dead person before, but I don't see how that would make a difference. Dead or alive, you're still located somewhere. This must be something very different. Very odd.'

'What the hell does it mean?' Simon asked.

'I don't know. But maybe you're right. Maybe Beth hasn't just run away. Sorry mate.'

Simon took a deep breath. It felt good, as if it was the first time that he'd properly breathed since Beth's disappearance. He enjoyed a flicker of relief as his uncle finally seemed to be taking the situation seriously. And they'd also discounted the idea that Beth could be dead.

'I wanted her to have just run away,' Paul explained. 'I was sure that she just needed space, it made so much sense. But this doesn't. There's interference somewhere, and we need to find out where she is.'

Simon's relief was short-lived as a sickening dread suddenly pulled hard at him. He realised that the very reason his uncle was now taking it seriously was because it was serious. Beth wasn't just trying to avoid him and she hadn't just needed some space. Something was wrong, very wrong. 'Okay, where do we begin?' Simon asked, standing to his feet, now desperate to be proactive.

'I don't know mate, let's think about this. If this was a contract, what would you do?'

'Beth's not a job at work!'

'It's what you do best Simon, get your head into gear.'

'Right. Sorry.' Simon thought hard, trying to line up his thoughts logically. 'The first thing to do is eliminate where she isn't. That should, hopefully, lead us to where she is.'

'Makes sense. How do we do that then?'

'Let's think where she could be. Anywhere. Doesn't matter how bizarre, if she could possibly be there, we need to eliminate it.'

'Good. Right, last night you said she could be at Gayle's, and then we also suggested hotels. But that's a huge job. How do we eliminate hotels in this part of the country? There are thousands.'

'Of hotels, yes, but how would she have got there? All the cars are here. Jim!' Simon shouted.

After a few seconds, Jim appeared at the doorway. 'Yes sir.'

'We have reason to believe that Beth might be in trouble and we need to find her fast. Could you please call all the local taxi companies, anyone who could and would come here, and see if they came to this address last night. And then, more importantly, if they did, where did they go next?'

'Absolutely sir. I'm on the case.' Jim headed off to start his task and Simon looked back to Paul.

'Gayle next,' Simon instructed.

'I know Gayle from long back, let me call her. I think you need to eliminate her folks.'

'How do I do that? Call them up and tell them that she's missing and ask them if they've seen her? They don't like me very much as it is.'

'We can't let anyone know that Beth is missing. Not yet. Especially if it's Malancy related.'

'You think it's Malancy related?'

'When it comes to you, Si, everything is Malancy related.'

'So what do I say to them?'

'You're the brainy one, think of something. Be subtle. I'm going to call Gayle.'

Paul walked out to get his mobile, leaving Simon alone to think. He needed a way of finding out if Beth was there, or if they'd heard from her, without actually asking them directly. He needed to speak to them about something that they wouldn't be willing to talk about in her presence. That would give him everything he needed, and they'd be none the wiser.

Then it hit him.

He hadn't got a clue what their number was, but luckily he had other ways of contacting someone. Who needed directory enquiries when they had incredible powers?

Simon picked up the landline and thought of her parents. He imagined their house and them in it, and he thought hard across the distance, closing the gap with his mind.

Suddenly the ringing tone sounded in his ear and he knew he'd been successful. On this anyway.

'Hello?' Alice answered at the other end.

'Hi Mrs... Alice. It's Simon here.'

'Oh hello. How are you?' she asked, although he could sense she wasn't exactly delighted to be hearing from him.

'Really good, thank you. I'm sorry to call you so late but I wanted to ask you something, if you've got a second?'

'Yes, go on. What is it?'

'I wanted to speak to you about Beth's birthday next week.'

'I had hoped she'd come home.' Her response, although not totally pleasant, did give Simon his first inkling that maybe Beth wasn't there.

'I'm sorry Alice, what with work commitments, I don't think we'll have time to make the journey up. But I am planning a surprise party for Beth at our house on the day of her birthday, and I wondered if you'd like to come? It would be nice to see you again and for Beth to celebrate with you.'

'Oh,' Alice said, clearly not expecting this. 'That's very kind of you. I'll have to speak to Frank, but it would be lovely to see Beth on her birthday.'

'Excellent.'

'Would we just come for the evening?'

'Nonsense. We have plenty of room here. I'll get Jim to make up a room for you.'

'Who's Jim?' Alice asked as Simon berated himself for his slip. He'd been careful not to talk too much about his wealth and lifestyle in front of them. He thought they should get to know him first as their son in law before they knew him as a rich and powerful person. It was too late now, though, and they'd know for sure next week. They'd also either be celebrating their daughter's birthday at a very last minute surprise party or they'd be learning the truth about her disappearance. He prayed it was the former.

'Jim is my butler,' Simon replied, quite to the point.

'Butler? You have a butler?'

'Who has a butler?' Simon heard in the background. It was Frank. They were both there, so if Beth had gone home, she couldn't be far.

'Your new son in law,' Alice replied to Frank, as if Simon couldn't hear.

'What's he need a butler for?' Simon heard Frank say.

'I don't know,' Alice argued back.

'It helps with my lifestyle,' Simon cut in. 'I used to spend a lot of time in New York and it was good to have someone here to take care of things.'

'I hope you won't be expecting Beth to spend a lot of time in New York. It's bad enough she lives in London.'

'No, Alice. That's all changed. We now live permanently here.'

'I'm very glad to hear it.'

'He's posher than we thought,' Simon heard Frank mutter through the line.

'Anyway,' Simon said, very eager to change the subject, 'I want to know if you have any ideas as to what I can get her as a present? Has she said anything to you recently?'

'Don't you know? You're her husband,' Alice jabbed at him.

'Yes, but no one can possibly know her better than her parents, surely,' Simon curtly replied.

'Very true. Well, we'll have a think and we'll get back to you.'

That wasn't what Simon wanted. 'Maybe Frank might have an idea?' he said, grasping at straws. 'Could you ask him? I'm eager to get it sorted, it's not long to go now.'

'Fine. Frank, he wants to know what he can get Beth for her birthday.'

'What about a Jaguar of her own?' Frank said in the background. 'Then she could lend it to her dad,' he chuckled. 'If he's got a butler, I'm sure he can afford a nice new car for our little girl.'

'I'm not telling him to get her a car,' Alice said, as if Simon was somehow on hold again.

'Why not? He's good for it, isn't he? What's the point in her marrying into wealth if he's not willing to spoil her a little on her birthday?'

Simon was now positive that Beth wasn't there. She'd never allow them to talk like this in her presence. He just needed to make sure that they'd not heard from her before he could go, but he had to endure their argument about the present buying issue before he could do anything. It was such a waste of precious time.

Finally Alice came back to him. 'Your father in law believes that you should get your wife something very special and something to keep her safe. Like a car.'

'Is that what she said she wanted? Has she spoken to you recently about cars?'

'No, you've just made Frank very jealous flashing that Jaguar of yours about at the weekend.'

Simon made a mental note to hide the Aston Martin when they visited. Then he pushed Alice a little harder. 'Oh yes, he did like it, didn't he. I was so sure that Beth said she'd spoken to you since the weekend about presents. Just thought we could share ideas, that's all.'

'No, as usual, I haven't heard from my daughter since we saw her last. We'd like to speak to her. Do you think you could get her to call us?'

'Of course,' Simon sighed. He'd got his answer. He wasn't sure whether it was good news or bad, but at least it was a definite result. 'Next time I see her. Thanks for the idea of a car. I'll keep it in mind.'

'Don't spoil her too much. Money can ruin people, you know,' Alice stated.

'Let the poor boy spoil her, Ally, it's about time someone in this family had a bit of luck,' Frank argued from the background again, and Simon once again had to listen to their rabbiting. He was now so desperate to hang up.

'You have our address, don't you?' Simon cut in.

'Yes, Beth's given it to us,' Alice snapped, still riled by Frank's meddling. 'Tell her I want to speak to her before next week. You make sure you tell her.'

'As soon as I see her,' Simon replied. 'I better go. See you next week.' He placed down the phone, utterly relieved that it was over.

Paul came back in the room, phone in hand. 'No luck, mate. Gayle's not seen her since Monday.'

'What did you tell her?'

'Don't worry, I just said Beth was going through a few things and I asked if Gayle had heard from her. I kept it vague. Have you called her folks?'

'Yes, she's not there.'

Jim entered the room shaking his head. 'I'm sorry sir, no luck. No taxi has been here at all. I've also checked the security camera footage from last night and there's no sign of any movement. I hope you don't mind.'

'Good thinking, Jim,' Paul encouraged.

'You did it very quickly,' Simon noted.

'I knew who to call. I promise you sir, she didn't get a taxi.'

'How the hell did she get out of here? This house is in the middle of the countryside. The nearest town is miles away,' Paul stated.

'I don't know, sir. But we're not on the right track yet, that's for sure.'

'Let's keep moving. On to the next thing,' Simon ordered. 'Between us, I want to call everyone in the office. They're the only people Beth has had any interaction with since moving down here, someone's got to know something.'

'You got the HR files here?' Paul asked.

'Let me just get my laptop.'

'I'll get the coffee on, Mr Bird. You're in for a long night.'

'Sorry, one more thing Jim, before I forget. Beth's

parents are coming next Wednesday so we need to make up a room for them. And we need to buy Beth a car.'

'Very good sir, I'll get it sorted.'

ELEVEN

Hours had gone by and Beth's mind had been consumed with nothing but questions about what Mr Taylor had told her. After making the shocking statement that in just a few days Malancy could vanish forever, he'd left the room and had left her utterly bewildered as to what the future could hold. She really didn't know what to make of any of it. It was another huge event in her life and Beth was finding it increasingly difficult to cope with anything.

Mostly, Mr Taylor's news made her very sad. Malancy meant everything to Simon. His life would be totally different if it was to vanish. Then she also had to consider how much she'd started to like the idea of having power; despite its capacity being a little overwhelming.

Her brain went round and round in circles as she tried to process yet another colossal situation, but whatever line of thinking she took, it always came back to the same woeful thought: there was nothing she could do about any of it. She was trapped in a room in the middle of nowhere with all magic blocked. She knew Simon would be looking for her, but she also knew that Mr Taylor and his peers would be doing everything in their power to stop him. She was completely stuck. It was all such a torturous waiting game.

Sitting on the edge of the bed, she rubbed her heavy eyes. She was now dizzy with tiredness and stress but there seemed to be so much happening, she just couldn't get any rest.

She'd been delivered multiple different meals that all turned up at the most random of times, and the majority of items placed before her were sugary foods that did nothing but amplify her already edgy state. It also didn't help that the pipes were faulty and she'd been warned that the water in the taps was probably quite unclean. It was okay boiled, but it meant that she was having to rely on cups of tea or cans of coke for beverages as there was nothing else available.

Then, if they weren't delivering her food, she was receiving bits and bobs of clothes to get changed into, or shampoo, shower gel, a brush or comb, she never knew what was coming next. And while she was relieved that she could freshen up, she felt no less a mess in the baggy white T-Shirt and ill-fitting pale jeans that she had little choice but to wear.

She had to get out of this place. Her head was throbbing through lack of sleep and dehydration and, with each passing minute, she was sinking into such deep turmoil, she was struggling to fight with reality.

It was now light outside. Beth had it in her head that it had been light for a while, but she couldn't really remember. She moved herself back into the centre of the bed and lay down again, facing away from the door. Things had been quiet for a while and she was hoping that all the goods had now been delivered and that she'd finally be left to sleep. She let her eyes drop shut and in an instant a dreamy state took over.

Not a minute later, though, once again, to her ever-increasing frustration, the door clicked open and Beth was woken up from her doze. She sighed heavily, feeling the anger rise in her gut, imagining it to be yet another plate of cookies or bowl of fruit. She heard the door close and then heavy footsteps walked over towards her.

She felt the person sit down on the edge of the bed behind her, and she knew it was different to before. Maybe it was that Mr Taylor, she thought, sensing this was more than just another ridiculous delivery.

'Hello Beth! I'm so pleased to see you again,' a slimy voice greeted.

Beth sat up in a panic. She set her eyes on a very unwelcome sight. Her heart started to pound harder than ever as she absorbed the man before her: a terrible man, a man she hoped that she'd never have to see again. It was Damien.

Simon was suffering from lack of sleep himself. They'd spent the previous evening phoning everyone that they could. To make it more manageable, they'd chosen to only call those people in the office who were most likely to have had dealings with Beth, and then to not cause too much suspicion, they'd claimed their call was a survey to find out what the person thought of Bird Consultants' first female director. This then meant that they could delve a little deeper into what relationship the particular individual had with Beth and when the last time they'd spoken to her was.

As strange as it no doubt seemed to the person on the other end of the line, no one would dare to question Simon or Paul, and they knew it. They also hoped that it was random enough to look more like a genuine interest than a cry for help.

Simon had not really cared too much about the exact responses to his questioning, he knew no one was going to criticise his wife's sudden and extreme promotion. He was far more interested in their tone of voice and how they spoke about Beth, searching for clues as to their guilt.

Despite the numerous calls they'd made, though, not one person had heard anything from Beth since she'd left the office on Tuesday, and Simon believed all of them.

After exhausting all options in his elimination plan, and as the early hours of the new day had started creeping in, Paul had insisted that they try to get some sleep. Reluctantly, Simon had headed to a very lonely bed. Sleep didn't come easily and when his tiredness finally did get the better of him, his slumber was far from pleasant. His night was plagued by dreams of Beth.

They'd had this incredible power between them. They were utterly invincible together and could control everything around them. All they had to do was mutter a few words and they could own the world.

It had been such a vivid dream and, when he woke, Simon felt quite ruffled. He needed to find Beth and to stop his imagination running so wild.

It was now Thursday morning and Simon was sitting at the breakfast bar in the kitchen. He picked at the toast that Jim had prepared, but he wasn't the slightest bit hungry.

Paul joined him, taking the stool to his right. Paul had just been in the living room. He'd been calling the office to leave a few instructions as neither of them were planning on doing any sort of work for the foreseeable future. Normal life was most definitely on hold until Beth was back with them and safe, that was non-negotiable.

Jim poured Paul a cup of coffee and he placed it down before him. 'Would you like another coffee, sir?' he then asked Simon.

Simon just shook his head. He was in deep thought. He was searching his mind for all the possible options that were left for them, but he couldn't hide away from the fact that there was only one remaining place that they were still yet to eliminate.

He turned to Paul and Paul just nodded, as if he'd read his mind. They couldn't talk in front of Jim, and they couldn't put off talking about it anymore. They both stood up and headed to the living room, shutting the door behind them.

Simon walked straight over to the window. As silly as it seemed, he couldn't help but check to see if Beth was out there. She might be walking up to the gates, having returned home. He was clinging on to such desperate hope, as futile as it really was.

'It's time,' Paul stated.

'I know. I just...'

'I suppose we should have gone to them straight away.'

'You were the one that said we should keep things on a need to know basis. And we both know you meant specifically to keep things from Malancy HQ.'

'You're right. And I still think we need to keep things from Malancy HQ in general. But we have allies there. People we can trust.'

'You mean Jane?'

'Jane and I go back a long way. I absolutely trust her.'

Simon thought for a second. He actually felt afraid. He knew in his heart that he was more likely than not to find answers at Malancy HQ, but Paul's confession on Tuesday about how much he'd been of interest to them had left Simon feeling particularly bitter about the organisation.

Then there was the timing of it. He had to conclude that Beth's disappearance was somehow linked to her powers. They would surely have presumed that he was going to be looking for her, and all of that made him very suspicious that they were walking into a trap.

He needed time to process it all before stepping in unprepared, but time just wasn't available. All they could do was proceed with caution. And at that moment in time, he was even going to be cautious of Jane, no matter what Paul said.

'Let's get this over with,' he finally stated, suddenly fearing that his procrastination could be costly to Beth. He walked to the door to call for Jim. When it came to travelling into London, Simon always relied on Jim.

'Yes sir?' Jim asked, walking towards the living room.

'We need to go into London. Leaving in five minutes.'

Simon assumed that his order would suffice and he headed to the bathroom across the hallway.

'We can't,' Jim replied, stopping Simon instantly in his tracks.

'I beg your pardon?' Simon asked as Paul came to join them.

'It's not that I'm unwilling, sir, please understand. I was hoping that I could get it sorted before I needed to tell you. I don't want to cause you any more problems.'

'What is it?' Paul nudged.

'It's the cars, sir. All three of them. They've been tampered with. They're not going to go anywhere for the time being. I can fix them, I just need time.'

'What do you mean, tampered with?' Simon asked, opening the front door to take a look. All three of his cars were sitting in the driveway, shining against the morning sun. 'They look fine to me.'

'I was doing my regular checks on them this morning, first thing, but I couldn't get the Lexus to start. A little suspicious, I tried the Jaguar and then the Aston too, but none of them would start. I haven't looked deeper into the issue yet, sir, I knew you'd be waiting for breakfast, and I was hoping I could solve the problem without you ever having to find out about it. I'm sorry, I didn't mean to mislead you, I just didn't want to cause you any further worries.'

'I appreciate your concern, but next time I need to know.'

'Of course, sir.'

'I'll check the cameras, see who the little buggers are,' Paul said, heading to the study.

'Already checked, Mr Bird. There are no disturbances at all. All night. It's the strangest thing.'

Simon and Paul shared a knowing glance. 'Go on then, Simon, you're the man,' Paul said, patting Simon on the back.

'You're good with car mechanics?' Jim asked Simon

with surprise.

Simon knew nothing about cars at all. He didn't need to. With his powers, everything was always taken care of, and he knew that was exactly what Paul had inadvertently referred to.

'He's just having a joke at my expense,' Simon covered, flashing Paul a fierce glare.

'Yeah!' Paul said, forcing a fake chuckle. 'I always wanted my boy to be good with cars. Still, he owns three corkers, so it's not all bad.'

Simon considered his options. Magic was most definitely involved, and he knew that he'd be able to sort it out in an instant, but how could he tell Jim that? He really hadn't got time to deal with this now. He decided to let Jim have a go at fixing the cars, and then the second he took a break or stepped away, Simon would nip out and reverse the spell, whatever it was. That was all he could do. It shouldn't take long.

'Jim, could you get cracking on the cars now? We urgently need to get into London.'

'Of course sir, I'm on the case.'

TWELVE

Beth scrambled off the bed and edged herself to the back of the room, far away from Damien. A flash of the last time she was alone in a room with him appeared in her head and she lost her breath with fear.

'Fair enough,' Damien said, holding up his hands in mock defeat. 'You stay there, I'll stay over here.'

'You went to jail!' she gasped.

'Not quite.'

'How?'

'Things are a little more complicated.'

Beth's heart was pounding and her whole body was shaking.

'I'm here to help the cause,' Damien stated.

'You make it sound like a charitable event.'

'Well it does affect the future of millions of people. Beth, the Malancy is far bigger than you or I, and whether you like it or not, Simon will try to get you to cast that spell. It's all he wants. He's nothing without the Malancy. But you need to consider all the facts.'

'Simon has every right to make the decision however he sees fit. So do I.'

Damien started to chuckle at this. 'You think you get a

say?'

'Well I should do, being that I'm a chosen one.'

'Then why do you think he hasn't told you?' This silenced Beth. It hadn't occurred to her once that Simon could have known about any of it. She'd assumed that he was as much in the know as she was. 'Oh Beth, you really are naïve. But it's kind of sweet.'

Beth tried to focus her brain. She needed to think of whether Simon could have known or not - if there were any clues - but her fuzzy, overwhelmed and seriously tired mind made it impossible for her to process anything.

Then the niggle that she'd been trying to bury away suddenly burst to the front of her thoughts. The words her mother had said, questioning how well she could really know Simon, echoed through her mind. She hadn't wanted to listen, she wanted to believe what was in her heart, but she couldn't deny that there were doubts. How well could she possibly know him in reality? How well did he know her?

'I can see you're a little confused,' Damien said, moving around to make himself comfortable on the end of the bed. 'Let me shed some light on the matter.' Damien took a second to consider his start point. 'First of all, let me clarify something. You need to know that from the very first moment I saw you, I was infatuated. You're so beautiful. And so ambitious. My sort of woman. I was thrilled that you'd started working for Bird Consultants. Well, until I found out that Simon had started to take an interest in you as well. I didn't know straight away that you were the chosen one. It took a while for us to even grow suspicious. But Simon, he must have known all along. Ask Mr Taylor. Simon would have felt the connection immediately. He'd been waiting for you for years, how could he possibly not know when he met you?'

Beth thought back to her first interaction with Simon in the kitchen at the office. Simon had treated her differently to everyone else. Maybe him coming to the kitchen had all been planned. She couldn't believe it, though. If only she could think straight.

'That's why I cast the spell,' Damien continued. 'That's why I turned him into a bird. To keep him away from you. Yes, okay, it was a little harsher than perhaps it needed to be, but I was a jealous man. How do you think I got my hands on bicantomene? And why do you think it took you alerting the Malancy HQ before they did anything? They can track the use of a dark substance before the spell's barely started. Didn't Jane tell you that?'

'That doesn't explain why you tried to rape me!' Beth spat.

'No, it doesn't. And there's no excuse for that. I wanted you to stay away from Simon. I was convinced that you were captivated by his money and power. That's what drives types like us, you can't deny it. I thought if I offered you more then you'd be swayed. But in your flat that day, I saw that you loved him. It hurt me so much. I was raw with jealousy! I didn't know what I was doing, I just wanted you to see how good we could be together. I didn't mean to be forceful, it just happened. But then when I saw how scared you were, I knew I'd messed up. That's when I left. I'm sorry Beth. Really, really sorry.'

Beth was quite taken aback by this confession, and even more so at the apology. She'd never expected it. It also kind of made sense. At least she thought. If only she wasn't struggling so much for clarity.

'Come and sit on the bed,' Damien soothed. Hesitantly, Beth edged forward and sat on the corner of the bed. She'd been feeling a little dizzy on her feet anyway. Damien shuffled along to sit near her, but not too close.

As much as she'd wanted him to disappear, Beth's intrigue was now taking over and she found herself actually willing to listen to more of Damien's tale. She was willing to listen to anything that could help to make sense of what was going on.

'I know this is hard,' he virtually whispered. 'You're not

only having to deal with your sudden found Malant powers, but you've just found out that the man you love, your husband no less, has been lying to you. I can't say that he doesn't care about you. I don't know what he feels. We both know Simon's not a nasty person. You can't blame him for wanting to keep the Malancy alive and for doing everything in his power to make that happen.'

Beth glared at Damien as a new fear trembled her. 'Are you saying that he's just been using me?'

Damien put his hands in the air as if to surrender. 'They're your words, not mine. As I said, I don't know what Simon does and doesn't feel, and it wouldn't be fair of me to speculate. He may feel a connection with you as a bi-product of your destiny, and that could translate to love, I suppose. Who knows? All I do know for sure is that his first priority is to get you to cast the spell with him. We all know it.'

'If that's all true, then why haven't we done the spell yet? What's he waiting for?' Beth was desperate to find the flaw in Damien's story.

A small smile grabbed Damien's lips. 'Tell me this. Was he happy about your powers?' Beth just nodded in reply. 'But I'm guessing that he told you to keep them on the down low until he could speak to Paul Bird?'

'Yes,' Beth hesitantly replied.

'Paul's all part of it. I'm thinking, Paul made a huge deal of it and told you to keep it completely secret as well. Am I right?'

'Yes,' Beth swallowed. The notion that Damien could actually be telling the truth terrified her.

'They were building up to it. They couldn't have known how you were going to react to your powers and the truth of who you are, so they've been playing it up, making a drama of it. The more important you feel it all is, the more likely you are to cast the spell. They're clever people. That's why I needed to get you out of there when I did.'

'You took me?'

'Don't hate me! I waited in your room.'

'How did you get in there? Why don't I remember?'

'I teleported. It was fantastic! It's a ridiculously difficult spell - well probably not for the all-powerful Simon - but there are so many of us working together. There are about two hundred and fifty of us. We all cast a spell together that knocked you out the second you entered the room and then they teleported us both out to this place.'

'Where are we?'

'Scotland.'

'Scotland?' Beth spat.

'We needed it to be far enough away that Simon couldn't easily find us. With that and the fact that we've blocked all magic, we think we're pretty tight. That just goes to show how dangerous Simon is. It takes more than two hundred regular Malants to counteract his magic.'

'Our magic.'

'Of course. You're his equal now. Don't you forget that, Beth. If and when he does appear, don't let him walk all over you.'

'Maybe I agree with him!' Beth snapped. She couldn't bring herself to think badly of him.

'Do you, though? Do you really? Don't you think that the Malancy power has been abused? Do you agree with what Bird Consultants does? What about Simon's rather tainted past?'

It was true, Beth had toiled with the morality of it all, from the second that she'd been told about the secrets. But now was not the time for her to be questioning it. She needed time for her brain to rest before she had any hope of making sense of any of it.

'I'm just going to say it Beth,' Damien suddenly blurted out, coming in closer next to her. 'Don't hate me for saying this. It's the truth. It's my truth. I don't expect anything from you other than acceptance. Okay?'

Beth just regarded Damien with confusion. Her brain was still reeling at the idea that Simon had been using her and she really just wanted Damien to leave. She wanted to wallow in self-pity for a while at the possibility of her marriage being a sham. She wanted a few moments to process all this new information.

'I was encouraged to marry you,' Damien started. 'The spell to continue the Malancy wouldn't have been possible to cast under the conditions of that contract. But I have to admit, I didn't put up much of a fight. The truth is Beth...' Damien glared into her eyes with deep sincerity. 'I've fallen in love with you.'

This was too much for Beth's tired ears and tears sprung into her eyes. She wanted to hate him and to slap him for insulting her but she was actually softening. He was becoming more agreeable the more that she sat with him. Despite all of her instincts telling her not to trust him, every word he'd uttered had made nothing but perfect sense. And she was far too exhausted to question any of it.

'I can't take this Damien. I'm just so tired. I just want to sleep. Every time I try to, though, you or some other bloody inconsiderate idiot walks in the room and disturbs me. Please can I sleep?'

'I'm so sorry, Beth. Of course. Here, I've got some sleeping pills with me.' Damien pulled a little food bag out of his jeans pocket that contained a few white pills.

'I don't like the look of them.'

'Don't be silly,' Damien soothed, picking up the half empty can of coke that Beth had left on the bedside table. 'Ever since you dumped me at the altar, I haven't been sleeping so well either.' She didn't know why, but his made her feel wretched. 'I don't blame you. I deserved it.' Damien grabbed two pills from the bag and handed them to Beth. 'Two should knock you out for hours.'

'I don't know. What if something happens?'

'Like what? You have two hundred and fifty Malants out there all looking out for your best interests; and one of them is in love with you.' For a moment Beth's heart sang as she thought he meant Simon. Then she realised that he meant himself and she looked down to the pills in his hand with disappointment. The idea of shutting all the world away suddenly seemed more appealing than ever. 'I promise, I'll wait outside and I won't move until you wake up. You just knock on that door when you're ready for food and I'll take care of everything.'

'I don't know.' Beth shook her head, but she was clearly weakening.

'I swear, Beth, nothing bad is going to happen to you. You'll see things far more clearly when you've had some rest.'

The word rest echoed in Beth's ears. It was all that she desired. 'I can sleep without the pills, Damien, if you just promise I won't be disturbed.'

'No can do, sorry. In about fifteen minutes they're about to start preparation for the next five hundred years. I can't tell you what it's all about, but it will be very noisy. You'll never sleep without a little help.'

Everything in her body was trying to warn her off taking these pills, but her mind was giving in, it so desperately needed sleep. She couldn't take the thought of any more disturbances. She grabbed both the pills quickly, without overthinking it anymore, and she washed them down with the cola.

'There you go. Now just rest your head and hopefully sleep will come.'

'Okay.' Beth crawled across the bed and lay her head on the pillow. She went to close her eyes when a question suddenly niggled her mind. 'Can I ask you something?'

'Anything.'

'How come you're not in jail? Did George Malant sort it out?'

'No.'

'Who then?'

'Who do you think? The most powerful person of them all,' Damien replied with a smile. 'Jane Parker.'

THIRTEEN

Beth rolled onto her back and sighed. She couldn't sleep. Damien's pills hadn't helped at all; if anything they'd made her even more alert. And now, as he'd warned her, it sounded like a brass band was playing in the next room.

Her mind flicked to Simon. Was he really a liar? Had he really been using her? It seemed so hard to believe. Even if he had known all along, no one could fake such a connection to another person, surely?

Then she thought to how he was her husband. Lie or not, she had promised to always be there for him and she'd meant it. If he desired to keep the Malancy alive, then who was she to argue? She wasn't a Malant, it wasn't really fair that she have an equal say. Simon had spent a lifetime with his powers, he'd built a business around them; they were all he knew. It wouldn't be right for her to refuse him that future.

Despite what Damien and Mr Taylor believed, despite the force of hundreds of Malants against him, Beth knew Simon would be looking for her, and she knew that his exceptional powers would be hard to contend with. Not only because of their relationship, but because the future of the Malancy was being threatened. She just had to sit tight and wait.

Feeling twitchy and uncomfortable, she got up and lapped the room a few times. Her body ached. A heady mixture of exhaustion and stimulation, lack of hydration, and an overwhelming anvil of information all weighed down on her and she could no longer even recognise her own thoughts. Reality seemed so far away.

She tried to lie down again, but the combination of instruments, shouting and banging from somewhere in the building was pounding against her already throbbing head. She put her hands over her ears, but it was no good. She didn't know how long she'd now been awake, but it was far too long. She had to get some sleep.

Hours must have gone by, and the noise finally stopped. Beth was curled up in a tight ball in the middle of the bed with tears blurring her eyes. Every muscle in her body was tensed up against the torment around her, and although it finally seemed quiet, she didn't know if she could trust it.

She waited in the same taut position, expecting it to start all over again, but as the silence stretched out and the peace seemed to settle, she slowly began to relax.

She unfurled herself across the bed, feeling her heart calm down and her muscles loosen. Without even having to try, without any hesitation at all, she found herself quickly drifting off, sleep finally having its way.

Sure enough, though, just as she started to dream, the door clicked open again and she was yanked back to reality.

'What now!' she screamed across the room, sitting up to find Mr Taylor bringing his chair in.

'That's not very polite, Bethany,' he said as he placed his seat down in the exact same spot as last time.

'Neither is disturbing someone every time they fall asleep. What's wrong with you people?'

'I can leave if you want. But I won't be back for a

while. Don't you have questions that you'd like me to answer? Or should I just go?'

Beth glared fiercely at Mr Taylor. She really wanted to tell him to get lost so that she could properly get some peace and quiet, but she couldn't let this chance go. He was the only one who could help clear the cloud of confusion that was giving her such a headache. It was a close call, but her need for answers just about outweighed her need for sleep. But it would have to be quick.

'Okay, stay,' she said, shuffling herself to the end of the bed to face him square on.

'Why, thank you,' he smirked as he took his seat. 'I take it you've been mulling things over since our last chat?'

'No, I've been far too busy,' Beth sarcastically scowled.

'How do you feel about it all?' he continued, ignoring her snap.

'Why do you care?'

'Your future peace of mind is important. We're not monsters.'

'What does that mean?'

'It's inevitable that when the Malancy has ended, you're going to feel partially to blame.'

'How can I be to blame?' Beth squealed, enraged by his accusation. 'You've kidnapped me and you're holding me against my will. I'm the last person in the world to blame for any of this.'

'You will feel guilty. Trust me, Bethany, that's how human emotion works. When you see Mr Bird powerless you'll look back and question all of the things that you could have done and didn't.'

'What can I do? I'm trapped.'

'That's the point. You can do nothing, but you'll feel guilty nevertheless.'

'That's such a stupid thing to say. I don't want to talk about this anymore, it's ridiculous. Can we get to my questions?'

Mr Taylor sighed. He was clearly miffed by Beth's

dismissive response to his concern. He hesitated for a moment, studying her. 'Very well.'

'Damien told me that Simon knows all about this. That he's known all along.'

Again, there was a small pause before Mr Taylor responded. 'Did he?'

'Is it true?'

'Does it matter?'

'Of course it bloody well matters!'

'Mr Bird is never going to want to lose his powers, and who could blame him? But do we always know what's best for us?'

'So he does know?'

'Do his powers make him happy?'

'Answer the question!' Beth demanded, anger rising within her.

'I am, you just don't know it yet.' For the first time Mr Taylor appeared to be losing his cool, ever so slightly. 'Work with me, I will give you everything you need to know.'

Beth sighed heavily. 'I guess I have no choice. What was your question again?'

'Do Mr Bird's powers make him happy?'

'Of course they do.'

'Do they?' Mr Taylor pushed.

'Why wouldn't they?'

'Think carefully Bethany. Do Mr Bird's powers make him happy?'

Beth did as requested and took a moment. She tried to cast her mind back to when she had last seen Simon. It felt like decades ago. Recalling her memories of him was getting harder as the tiredness was starting to trick her brain, but she eventually decided that she'd never seen him unhappy with his powers. He'd said they could be fun. But then she remembered his troubled upbringing and how he'd struggled to fit in. It wasn't much different twenty years on.

She'd felt first hand how awful it was to have people be physically chilled by your presence. He'd had a lifetime of that. The only difference that he'd ever known was Beth. In fact the truth was that Simon's powers had affected every relationship that he'd ever had, with anyone. His powers had controlled his whole life in one way or another. Until he'd met her, he hadn't been happy at all.

'No,' she replied, much calmer now.

'He might think he's happy now, but he's spent the last three decades in the most miserable state. Trust me, we witnessed it.'

'So what are you saying?'

'Mr Bird's powers are all he knows. He doesn't know any other way. Of course he's going to do everything he can to hold on to them. Anyone in his situation would. But if he could step out of his own shoes for a second and see things from your perspective, would he still want his powers? Given the choice, would you tell him that he had to keep hold of them?'

Beth thought hard about this question. She had to admit, a life without the Malancy wouldn't be so bad. To have a normal husband that was never in danger of turning into a bird; it was quite an inviting prospect. She looked to Mr Taylor. 'I don't suppose Mr Bird needs his powers. They have been quite a curse to him at times. In his own words.'

'I know you love Simon, and you'd do anything for him, but sometimes we need to do things for our loved ones that are the best for them and not necessarily what they want. Do you understand?'

'But if I agree with you, then it means that Simon loses all he knows. He'd be out of business.'

Mr Taylor smiled at this. 'Mr Bird's powers are purely physical. They don't affect his brain. He's one of the most intelligent men that I've ever come across. His ability to work through problems is outstanding; he can take his hand to anything. Just think, a life without powers would open up his world and offer him far more than he's got now. That's the true gift.'

'How?'

'With a mind like Mr Bird's he could do anything. He could go to university, like he always wanted. I think he's wealthy enough not to work for a while, don't you? He and Mr Bird senior.'

'I'd be out of a job too!' Beth suddenly realised. 'We all would.'

'Not for long. Entrepreneurs like you Birds always land on your feet. I could see Bird Consultants diversifying and opening up as a more legitimate consultancy. Couldn't you? And wouldn't that be better?'

Beth felt a little tinge of excitement at the prospect of starting up a new company with Simon. Rather than being in charge of admin, she could be joint CEO and they could rule together.

Mr Taylor continued, 'The irony is that Mr Bird's Malant abilities have actually been holding him back. All we're doing is setting him free. Him and many Malants alike. It's the moral thing to do.'

That one word – moral – pricked up Beth's ears. This was the moral decision. Simon would be far better off. Of course he wouldn't want it, but she would be there to help him start his new life. Their new life. This was the best thing for both of them, she was sure of it.

The topic of morality led Beth to a new question. 'Is it true Jane Parker is behind all of this?'

Mr Taylor paused again, revealing nothing as to what he was thinking. 'Something else Damien told you?'

'Yes.'

'Jane has been instrumental to our plans, it's true. I told you, we have the complete backing of the head of the Malancy, and there are many other people from Headquarters who are also involved.'

'She wants the Malancy to end as well? But wouldn't that put her out of a job too?'

'George Malant is a good man and he is ensuring that all employees of the Malancy government will be well looked after.'

Beth sighed as the pieces of the jigsaw finally started to slot together. Her body began to relax as she reasoned that her being trapped in that room wasn't such a bad thing after all. It could all work out for the best. 'How much longer have we got to wait?' she asked.

'Six days. In six days this will all be over. Six pm next Wednesday is the deadline and then we'll take you back home and you can continue with your life. We won't disturb you ever again, you have my word.'

'I have to stay here for another week?' Beth's heart sank.

'Perhaps we could arrange a television or something? Shall I see what we can do? Your comfort is our prime concern.'

'Then why won't you at least let me sleep?'

'I can do that. I'll leave you now. I'm sure the preparation downstairs won't be too loud.'

'What preparation?' Before she'd finished her question, the shouting and playing commenced again. 'Can you tell them to shut up? Just for a little bit?'

'I wish I could, but their practise is vital. Don't worry, you'll have plenty of time to rest properly soon. Just relax for now. I'll see about that television.'

* * *

Back down in the south of England, Simon was pacing around his living room. Jim had spent hours meddling with the cars, but there was still no resolution. Not surprisingly, he'd been unable to find a single problem with any of them and his stubbornness was getting irritating.

'He's on the phone again!' Simon hissed from the window.

Paul sat more casually on the settee. 'It must be his cousin again.'

'I don't care how much of a car genius he is, we both know he's never going to be able to fix them.'

'What are we supposed to do?'

'If only he'd have a break. Who can go that long without needing the toilet?'

'Simon, calm down.'

'No! Beth's life could be in danger and we're stuck here. It's been long enough now. What about getting a taxi?'

'You need to get your hands on those cars, Simon. This has to be related.'

'Don't you think I know that? I should have been able to sort it out by now. His determination is really starting to piss me off.'

'Be grateful that you've got such a dedicated butler.'

'Dedicated or just plain difficult?'

'You've taken him out, what, three bottles of water. He'll definitely need the loo soon.'

Simon took a deep breath. 'Sod this, I can't take it anymore.'

'Don't do anything you'll regret!' Paul shouted, but Simon was already heading out the front door.

'How's it going, Jim?' Simon asked as he approached the Lexus. Jim had his head buried in the bonnet.

'I'm getting there, sir. Things are slowly starting to make sense. Someone was very keen to keep you at home, that's for sure.'

'Come and have a break,' Simon suggested.

'It's fine sir, I know how eager you are to get to the city.'

'It's too much now, Jim. You need a break.'

'I'm fine, sir.'

'It's not a request. Take a break.'

'I'm putting the kettle on!' Paul shouted, suddenly appearing at the door.

'But sir...'

'I mean it, Jim. I want you to take a break.'

'I think I've cracked it.' Jim suddenly jumped into the driver's seat. Within seconds the engine started.

'You did it?' Simon queried with total confusion.

'I can't explain it. I tinkered enough and eventually it all fell into place. Just like magic.'

'How true,' Simon muttered. 'Go clean yourself up then, we've got to get on the road.'

'No time for a cup of tea?' Jim enquired as he closed the bonnet, much to Simon's horror. 'I'm just kidding, sir. I'll be ready in a few minutes.'

Jim disappeared into the house and Simon turned to Paul with relief. 'Well then?' Paul asked.

Simon moved over to the Aston Martin and gently placed his hand on the bonnet. He could feel a magic within it. 'It's Malant interference, that's definite.'

'What sort of magic?'

'This is so weird. It's very simple magic. It's just enough to stop a non-Malant turning on the engine. Any Malant could have fixed it, it would hardly be an obstacle.'

'But why?'

'Maybe it's not related to Beth's disappearance after all. Maybe it was just a prank. Somebody scared of me.'

'Why did no one appear on the cameras then?'

'You could do this sort of spell long distance, if you so desired.'

'I don't know, Si, let's keep our minds open on this one.'

'At this moment, I think I'm open to anything.'

Paul nodded. 'I've just got to take a leak and then I'll be ready to go.'

As Paul headed into the house, Simon moved to his Jaguar. He placed his hand on the bonnet and took away the magic. He couldn't figure out how Jim had fixed it; unless the spell had somehow worn away. There was no time to think over that now, though. All that mattered was getting Beth back, and his car troubles were clearly not giving him any clues.

Jim reappeared in a change of clothes, back to his much smarter self. 'I'm ready whenever you are, sir.'

'We're just waiting for Paul.'

Jim nodded and moved towards the Lexus. He patted the bonnet as if it was a well behaved pet and then looked to Simon hesitantly. 'I don't want to talk out of turn sir, but can I make a suggestion?'

'Of course.'

'You may have only known Mrs Bird for a short while, but it's hard not to notice how close you two are. It's obvious that there's a significant connection between you.' Jim really emphasised the word connection and Simon listened intently. 'I can't help but think that the answer to her disappearance is somehow deep within you. Maybe if you look inside yourself, deep, deep inside yourself, you might find what you're looking for. People never just vanish. I bet there's a clue that's so obvious, perhaps even too obvious to see. Deep, deep down inside yourself.'

'Are we ready guys?' Paul said as he shut the front door.

'Yeah,' Simon replied, distracted. Jim's words had struck a chord with him. Maybe he did know more than he cared to think about. Maybe Beth had given him a clue.

'You coming, Si?' Paul asked, getting in the back of the car.

'Yeah.'

'Whereabouts are we going then?' Jim asked as the gates slowly opened.

'London Bridge please,' Paul answered, seeing Simon still lost in a trance. 'You all right, Si?'

'Yes. Of course. Just thinking about Beth.'

'Let's hope we get some answers in the next few hours.'

'Do you think we should call Jane to let her know we're coming?' Simon suggested.

'Not at all. She'll always be happy to see us. Besides, if

she doesn't know we're coming, no one else can either.'

'Good point. We need the upper hand now more than ever.'

FOURTEEN

Beth had managed a whole three minutes of sleep this time before Damien brought her back to reality again with his presence.

'This is getting ridiculous!' Beth hissed as Damien sat down on the bed next to her. 'Can't you give me some time to rest? Just an hour. I'd give anything for an hour.'

'I gave you sleeping pills!' Damien argued in his defence.

Beth just shook her head. 'What do you want?'

'Just to see how you're doing.'

'I'm pissed off as no one will let me sleep!'

'Mr Taylor said you had a good talk.'

'So?'

'He's really worried about you, you know.'

'That's nice.'

'And so am I.'

'Then let me sleep and I'll be fine.' Beth threw herself back on the pillow and tried to block Damien out.

'I know that Mr Taylor asked you to consider the future. How you might blame yourself. But there are other things you need to think about as well.'

'I don't care.'

'I'm worried how you're going to handle things after the Malancy has gone. Your life is never going to be the same again.' Beth rolled her eyes at how obvious this was. 'Simon's going to be livid, you know. But more than that.' Damien hesitated. 'I think you need to consider the fact that your marriage might be over after this.'

Beth sat up and glared at Damien, anger and fear striking through her like lightning. 'How dare you!'

'I hate to say it, Beth. I don't want to hurt you but I think you need to be prepared for the fact that your use to Simon will have gone.'

'My use?'

'Like I said to you earlier, I don't know how Simon feels, no one can but him; but tread carefully. When he loses his power, your relationship is not going to be the same.'

'You don't know Simon. He would never just use someone.'

'I hate to say this Beth but I've known Simon since I was at school, you've only known him for a few weeks. He's used people all his life. That's how he grew his business. He once forced a man to recommend Bird Consultants or he threatened to scar the man's wife for life.'

'You mean the lady who wanted the necklace?'

'He told you?' Damien looked quite surprised.

'Of course. We're honest with each other.'

'Are you sure about that?'

Beth wanted to argue but it was becoming increasingly difficult. Her negative thoughts were casting too many shadows and she was finding it hard to hold on to any positivity.

Her mother's words echoed in her mind again. Maybe it really had been far too soon for them to get married. She wanted the romantic dream but the stark reality was so much easier to believe. Whatever was going on, there was no question that things weren't as Simon had led her to believe. That she was sure of.

Tears sprung into her blood shot eyes. She felt like an emotional wreck. She moved to the side of the bed, away from Damien's stare, and sobbed.

'Don't cry,' he said, shuffling along to put his arm around her. 'There's no need to cry.'

'No need to cry? Nothing is as it seemed.'

'Is that so bad?'

'Yes! If what you say is true, then I've lost my husband, my job, my house; everything.'

'You haven't lost anything. You've gained. You gained the knowledge that your so called husband is a user and a liar. You've realised that you have the ability to be a director of a company, but you get to start one with a moral standing. And as for living, there's always a spare room at my house.'

'Shut up, Damien,' Beth said, knocking his arm away. 'How am I supposed to start up my own company? I have just a few weeks' experience, with no money and no idea what I'm doing. I shouldn't be in that stupid job.'

'I think you're forgetting that you have a husband who's a millionaire.'

'It's never been about the money, I don't care about that.'

'But no matter what, half of it is now yours.'

Beth stood up as she felt her heart break at the idea of no longer having Simon in her life. Her tears were relentless and she moved over to the window. She needed some space from Damien, he was confusing her far too much. She had to think clearly. Was Simon really using her?

She thought about their marriage. If he really was intending to leave her then wouldn't he have stopped her having access to his money? Maybe he already had? Or maybe he never intended on the Malancy being a threat and he'd assumed that they'd just easily cast the spell and then they could stay married? He did yearn for companionship and she was the only one who could stand to be around him.

Her sob deepened as she realised that whichever way she looked at it, he was still using her. It just couldn't be true.

'Beth, please,' Damien said, heading towards her.

'No!' she ordered. 'Just give me a minute.'

Damien sat back down on the bed.

Beth looked out at the sun drenched hills ahead of her. She hated the sight of grass. Her London escape was supposed to take her away from all that, but she suddenly feared that no matter where life would lead her, she was inevitably doomed to failure.

She'd been foolish enough to believe that the last few weeks had been the best of her life, that she was somehow finding herself. But the reality of the dark world that she'd actually entered made her now feel more lost than ever.

Sitting in the back of the car, Simon had barely said a word since Jim had spoken with him. Jim had been right, Simon did feel a connection with Beth, one he'd never thought possible. Simon had been so determined to look at the rest of the world for answers, he'd failed to look inside himself at all. He knew her. Despite the fact that they'd only met a couple of months before, he really knew her. They had a connection so deep, it was as if they'd always been destined to meet. He couldn't explain it. Maybe, just maybe, there was something that he hadn't thought of yet that could help them solve this mystery.

He let himself relax a little and he put his mind to his wife. Closing his eyes to properly focus, he let all other thoughts fade away until there was nothing but Beth left. He thought to her beauty and her alluring scent, then he thought to her warmth, and how he'd grown to feel so close to her in recent days. How them getting married had changed so much of both their lives. He thought of their first meeting and how she'd been so carefree in the way that she'd spoken to him. Then his email to her and how she'd come up especially to see him in his office.

His mind moved on to consider every glance they'd shared and every laugh they'd enjoyed together. Their first date, their first kiss, the first time that he told her he loved her. As the intensity of her image grew wildly in his head, he could feel a vibrancy building in his chest.

Then, out of nowhere, she appeared in his mind like a film. It was like he was looking at live imagery of her, more than just a memory. Then he realised, that was exactly what he was doing. He could see her exactly as she was at that very moment. He'd located her.

'Stop the car!' he shouted.

'What's the matter?' Paul asked with great concern.

'Pull over!'

'We're on the motorway, sir,' Jim replied.

'I don't care. Let me out!'

'What is it?' Paul queried with urgency.

'I can see her. I've just seen her.'

'What do you mean?' Paul urged. Simon opened his mouth to respond, but catching Jim in his sight he knew he could say no more.

'I know where she is. It's just an instinct, but...'

'Where we going?' Paul asked, ready to support his nephew as Jim pulled into the hard shoulder and stopped the car.

'No, Paul. I have to go now. Just go home and I'll be in touch.' With that Simon jumped out the car away from the traffic and ran as fast as he could into the field alongside the road. He ran far away from the car, so deep into the grass, so determined to be out of clear view. Then he dropped to his knees.

He could see a farmhouse ahead of him and he knew that he'd have to be quick before anyone noticed that he was there.

He focussed hard again and breathed in Beth's essence. He had to concentrate, he had to see her again; he needed this to end. She appeared again in his head, so vividly.

He gasped as he saw how tired and sad she looked. She had big bags under her eyes and her cheeks were so puffy from where she'd been crying. It wounded him that she seemed so downtrodden, he just prayed that she was at least unharmed.

He turned his mind to where she was. She was staring out a window. He followed her gaze and saw that she was looking out at hills. It gave nothing away, it could be anywhere.

Knowing he needed more, he opened up his mind. He pulled back from her location, like zooming out on Google Maps, and he took in her complete surroundings. Then he saw where she was. She was in Scotland. The Scottish Highlands to be more precise.

It didn't matter what her exact coordinates were because Simon knew exactly what he needed to do. He hadn't done it in years, and last time it had taken away all of his strength, but even if he had to catch his breath upon arrival, it was still by far the quickest way that he was ever going to be with her. He had to get to her.

Simon stood up tall and looked around. There were trees in the distance, but he needed to work fast. In the middle of all the farmland, he knew there was no hope of finding a stone. His best bet now was the earth itself.

He knelt back down and pulled away at the grass, finding the hard soil below. He dug his fingers into the earth as best he could, trying to tap into its power. Then he closed his eyes.

He focussed hard on the large house that Beth was kept in. He thought to the building as he converged all of his emotions together and channelled the essence from the soil that now coated his hands. He churned all of the power into a tight ball in his chest, tensing every muscle in his body, not leaving one pore to breathe freely, as he utilised every element that he could.

The earth glowed red around him as the greatest spell

known to the Malancy started to work. Then Simon's arms, torso, legs and head all soaked up the radiance of the power until he was a scorching flame of fire. He burned vibrantly, a glowing beam lighting up the entire field, until suddenly he vanished.

With a flash, Simon found himself outside the house that Beth was in. He stood up quickly to absorb his surroundings, quickly realising, to his horror, that he was at the front of the building. He'd meant to go around the back. He'd meant to be more surreptitious. He was so out of practice, and he'd been so desperate to get here so quickly.

He fought for his strength, suddenly fearful of how conspicuous he was, but the spell had left him with nothing. He fell to the floor, barely conscious.

Within seconds, dozens of men circled around him. He battled with his mind, trying to make sense of how many boots were racing before his eyes, but there was nothing he could do. He'd used everything he'd got to find his way to Beth.

He tried to concentrate on everything that he could, to take in any clues as to who was there and what they wanted, but the exhaustion was beating him.

As the army picked him up and dragged him towards to the house, Simon lost his battle, and the last thing he saw was a smartly dressed man greeting them at the door.

FIFTEEN

'Come back and sit next to me,' Damien said, patting the bed to his side. Beth turned around, all out of tears, and slowly did as requested. 'I hate to see you like this,' he said as he curled her hair behind her ears.

'Don't!' she warned, knocking his hand away.

'Sorry!' He put his hands up as if to surrender. 'Look, I've made some terrible mistakes when it comes to you and I... I need you to see the good I meant.' Beth looked to the floor and sighed. She was fed up of listening to him now, all she wanted was peace and quiet. 'If you remember, that day when I visited your flat, I actually came with a proposal.'

Beth shook her head, actually quite sickened by the memory of that fateful day. 'All I remember is that you tried to rape me.'

'I've explained that. That wasn't my intention. You just get under my skin. You drive me wild, Beth. But nothing like that will ever happen again. Seeing the fear in your eyes was a sobering experience. I've learnt to control myself far better now.'

'You shouldn't need to see fear to know you're doing wrong,' Beth corrected.

'I actually came to your flat to offer you a job,' Damien continued, seeming to have not heard her last comment. 'I wanted you to join me on the board of my new company.'

'Are you serious?' Beth glared at him.

'Never been more so.'

'I think what you actually said was, I could sit side by side with you, or wherever else I wanted,' Beth cringed.

'I thought that's what you wanted to hear. I thought we were alike.'

'Well we're not.'

'Actually we are. I was right from the very beginning. You're ambitious, aren't you?' Beth shrugged. 'You want to succeed just as much as I do. I can see it in your eyes, you're hungry for it. Well how about no more back scratching, but instead we tackle the future together, fifty fifty?'

'I'm not going into business with you.'

'You think you're going into business with Simon?'

'Possibly.'

'He's a loner, Beth. Always has been.'

'Oh yeah, what about Paul?'

'That's different, he's family.'

'So am I!' Beth stated, although as soon as the words came out, they hurt her.

Damien just raised his eyebrows and Beth could feel the sting of tears rising up once more.

'Beth, darling, please don't cry.' Damien pulled her in next to him and she let him. She cried on to his shoulder and for the first time she didn't fight it. 'Whatever happens, you've got me. We can be friends, can't we? I know what it's like to have the bug, to have the need to succeed. I think I know you better than you realise.'

'Mr Rock,' a black clad man said, suddenly bursting into Beth's prison.

'What is it?' Damien asked, clearly unhappy with the disturbance.

'We need you.'

'Sorry Beth,' Damien sighed. He wiped a tear away from her cheek with his finger, sending shudders through her. She needed to start thinking clearly. What was she doing letting Damien comfort her? Simon was the one who should be comforting her.

Damien left the room and Beth remained on the side of the bed, expecting his disappearance to be short term. She waited and waited, her tears slowly drying up, but nothing happened.

What felt like an age went by and still no one came back into the room. Then she realised it could finally be time for her to get some sleep. Whatever he'd been called for, it had brought with it absolute silence, and Beth needed to make the most of this opportunity.

She curled up in the centre of the bed, laying her head firmly against the pillow, and she closed her eyes. Despite her desperate need for sleep, she was so ready for some sort of disturbance, it made it hard for her to relax. After a few minutes, though, she eventually drifted off and dreams of Simon flooded her mind.

They were together, holding hands. They were powerful, really powerful, as if nothing could stop them.

'Beth.' The sound of her name cut through her dream like a knife and she was yanked right back to reality. 'Wake up.' The annoying interference of Damien caused her body to tense up, but she was too tired to react. She just groaned. She hadn't got a clue as to how long she'd been asleep, but it didn't feel like very long. 'We need to talk.'

'What now?' she sighed, still refusing to wake up properly.

'We need to be quiet and we need to be quick,' he warned in hushed tones.

'What are you talking about?' Beth opened her eyes to look at him, suddenly curious. She saw him holding a document. 'What's that?'

'I've just found out something terrible. But I'm going to look after you. This contract will look after you.'

'Contract?' Beth looked again at the document in his hand. She sat up properly, trying to comprehend the new situation that had now presented itself out of the blue. Just like the contract before her almost marriage to him, the paper in his hand wielded a slight golden tinge.

'No one knows I've got this. I've just put it together. You have to sign in.'

'Oh no! I'm not signing any more of those things.'

'You don't understand. Your life is in danger.'

'What are you going on about?'

'I wasn't supposed to find this out, but I just overheard some of the men talking. I didn't know, you have to believe me. After Wednesday, after all of this is over with, they're not going to let you go. They're going to kill you.'

'What?!' The blood drained out of Beth's face as the revelation shook her. 'Oh my God! Am I safe now? Why are they waiting until Wednesday? What's stopping them from just killing me now?'

'They can't kill a chosen one before the deadline. They don't know for sure what will happen. They're worried that your death might cause the spell to be cast anyway, so they can't take the risk. You're safe until six o'clock on Wednesday, but after that, they'll have no purpose for you anymore. It's better for them to just get rid of you.'

'But Mr Taylor said-'

'Of course he did. What else was he going to say?'

'You have to help me get out of here,' Beth gasped, jumping off the bed.

'There's no way out, Beth. Trust me. They have this place pretty well covered. But what they don't have are the skills of a Bird Consultants employee. Or ex-employee... as I well deserved.'

'What do you mean?'

'In this contract it states that after Wednesday, anyone who tries to take your life or cause you long term physical harm will find the results turn on themselves.'

'What? Are you saying that if someone tries to stab me,

they'll end up stabbing themselves?'

'Exactly.'

'Damien, that's horrible.'

'So is deciding to take your life.'

'I didn't think that you could do that. I thought the contracts had to be ethical.'

'The contracts can be whatever I make them. The ethics come from Simon and the Malancy government. But even with his uppity moral standing, I hardly think Simon would have an issue with this. I mean, he might not love you, but he'd never want to see you harmed.' This comment jabbed Beth right in the heart. 'And if the Malancy government ever tried to overturn it, they'd have to admit that they wanted to kill you. I know those at the top are against you, but still, not everyone's corrupt. This would put their actions in the public eye.'

'So this would make me safe, once and for all?'

'Yes Beth. I promise.'

'Can I have a look?'

'Just sign it here.' Damien quickly flicked through to the last page before holding out a pen for her to use.

'I want to read it.'

'There's no time, Beth. They're coming. If they find out I've got this contract before you sign it, they'll rip it up. They'll stop me seeing you. This is your only chance at survival.'

'But I-'

'Beth, they're coming.'

Just then, Beth heard footsteps behind the door. She looked to Damien, her heart pounding with fear. 'This is your last chance at living, Beth.' She heard the door handle slowly turn and her breathing extinguished. With no ability to think straight and her body pounding with exhaustion, dehydration and now terror, she grabbed the pen from Damien's hand. 'Are you sure?'

'This contract is the only thing that can save you. You must sign it.'

The handle had now completely rotated and the door was creaking open. With her whole body shaking, Beth knew she had no more time. She signed her name on the dotted line.

'Is everything okay in here, Mr Rock?' the man at the door asked. 'It's gone very quiet.'

Damien grabbed the document and shoved it under the duvet. 'Everything's just perfect, thank you,' he nodded.

'Are you sure?'

'Positive. I'm just keeping Beth entertained, as Mr Taylor requested.'

'Very well.' The man left them, shutting the door tightly behind him, and they both sighed with relief.

Damien pulled the document up from under the sheets. It was now glowing a golden light and had completely sealed itself in a film that rendered it operational. There was no going back.

'You're safe now. Stop worrying.'

'How can I not worry? I just want to get out of here. I just want to be able to clear my head and get back to my old self.'

'Well I have to partly apologise for your lack of sleep. Or at least apologise on behalf of my rather spiteful colleagues. It seems that they've played a rather nasty trick on us. They swapped the sleeping pills that I thought I was giving to you for caffeine pills. I'm so sorry.'

Beth shook her head. 'At least that explains how alert they made me.' She couldn't help but feel hurt. These people, who didn't even know her, were being so cruel. What had she done to them? It wasn't her fault that she was a chosen one. She wasn't even a real threat to them.

'I have the right pills now. Let me give them to you. Oh and I do have a little bit of good news for a change: the pipes have been fixed.' He pointed to a glass of water sitting on the bedside table.

Beth immediately grabbed it, she was so thirsty. She knocked back the whole glass in seconds. 'Thank you.'

'That was supposed to be for your pills,' Damien smirked. He took the glass to the door and asked someone outside to bring them another one. 'We'll let you get some sleep now,' Damien whispered, walking back over to Beth.

A man came in and placed another glass of water on the bedside table and Damien pulled out a small food bag full of white pills from his jeans pocket.

'I don't need sleeping pills.'

'Do you want to sleep?' Damien asked.

'I think you know the answer to that.'

'Then I promise you, these pills are exactly what you want. It's going to be noisy again. They'll help you block everything out.'

He took two out of the bag and gave them to Beth. She looked at them and in that instance she knew she just didn't care anymore. Sleep, awake, here or somewhere else, the pain inside of her was still going to throb. She'd never felt so low and unhappy. She picked up the water and swallowed the pills all in one go.

'Come on then, let's get you comfy.' Damien picked up the corner of the duvet.

'Is it clean to get under?' Beth asked, sure that the last person to sleep in the bed must be about two hundred by now.

'Of course it is. It's just the natural charm of the place.'

Beth, reluctant but also desperate for rest, moved herself under the duvet. She curled up in a ball and placed her head down on the pillow.

'Sleep tight now, Beth. We won't be far. We'll see you soon.'

SIXTEEN

Nearly a whole day passed by and both Beth and Simon remained unconscious. Then, as afternoon melted into evening, Simon finally stirred.

He opened his heavy eyes, trying to wake himself up, trying to counteract the grogginess that weighed down on him. He sat up and looked around, suddenly aware that he recognised nothing. His surroundings were deeply old fashioned, like a bedroom at some terrible museum.

He got up off the bed, very confused, and headed to the window to get a better idea of where he could be. He saw the lush greenery of the highlands ahead of him and his mind flashed to Beth.

Of course, he'd teleported! It all came back to him like a vivid dream. This was the view that he'd seen through her eyes. He was near her.

He turned around and found a door. He slowly edged over to it, the weariness from the teleport still impeding him. He placed his hand on the knob but it wouldn't budge. As mere locked doors had never been a hindrance to Simon, he simply moved his hand to the middle of the panel and summoned his power. Only nothing happened. His power could normally unlock anything, he'd never had so much as a small hiccup before, but this time the door remained firmly shut.

He tried again, telling himself that it was just the result of over-exertion after teleporting, but no matter what he did, it rendered the same result and the door refused to budge. He could feel the power within him, he knew he hadn't lost it, but it wasn't working.

He turned to the window to try a different tack. He placed his hand on the glass, summoning his power once more, but it remained completely unaffected. He could do nothing.

Now a little more frustrated, he turned to the bed. He stared hard at one of the pillows, as he'd done so many times in the past, and he tried to flick it up. But again nothing happened. He focussed hard, convincing himself that his fatigue was to blame, but no matter how much he pushed, his magic was useless.

Then he became worried. With no magic, he was well and truly trapped.

He sat back on the bed and tried to catch his breath. All the effort was leaving him quite dizzy.

He tried to clear his thoughts. He needed to figure this out. With soft breaths, he calmed himself and he allowed his mind to empty. With each soothing inhale his head started to de-clog and he regained some composure.

It was then that he noticed the silence. It was as if he was completely alone in the world, all except for a dull beating sound in the distance. It was a steady beat, not changing its speed or pitch, just serenely seeping through the walls as if it sent a soothing message.

He listened intently, trying to work out where it was coming from. Whatever the noise, he knew it was a good sign, he could sense it.

As he concentrated on it, the beating got louder, but not in its effort, more as if someone was now letting the sound in; like they'd removed the muffle so it could more clearly resonate. It was coming from above!

Totally confused as to what it could be, Simon stood on the bed and focussed. It was like a ticking clock; a throbbing, regular beat. And something about it warmed him.

It was Beth. It had to be. He knew that sense of warmth and it only came from one person. It must be Beth's heartbeat. He could hear Beth's heartbeat!

He listened on, so reassured to know that she must be directly above him.

After a few minutes, he sat back down on the bed and felt a new surge of determination. It also gave him comfort to know that if he could hear hers, then she should be able to hear his heartbeat in return. Surely that should bring her hope. She must be so worried being trapped in this stale building in the middle of nowhere.

Simon then realised that Jim was right: they had got a significant connection. It was like nothing Simon had ever known. She was so close. He was so close to getting to her. He just had to get out of that room.

'Hungry, Mr Bird?' a tall, well built man suddenly said as he entered the room. The man threw a plate of dried toast to the floor and then followed it with a glass of water, the edges of which splashed out as he slammed it down. He then banged the door shut, leaving Simon alone once more.

Simon looked at it with disgust. He didn't know who was keeping him there, but whoever they were, they clearly didn't like him very much.

Straight above him, Beth had slept soundly, non-stop since Damien had given her the pills a day earlier.

It was just after quarter past seven in the evening, and Beth had barely moved. She was in such a deep sleep; too deep a sleep. It was as if someone hadn't wanted her to wake up.

Then suddenly Beth was snapped awake. She sat upright as if something had jolted her. It was like lightning had stung her and she shivered. Then she felt herself momentarily lighten, like a weight was drifting away from her. She was free from something. Something good had just happened.

At the very same moment, Simon suddenly felt more alert too. It was as if his strength had just been bumped back up to maximum capacity and he felt renewed and revitalised.

If only he could get his powers to work. Feeling this new sense of energy, he set out to try again.

He tried the door first. He placed his hand in the middle of the wood and concentrated hard, summoning all of his emotion in a bid to budge it open. But, just like before, absolutely nothing happened.

He then turned to the windows. He knew how to summon his magic, it was like a second nature to him, he didn't even have to think about it anymore. But placing his hands on the glass did nothing but smudge the window.

Determined for something to work, he headed to the bathroom. He tried to turn on the taps without touching them, but they didn't so much as seep a drop. He came back to the bed, trying to flick the pillows, the sheets, anything that could be moved, but everything remained completely inanimate. No matter how hard he pushed, everything was resistant to his force.

In every sense, it was as if his powers were gone. But he knew they hadn't. He could still feel the magic flowing through him, just like always. He felt no different.

He sat back down on the bed and thought through the logic. If he still had power but it wasn't working, the only rational answer was that his magic was somehow being blocked.

Simon paced the room, trying to figure out how to overcome a spell that blocked spells. He was far more powerful than anyone he'd ever come across, how could any magic overpower him like this? He needed to think.

Without his magic, he felt utterly useless. He had to find a way to escape. He had to get to Beth and he had to get them both away from this place once and for all.

'Beth, you're awake?' Damien said with great surprise as he entered the room.

'How long was I asleep for?' Beth asked, feeling incredibly groggy.

'Not long. You must be exhausted still.'

'I feel awful.' Her whole body felt heavy, and even just picking up her arms was a major effort. It was if in so many ways her body was still asleep – and her brain wasn't far behind it - but something had forced her awake. She was now trapped in a half dreamlike state and it felt sickening.

'That's not surprising. Let's get you back to sleep. I have more pills.'

'No, thank you, Damien. I think I'll just sit up for a minute.' Beth struggled to sit up, determined to try and force herself properly awake. She had never felt so tired and heavy in her whole life. Rather than giving in to it though, the small part of her brain that was actually tapped into reality was telling her to fight it. 'I was having the weirdest dreams.'

'Oh?' Damien asked, although Beth was too tired to notice the deep concern that struck his face.

'About Simon.'

'You must be feeling guilty,' he quickly jumped back with.

'We were so powerful.'

'Just as he wants.'

'I suppose.' Beth felt sadness tug at her. 'I felt so close to him in my dream, but it's not real is it?'

'That's what your dream must have really been about. It was trying to tell you that he isn't right for you. You want to have power in your own right, power you've earnt from hard work, not something that's been gifted to you dishonestly. Remember that when you next dream of Simon. It's not moral.'

'It's not is it,' Beth agreed.

'Now, rest your head.'

'What is that beating sound?' she asked, sensing a new irritation. She wished she could just get some peace so she could properly get a grip of her thoughts. 'What are you up to now?'

'What sound?'

'It's like a really loud clock. But more emotional. If that makes sense.'

Damien's eyes widened. 'It's me,' he said quite suddenly. 'You can hear my heartbeat. We've bonded. That's what happens when two Malants bond.'

'I'm not a Malant.'

Damien looked at Beth cautiously. 'You have Malant powers.'

'Why couldn't I hear Simon's heartbeat then?'

Damien's gaze turned to a more sombre one. 'You tell me. But you can hear mine now. Who else's could it be?'

Beth felt her sadness triple in potency. 'How could I have bonded with you more than Simon?'

'I think we both know the answer to that, Beth.'

'No.'

Damien sat down on the bed and squeezed Beth's hand. 'Does it feel bad?'

'No. It feels warm and comforting.'

'That's all the answer you need then, isn't it?' Damien curled Beth's hair behind her ear and this time she didn't flinch, she didn't have the energy. Silent tears flowed down her cheeks as the truth of her marriage cemented itself in her head. The facts were laid out quite clearly.

'Come on,' Damien soothed, edging in closer to her. 'I thought you were a glass half full kind of girl?' Beth tried to lift her chin. At least she knew the truth. Ironically, being kidnapped had been the best thing that could have happened to her.

As she once again lost herself in the fog of her thoughts, she barely noticed Damien slowly, inch by inch, getting in to bed next to her.

SEVENTEEN

Simon looked at his watch. He'd been stuck in his prison for a day now and it was really starting to panic him. He had to calm down and think straight. He wasn't powerless, yet he was completely powerless at the same time; it was so frustrating.

He sat down on the bed and tried to compose his thoughts. He'd always told himself that if you couldn't work something out, then it meant you weren't thinking about it properly. He'd learnt that lesson years ago, and he needed to put into practice that very idea now.

He decided that he needed to think through one thing at a time. Firstly, the day was Friday. It was just after eight o'clock. This very thought stopped him in his tracks. He'd now been married for two weeks. It had been exactly two weeks since Beth and he had stood in Malancy HQ and had exchanged their vows.

A wave of sadness crashed through his soul as he remembered how happy he'd felt. He'd been so sure that defeating Damien and declaring his eternal love to the most amazing woman that he'd ever met was the fresh start in his life that he'd always dreamed of. He'd been positive that all the gloom was finally far behind him. How wrong he'd been. It was now hard to believe that there was ever going to be a time when he wasn't doomed to misery.

A new thought then occurred to Simon. A fortnight since the wedding meant it was a fortnight since the contract had been signed. They were now free. That dreadful contract that Beth had been left with little choice but to sign, the one that had ultimately resulted in their hasty marriage, must now be voided following the actions that he and Jane had put into place.

That must have been what had jolted him not so long ago. It must have been what had helped him regain his strength again. Beth surely would have felt it too. She must be so confused. How he wished he could explain it to her. Those contracts were such powerful forces.

Frustration tore away at him. He was so close to Beth, he'd travelled so far, but he still couldn't connect with her; well not on a physical level anyway.

Like lightning, a new idea suddenly sparked in his head. He'd been stuck in a powerless state, but he was far from powerless. He could hear Beth's heartbeat, he could sense her warmth nearby; the magic was within him, it was within them both.

Then it all made sense. Magic was running through him, he just couldn't project it out from himself. But he could use it internally. He could make himself stronger. As long as it only affected him and not anything around him, then it wouldn't be a spell, it would just be a matter of his own personal strength taking charge.

He stood up to test his theory. Moving to the end of the bed, he summoned the force within him. His power soared through his veins like electricity and he felt strength pulsate every inch of his body.

He focussed his mind on their captors. His anger rose at the thought of how these disgusting people had taken his wife away from him and had caused her so much upset, and it surged the power within him.

Simon placed his hands on the base of the bed, and

with one easy motion he lifted it from the floor. He held it high in the air, effortlessly, the force within him merely channelling the amalgamation of negative emotions that enflamed his soul. He slowly brought the bed back down to the floor again, and he sighed with relief. It had worked.

Next stop was the door. He wasted no time in wrapping his hand around the knob before summoning his power one more time. But before it had started to flourish inside of him, he stopped. He suddenly realised that he had no clue as to what was on the other side. What if there was an army waiting for him? What if they'd figured out that he could still have powers? He couldn't take the risk of being on the back foot. He needed to make sure that he had the upper hand.

He sat back down on the bed to plan his next move properly. There was no way they were going to get the better of him, whoever they were, and he wanted to be sure that he was absolutely in control. He'd made one mistake so far on this mission, he wouldn't be making another one.

Damien had managed to worm his way in so much, he was virtually snuggled up next to Beth in bed, but she had hardly seemed to notice.

'I know the contract was harsh,' Damien muttered.

'The contract?'

'The one I made you sign before you married me. I could tell you a lie about how I wanted to protect you and all that, but the truth was I just wanted you all to myself. I couldn't take the thought of you leaving me. I wanted to give us a chance. We're peas in a pod, you and me, and I knew that one day you'd see it too.'

'Right,' Beth said, not really listening. All she could think about was Simon. Processing her thoughts had become a cumbersome task. She had no chance of dealing with more than one issue at a time, and her relationship with Simon was most definitely top priority.

'I was never just going to marry you and then treat you like crap, you know. We would have been a true partnership, whatever the contract said.'

'Yeah?'

'I had a honeymoon planned.'

This caught Beth's attention. 'A honeymoon?' She suddenly seemed to notice that Damien was right next to her but she was too tired to let it bother her.

'We were going to Florence.'

'Florence?' Beth's eyes lit up.

'Have you ever been there?'

'No, but I love Italian food. I've always wanted to go to Italy.'

'It's an amazing city. To me, it's far more romantic that Paris or Rome. It's so intimate and friendly. You would have loved it.'

'You really had that planned?'

'I deserved to lose you, Beth. But hopefully in time you'll come to see me in a different light.'

Beth looked deep into Damien's eyes and for a moment she saw compassion. He seemed more human in that moment than she'd ever believed he could be. For the first time she actually started to warm to him.

Simon felt lost. It was so unlike him, but there was so much at stake. He was still sitting on the bed contemplating his options, but he couldn't devise a plan that didn't leave him potentially vulnerable.

Suddenly, out of nowhere, the door flung open and the same man as before threw a plate of beans on toast to the floor. Within a second, Simon's brain snapped into gear and he saw his chance. It was now or never. If he could make himself strong, then he could also make himself fast. There was no way they could see this coming.

Before the man even had chance to slam the glass of water down, Simon zipped to his exit. He smacked the door in the man's face on the way through to prevent him from raising the alarm, and he escaped his prison.

He fled out into a surprisingly empty corridor. He was free, and no one for the moment seemed to know about it. All he had to do was find the stairs, find Beth, and then they'd have to fight their way out of there. Once outside, though, he knew that he'd be able to teleport them away together. They'd just need a strong enough element. If he could just get them outside, he knew everything would be okay. He had to at least get them outside.

'Whatever happens in the future, Beth, I'm always here for you. Don't forget that,' Damien whispered, now millimetres away from Beth's lips.

She wasn't quite sure what was happening, nor if she really liked it, but it was the most secure that she'd felt in days. Her bitterness and anger towards Simon was eating away at her, and Damien's currently comforting words were giving her the respite that she so desperately desired. For just a moment, it didn't hurt quite so much.

As she looked into Damien's eyes, now so close to her face, she knew that he was going to kiss her, and she didn't back away. She wasn't sure why. Perhaps to get revenge on that using git who had the nerve to call himself her husband, perhaps to try and start afresh and put her marriage behind her, perhaps even to know if she had indeed developed the bond with Damien that the ticking sound implied. Whatever the reason, she didn't fight him.

His lips met hers and she immediately noted how rough they were and she felt dead inside. The warmth and wonderment that she enjoyed when Simon kissed her was now on the other side of the world, and Damien's lips were as cold and callous as the man she remembered him to be. At that very second she felt sick as the realisation of what she was doing hit her.

A man suddenly came flying sideways through the door, landing heavily on the carpet at the end of the bed, and the whole atmosphere charged with urgency.

Beth and Damien sat up straight in shock to view the wounded man lying in pain on his side, then they saw Simon moving quickly towards them from the door. He grabbed Damien by the collar, yanking him out of the bed. He threw him across the room, leaving him to smack unevenly against the wall.

Beth flopped out the other side of the bed, her heavy limbs making it hard for her to move. Despite all of her wishes, the last person she ever really expected to see was Simon, and now he was there, she had no clue how to feel about it.

All that she did know was that she felt sick and confused. She also felt utterly ashamed of herself for kissing Damien and she couldn't help but pray that Simon hadn't seen their lips locked together.

Beth closed her eyes for a second as the incredible warmth that Simon always brought with him wrapped itself around her. She'd almost forgotten how much his essence consumed a room and she recalled how much she used to melt into it. It saddened her as she no longer felt that way. It was no longer enjoyable. It brought with it doubt and perplexity. Who was this man and what did he really want from her? Was he really here to force her into casting a spell with him?

Beth backed herself against the far wall, but Simon was quickly upon her. 'I'm so sorry, Beth,' he said with such conviction. The sentiment in his voice left her weak. He reached out for her hands, but she hid them away. 'We need to leave, give me your hand,' he ordered.

'No,' she fought.

'Beth, we need to get out of here.'

'I know why you're here.'

'I should hope you do. We need to go!'

With the door now wide open, Beth could hear footsteps approaching. It was far from one or two men, an army was on its way.

'Oh God,' Simon whispered, turning to the door. Beth

had never seen him so scared. Thrown by his uncharacteristic fear, she momentarily forget her resistance and he grabbed her hand tightly.

As their skin touched, a spark fizzled between them. They both looked down to see their interlocked palms glowing red.

A smattering of hope dashed across Simon's face and Beth could tell that he'd understood what this meant, but she was now even more confused. He grabbed her other hand and there was another fizzle, then within a second their hands started to blaze.

'Are you ready?' Simon asked her. Beth didn't know what to say. He glared deep into her eyes. 'We only have seconds. Think of somewhere. I don't care where you want to go, but think of somewhere far, far away.' Beth couldn't absorb all that was going on. So many men were now in the room and they were pointing guns right at them, demanding their surrender. So much action, so much confusion. Her mind couldn't process it. 'Do it now!'

'What?' Beth gasped. She didn't even know if she wanted to leave. Was staying with Damien better? What was Simon going to do to her?

'Think of somewhere!' Simon demanded. She looked again at the guns ahead of her. This was worst case scenario for the anti-Malants, but Beth knew they couldn't kill them. 'Think of somewhere!!' Simon screamed, his eyes now burning with terror.

Shuddering, Beth looked at him. His eyes were so fiercely red; this was a new level of fear that she'd never witnessed in him before. She couldn't bear to see him in such a state. No matter what he'd done, she couldn't help how much she loved him. Without another thought she closed her eyes and she imagined the first place that came in to her mind.

A fiery glow wrapped itself around them and instantly they vanished.

EIGHTEEN

The quickest flash of red dazzled Beth's eyes and everything changed. One second they were in a dark, damp room, the thud of men marching towards them echoing off the walls; then, literally not one second later, they were hit with near peace. The sounds of distant cars and indistinct chatter were now all that could be heard. It was warm, incredibly warm for the time of night, and Beth took in her dark surroundings.

They were in some sort of small side street. The sky was clear and the stars were so bright. It was beautiful.

She was pulled from her thoughts as Simon suddenly hit the floor with a bang in front of her.

'Simon!' she gasped, touching his face, but he was completely unconscious.

A young couple shouted something at them from the end of the street. Beth couldn't understand a single word they were saying as they ran towards her, but the concern across their faces and their pointing towards Simon told her enough.

'He's okay. Just tired,' she said, gesturing sleep with her hands against her cheek, but as soon as the couple got close, they immediately backed away. Beth knew that retraction, she knew that look. It was that familiar fear of the chilly aura, which must now be doubly potent with both her and Simon emanating it.

She put her thumbs up and smiled, giving them the green light to walk away, and they couldn't do it fast enough.

She knelt down beside Simon, so grateful they were in a quiet street and away from lots of people. She took a deep breath and tried to remember what had happened. Her head was still so foggy.

Simon had come in to find her. It had been terrifying. He'd grabbed her hand and had told her to think of somewhere. They must have teleported. Where were they? Of course, Florence! That's where they were. Damien had been talking about it and he'd put the idea in her head. It was all that she'd been able to summon that was far away. They were in Florence.

Now slightly happy that at least she had their whereabouts sorted, she next tackled Simon's unconsciousness. Damien had told her that teleporting took a great deal of power, it must have knocked Simon out it required such intensity.

Beth needed him to be awake, though. She suddenly felt very alone and very vulnerable. What on earth were they going to do in this totally unfamiliar, foreign city?

More strange looks were sent their way as people passed by the end of the small street they were in. But only at one end. The other end seemed much quieter.

With her limbs still heavy and aching, Beth stumbled to the quieter end of the street. She had to find the strength to get them out of this.

At the end she found a beautiful little courtyard that led up to the front of a small hotel. It was delightful, with a few people sitting outside sipping at cocktails and wine.

She hobbled back to Simon. If she could just get him to wake up for a short while and make it to that hotel, then they would be safe. They could have time to think about everything.

'Simon,' she muttered, tapping his face, but he didn't move. She shouted a little louder, but still nothing. She was reluctant to make a scene and draw too much attention, so she tried a different tack.

Inundated with such frustration and anger, she grabbed hold of his hand and tried to yank him up, but her heavy arms were a hindrance. She wanted to scream and cry. How could he do this to her? At least with Damien she was safe and she knew where she was. Well, sort of. At least she wasn't stuck on the street of a foreign country all alone in ill-fitting clothes, feeling a complete mess.

She grasped his hand so hard and willed him awake, using all the force within her. So confused and desperate, she didn't notice their hands once again glow red as their mutual power surged. As a tear slipped down her cheek, she couldn't see Simon's eyes slightly open. 'Beth?' he whispered.

'Simon!' Beth gasped.

'Where are we?' he asked with a croak.

'Florence.'

'Florence?' he spat, trying to sit up. He leaned against the wall behind him. 'Why Florence?'

'It's a long story.'

'I'm sorry. Teleporting always drains me completely. It's something I do very rarely, but I had to get you out of there.'

'Oh I know you did!' Beth sneered.

'What?' Simon breathed. Then his face softened. 'I'm sorry. I didn't think we'd be stuck on a street somewhere like this. I'm not doing very well with my teleporting at the minute.'

'There's a hotel around the corner. Do you think you can make it? Have we got money?'

'My wallet's in my pocket,' Simon said, reaching into his jeans to reveal their funds. Then he looked into her eyes. 'Your power is fuelling me. We're so strong together,

Beth. If you hold my hand, I can make it.'

Beth shoved the wallet into her own pocket and then, channelling all her force, she helped Simon to his feet. She wasn't surprised that their joint power was so strong, but it didn't make it right.

They slowly made their way to the end of the street, through the courtyard, past the curious gazes of the leisurely drinkers, and into the air conditioned relief of the hotel reception.

It was a small but elegant reception area, with a bar hidden away to the right and a few seats placed towards the back near a bookshelf.

Ignoring the glares of those around her, Beth led Simon to the seats, knowing he hadn't got the strength to do much else but rest. He could barely prop himself up without her aid. It was all over to her now.

Standing up tall, despite feeling an utter wreck, Beth feigned dignity and strode over to the reception desk. She didn't know where she was finding this strength from, but she was grateful for it. She was greeted by a middle aged man with small spectacles and an inquisitive glare.

'Buonasera,' he said, not that Beth had a clue what it meant.

'My husband and I would like to check in for the night, please.' She spoke slowly, hoping that the man before her could understand her English. She followed his glare as he studied Simon, who was now slumped forward, barely conscious again. 'Make that two nights, please,' she corrected.

'We would love to help you, however, unfortunately, we only have the main suite left. The hotel is extremely busy at the moment,' the man responded with excellent pronunciation.

'That's fine, we'll take that,' Beth nodded, relieved that money was no object for them. She noted how at times like this she would normally feel a tinge of guilt at spending Simon's money, but all of a sudden she just didn't care.

The man glared at her. 'It's very expensive.'

'That's not a concern. We'd like the room for two nights, please,' Beth confirmed.

'It's two thousand five hundred Euros per night,' he added, clearly expecting a stark reaction.

Before this day, Beth would have probably dropped to the floor with shock at paying this much for a hotel room. When he said very expensive, she was thinking more like four hundred pounds. This was off the scale of expensive. And she'd asked for them to stay for two nights!

Before her face had the chance to flinch, though, she told herself that this was mere pocket money to Simon. She knew that he'd laugh at her for hesitating if he was conscious, so she decided to plough on regardless.

'Like I said,' Beth continued, her composed tone masking her vigorous heartbeat, 'we'd like the room for two nights.'

The receptionist fought hard to hide his surprise, but Beth noted his fleeting flinch. 'You'll need to pay in advance,' he insisted.

'Pay in advance?' Beth queried. She felt a sudden flush of anger as she knew that the other guests wouldn't be paying in advance. Then she looked down at herself and she forgave him. She far from looked like the millionaire she was implying that she was; that she knew she was. She decided to give in.

She pulled Simon's wallet from her pocket and looked through his cards. Then suddenly she stopped. What was she thinking? She turned to the receptionist. 'One moment,' she smiled and then she rushed over to Simon.

She grabbed his hand, bringing him back to life. 'I need your pin number.' He whispered the number in her ear and she quickly darted back over to the reception. She handed Simon's debit card over.

With scepticism plastered across his face, the receptionist slotted the card into the machine and then handed it over to Beth. It now required her pin and was asking for her to confirm the payment of five thousand Euros.

Beth swallowed. She'd never paid that much for anything in her whole life, let alone two nights at a hotel. She shakily typed in Simon's pin, making herself seem even more like a fraud, and she waited patiently for it to go through.

The receptionist eyed her suspiciously, so ready for the card to be declined. There was a moment of great tension as the technology before them held her fate. Then suddenly the transaction processed and the receipt printed, everything having gone through without a bump.

Beth almost sighed with relief. The man's clear scepticism as to their credibility had been so strong, she'd virtually doubted it herself. But, she told herself, they were totally legitimate. They were just teleporting people with super powers fleeing a kidnapping from another country in dire need of some well-deserved rest. What was there to sigh about?

The man stared at her for a moment, still clearly quite suspicious. Then he passed her a document and a pen. 'Please could I ask that you to fill out your details.' Beth's hand was still shaking as she took the pen and paper from him, he made her feel so guilty. She completed the form with their basic information, and then she pushed it back over the desk. The end was in sight and she couldn't wait to get to their room.

'I just need to see your passports.'

'Passports?' Beth queried, now not able to hide the panic in her voice.

'It's quite standard for tourists,' he stated.

'Of course,' Beth said. 'My husband has them.'

This was where she hated magic. They were now like illegal immigrants, weren't they? You weren't supposed to travel without passports, without passing the right controls. It surely wasn't legal to pop around, teleporting and landing wherever you liked. Then again, Beth felt quite positive that there wasn't an actual law against it either, it really wasn't an everyday occurrence.

'He wants to see our passports!' Beth hissed as she grabbed Simon's hand again, bringing him back to reality.

'Don't worry,' he mumbled.

'What are we going to do?' she flapped.

'It's fine.'

'We never should have come here. How are we going to get home without passports?'

'Beth, it's fine!' Simon asserted. 'Just use your powers.'

'My powers? Can't you do it?'

'Look at me Beth. The only thing keeping me awake is your touch. You have to do it.'

'But how?'

'Just imagine them. Summon all your emotions, like you've done before, but as you do, imagine our passports. Hold out your hands and will them here. It's very easy.'

'I'm sure it is for you!' Beth barked at him. Then, realising she had no choice, Beth let go of Simon's hand and prepared herself. She turned around to see the receptionist glaring at her. 'Just trying to remember where we put them,' she grimaced with all honesty. Then she turned back around so she was completely facing away from him and she closed her eyes.

She held her hands out closely in front of her and did just as Simon had told her. She pulled all her fear and anxiety together, all of the exerted emotions that had troubled her for the last few days. Her focus sharpened as she channelled her energy and tried to imagine their passports.

She let the image of them fixate in her head. Then, slowly, the picture of their passports became more vivid in her mind as the force within her intensified. Suddenly it reached a peak, and as the power surged through her veins, her eyes popped open. Two passports were, out of nowhere, sitting in her hands. They'd just appeared from thin air; it truly was magic. She wanted to jump for joy.

She checked them quickly and they were both the right documents. The end of this ordeal was almost in sight, it had to be.

'There you go,' she smiled, handing the passports over to the receptionist. His face flinched as once again Beth had shocked him. He studied them both carefully, and then he glared back at Beth.

'Bethany Lance?' he queried.

Beth kicked herself. She'd written down Bethany Bird on the form he'd given to her. Although the truth here was all that mattered. This was finally explainable.

'We've just got married,' Beth replied.

'So this is your honeymoon?' the man asked, his eyes lighting up for the first time.

Flashes of the truth popped into Beth's head before she realised that a lie here was her only option, as much as she hated herself for it. 'Yes,' she agreed.

'Congratulations!' the man smiled. 'Is your husband okay?' He looked to Simon who was now half way to the floor.

'Jet lag!' Beth said, thinking it's not quite a lie. His issue was travel related.

'From England?' the receptionist asked with clear confusion.

'No!' Beth giggled, extending her pretend humour while she summoned up yet another lie. 'We've just come back from America. We had a few days in Las Vegas,' she added, not sure where on earth all of this rubbish was coming from.

'How lovely!' the man smiled. 'I too suffer from jet lag, it's terrible.' Beth could see his expression had softened a great deal now that their story was starting to make sense. 'Well, everything's fine here. We'll look after your passports. Do you have luggage?' he asked, looking around.

Beth panicked again. Teleporting was severely hard

work. 'No,' she replied, trying again to think of a lie. She'd always known lying wasn't meant to be easy. 'We lost it. At the airport. That is the airline lost it. It's still in Las Vegas.' This was getting ridiculous now. Beth had never been caught up in such a web of lies and she felt quite sick.

The anti-Malants were right. All this magic was quite immoral and if Beth had doubted if before, she suddenly knew that she wanted to be rid of these powers as soon as possible. Wednesday could not come quickly enough, and there was no way that Simon was going to convince her otherwise. The Malancy had to end.

'I'm very sorry to hear that,' the man responded. 'Can we help in any way?'

'No, it's fine. It's all going to be sorted. We've just had a really bad day and we just want to get to bed.'

'Of course. Please,' he said, handing Beth the plastic card that was to be her room key. 'My colleague will show you the way.'

A porter suddenly appeared next to her, dressed smartly in the hotel's elegant light grey uniform. 'Please,' he said, gesturing the way to the lifts.

'Thank you,' Beth said to the receptionist, taking both the keycard and Simon's debit card from him. She then walked over and grabbed Simon's hand. 'We just need to follow this man to our room,' she said, helping him to his feet.

He struggled up and they both wearily followed the porter to the lifts. He took them up three floors and then led them down a bright, clean corridor to the very end. They were finally at their suite.

The porter showed them into their room. It was enormous. The separate bedroom and living room areas had stunningly upholstered, golden furniture, all of it looking not a day old. The huge bathroom was blessed with a bath big enough to swim in; it all exuded utter luxury.

He'd shown them around and now the porter was

waiting awkwardly by the door. 'Will there be anything else?' he asked.

'No, thank you,' Beth smiled, but he was yet to leave.

'Here,' Simon muttered, struggling into his pocket and pulling out a ten pound note. 'Forgive us, we're yet to change our money.'

'Thank you,' the porter nodded, humbly taking the note. 'It is very kind of you.' He then left them in peace.

Simon struggled straight into the bedroom, and, just kicking off his shoes, he clambered into bed. 'I'm so sorry, Beth,' he said before closing his eyes and losing consciousness again.

Beth stood at the end of the bed. They'd made it this far, but she still felt very alone, very scared and completely out of her depth.

NINETEEN

Not sure what to do with herself, Beth headed out to the large balcony area to get her first proper glimpse of the city. The night was so warm and she breathed in the relaxed atmosphere. It was her first time ever seeing Florence and this stunning hotel just happened to be in the heart of the city, which allowed for a breathtaking view.

In front of her was a sea of buildings all closely packed together. Beautiful architecture was dotted sporadically across the crowded landscape, and at the epicentre of the view stood the Duomo. It was a building that Beth had seen many times from images of Florence and it looked just as spectacular in real life, even at night. It was lit up brightly against the clear black sky; an exquisite vision of brilliance that Beth had never imagined such an old building could have.

She took a while to absorb the beauty ahead of her in the hope that it might help settle her nerves, but she couldn't shake her anxiety. She headed back into the bedroom a little deflated.

This truly seemed like an amazing city, somewhere she'd always dreamed of coming to. When Damien had mentioned the idea of taking her to Florence on their honeymoon, it had caught Beth's imagination instantly. Italy was one of the places that she'd always wanted to visit, but being here now was bittersweet. Instead of being able to enjoy it, she just longed for home and for things to be back to how they were before. How she knew they would never be again.

She looked at Simon fast asleep in bed. He seemed so peaceful. It was hard to believe that he could be the man that Damien had portrayed, but he certainly wasn't the man that Beth thought he was. He wasn't the Simon she'd so foolishly fallen in love with. As she looked at his face just poking up from the duvet she couldn't help but feel heartbroken.

She felt the sting of her heavy eyes and she forced herself to shake away all negative thoughts. Instead she focussed solely on getting some sleep. At least now she was guaranteed some proper rest. No one knew where they were.

She happily stripped herself of the awful clothes that she'd been left with no choice but to wear and she flopped straight into bed next to Simon.

The bed was deliriously comfortable. She melted into the mattress and wrapped the soft, fluffy duvet all around her. Within seconds she was asleep.

It was far from the peaceful sleep she'd wished for, though. Strange dreams haunted her mind. Both she and Simon had great power, more power than either of them knew was possible. They were ultimately in control of everything and nothing was too big for them to conquer. They just had to cast a spell and the world was theirs.

Beth woke up with cold chills. The dream had been so vivid and so distressing. It was clearly a reflection of the recent revelation of what her life could become.

Then it hit her. Everything had changed. Before now she'd only been troubled with how she felt about a situation that had ultimately been taken out of her hands, and that was big enough. But now she had to actually make the decision herself.

In being rescued, it now meant that the Malancy's fate lay completely in her hands. Simon's choice was made, there was no way that he'd want the Malancy to end, but he couldn't do the spell without her. So the decision was now just hers. What was she going to do? The night before she'd been adamant that she wouldn't cast the spell, but it wasn't such an easy choice. No wonder she'd had such a disturbed night's sleep, this was a monumental responsibility.

She looked at the TV ahead of her and saw a little digital clock below it. Finally she could tell the time; a small gift that she'd been denied for days. It gave her so much peace of mind to see it. It was nearly seven thirty in the morning and the sun was already gleaming its warmth through the windows.

Beth turned to see Simon still fast asleep next to her. In fact he was in exactly the same position as he'd been in the night before. He couldn't have moved.

She didn't know what to do. She wanted to wake him, but she knew as soon as she did they'd have to talk. They'd have to discuss the end of the Malancy and Beth would have to tell him how she felt about it.

She got out of bed, deciding it wouldn't hurt to let him sleep a bit longer, and she looked in the wardrobe where she'd seen a comfy, white dressing gown the night before. Throwing it around herself, she felt her stomach grumble. She was hungry, very hungry. She couldn't even remember the last time that she'd eaten, but it must have been quite a while ago.

She didn't really like the idea of going for breakfast on her own. She knew the staff would all be wondering where Simon was and she didn't want to bring herself any unnecessary attention, especially as they all believed it was their honeymoon. Instead she decided to order in.

She picked up the phone in the living room and dialled for room service. 'Hi, could I order breakfast in my room, please?'

'Of course. Did you place your order last night?' a male voice replied.

'Err... no. I didn't know what I wanted then.'

There was a short pause before the voice continued. 'No problem. Please, what can I get for you?'

'Everything. Just bring me up everything you have. We're very hungry.'

'Of course. And coffee?'

'No, actually could I get tea, please?'

Again there was a short pause. 'Yes, no problem.'

'Thank you very much.'

'Would you like a newspaper too?'

Beth was all poised to decline this offer before realising that it actually might be good for her to get a grasp of what day it was. 'Yes please. Anything English will do. Thank you.'

'You're welcome.'

Breakfast soon arrived and Beth was spoilt rotten for choice. She also finally got back on track with time. The newspaper revealed it was already Saturday. She'd spent far too long trapped in that horrid room.

Finishing her mountain of food, next she decided to enjoy a bath and properly wash off the week. It took well over thirty minutes to fill the tub, but it was worth it.

Once she was completely refreshed, she looked in the mirror. Her face seemed so pale and her eyes so grey. She needed perking up; she needed fresh air. She'd been stuck inside now for too long and she had to get out.

She headed back into the bedroom to check on Simon, but he was still comatose, in exactly the same position. She toyed with the idea of trying to wake him again, but she just couldn't bring herself to do it. The longer he stayed asleep, the longer she could avoid him. Not only did she still not have a clue as to what she was going to say to him, she was terrified of what he was going to say to her.

Determined not to let her loneliness get the better of

her, and determined to take control of something, Beth made the quick decision that she would venture out on her own. She didn't need anyone else. And it might give her chance to clear her thoughts. How she desperately needed that.

Having decided to make something of her day, it suddenly dawned on her that she was completely without essentials. For starters, she'd got nothing to wear. All she had were those smelly, horrible bits that the anti-Malants had given to her, and there was no way that she was going to wear them again. She was in the most fashionable country in the world, she couldn't leave the hotel wearing that tat. But what could she do? She had to go out to get clothes, yet she had no clothes that she was willing to go out in to get them.

Then there was the issue of her awful breath, her gloomy face, sun tan lotion, deodorant; the list of things she needed was endless.

It was then that she realised that she had the power to get all of those things right at her fingertips. If she could summon up her passport, she could easily summon up an outfit and a few toiletries.

It was wrong, though. She was contemplating bringing about the end of the Malancy, yet at the same time she wanted to use her magical ability to her own advantage. It was immoral.

Or was it? Even if it was all to end in just a few days, where was the harm in her utilising her powers while she still had them? Wasn't it her right? Besides, who was ever going to know? She made a pact with herself that she'd just summon up the important bits and then she'd buy anything else she needed from the city that morning.

Forty five minutes later and Beth looked stunning. She was wearing a blue stripy shift dress, her face was aglow with factor thirty sun tan lotion and a splash of make-up, and her hair was swinging freely with an after-straighteners radiance. She'd also summoned up her little black handbag so she could easily carry Simon's wallet with her.

Now ready for action, she felt a tug of guilt. She moved over to the bed to see Simon still out cold. She needed to at least check he was okay.

She nudged him but nothing happened. She tried again, a little harder, and then, when still nothing happened, she shook his shoulder quite vigorously.

'Simon!' she urged, but all the response she got was a vague groan and that was it.

The groan at least gave her some indication that he was just exhausted and nothing else was wrong. She couldn't help but feel a little relieved, not only that he was all right, but that she could legitimately put off talking to him for a while longer.

She quickly grabbed the notebook and pencil from the bedside table, scribbled a note to say she'd popped out for essentials should he wake up in her absence, and then she headed out of the hotel and into the gorgeous sunshine of Florence.

She had no clue where she was going but with her usual confidence she marched on with a smile. This was a new adventure, and for the first time in a long time, she felt back to her old self.

Within minutes she'd stumbled across a cashpoint. She withdrew fifty Euros just to cover herself, despite being plagued with guilt at using Simon's card; but they were married and she knew he'd have no issue with it.

Heading on, her first mission was to buy some clothes, and it wasn't long before the glamorous shops of the city were in sight. She walked past Armani, Dolce & Gabbana, Gucci and Versace, just to name a few of the designers that she'd only ever viewed as too expensive for her in the past. She glanced in the windows with a new realisation that she could actually afford these clothes now, but it felt so wrong. It didn't feel like her. She'd never worn a name in her life, and it wasn't the time for her to start now. Not even when in Italy.

She carried on, past a few more shops and down a few side roads, eager to see where the city could take her. Then she stopped. She was sure that she'd been heading away from the Duomo, but somehow she'd found her way back there and she was once again standing at the bottom of the beautiful building.

The sudden rush of tourists was quite stark in comparison to how quiet the shopping area had been. There were people everywhere, taking photos, mingling around, following guides and generally taking in the view.

She slowly walked on, absorbing the bustle of this tourism hub. She reached the end of the square and looked around for inspiration as to where to go next. To her left she noticed a more pedestrianised road and she decided to head in that direction.

This was far more like the high street that she'd been looking for. The shops were more reasonable in price and after a couple of hours of mooching, trying on and generally enjoying herself (ignoring the wary glances of those who had sensed her chilly aura), she'd happily spent a relatively small amount of Simon's money on three new outfits for herself, some summery clothes for him and a stylish overnight bag for them to put everything in during the journey home.

Feeling quite proud of herself, she made her way back to the hotel.

It was now lunchtime and she was very hopeful that Simon would finally be awake. Her fear of speaking with him was slowly morphing into a nauseating need to get it over with. She let herself into their suite and headed straight to the bedroom. Any hope was quickly diminished, though, when she found him, not only still asleep, but still in exactly the same position.

Sure that it couldn't be good for him to have not moved for so long, she pushed him over onto his other side. Without really intending to, she pushed him quite hard and nudged him a few times in the process, but despite her best efforts, other than a faint murmur, he remained completely unconscious.

She took a deep breath. Her inner torment at how much they needed to speak and how much she wanted it all over with was now growing. She rocked him again and called his name, trying anything to get him to wake up. But nothing seemed to work. He just groaned again but that was it.

Beth sat on the side of the bed, deflated. Her spirit was teetering, and for just a few seconds she almost caved in. Tears stung in her eyes as she felt everything around her falling apart.

Then she looked out and saw the glorious city ahead of her. She took another deep breath. Her life was soon to change forever – again – but this time she didn't want it to change. She wanted what she had before. She wanted to be Mrs Bird and carry on with her job. The thought of it ending was too much for her to handle.

Beth picked herself up and, after quickly glancing at Simon once more, she headed back towards the door. Being here was a rare opportunity and she had two choices: sit and wait for Simon to wake up or make the most of this incredible city. It was her last chance to pretend everything was normal. She was still Mrs Bird for now.

As she walked out again into the heat, she decided next on her agenda would be the tourist attractions. Well, after lunch. Her stomach was grumbling again.

She'd seen a little panini bar that morning and was on her way there, when she suddenly realised where she was. Never in her life had she had the chance to taste a true Italian pizza. Why on earth was she looking for a sandwich?

Not at all bothered about eating on her own, Beth searched for a suitable restaurant where she could sit outside and enjoy the city around her. Most of the places near the tourist spots were heaving, so she headed down a few side streets, and she soon found a delightful looking restaurant that seemed just right. She grabbed a seat by the road, as instructed, and let the sun kiss her skin while she scoured the menu.

She'd been so ready for pizza, but suddenly spaghetti bolognaise jumped out at her. A true favourite of hers, she couldn't waste the opportunity to taste it in its homeland. As silly as it may have seemed, it was an exciting moment for her.

She enjoyed every mouthful, its fresh taste light years from anything she'd tried at home. She finished the meal off with some homemade gelato and a cheeky glass of vino rossi, and for a moment she could have believed that she was on holiday.

Then she decided that's exactly what she needed to believe. She used every ounce of strength to forget the reality of her situation and for a few hours she convinced herself that she was there with her husband on a business trip. He was meeting with clients while she took in the sights. It was easy and could possibly be true. And it made her feel so much better.

With her new-found survival technique, she set herself up for an afternoon of tourism. She first made her way to see Michelangelo's David and then she headed on to climb the Duomo. Although most of her time had been swallowed up waiting in queues, she couldn't deny how lucky she felt to have had this amazing opportunity. No matter what niggled at the back of her mind.

Completely exhausted, it was nearly eight o'clock when she finally stumbled back to the hotel. She headed straight to the bedroom, so sure that Simon must now be awake; but he still wasn't. He was still out cold.

That was it. In that second, seeing him still asleep, knowing that they still couldn't speak, and no longer able to deny how alone she felt, she lost the battle within her. Her determined high spirits suddenly crashed down around her. It had taken so much work for her to keep her worries at bay, but she couldn't fight them anymore.

As if the weight of her woes was too much to bear, she sat on the bed and put her head in her hands. The terrifying prospect that this could be the last week that they'd spend together echoed in her mind. Would he really leave her if the Malancy ended? Maybe she should cast the spell with him after all? But then there was no guarantee that he'd stay with her whatever happened. Either way, once she'd served her purpose, what was going to keep them together? Love?

She loved him so much. She couldn't escape the breathlessness that she felt just being in his presence. But if he didn't feel the same way, there was nothing she could do about it.

Yes, he might stay with her through pity or desperation, but she didn't want that either. She just wanted the love that she'd come to believe that they'd had. It was too painful to consider an alternative.

She'd had her day away from it, and she'd needed it quite badly, but inevitably she couldn't escape the reality of her situation for long. Tears swelled up in her eyes as she contemplated a life without Simon. It just wasn't fair that he'd promised her his love and then he was going to so cruelly take it away.

Why couldn't he wake up! They needed to talk about it. Now that they both knew the truth, they'd have to discuss it. He would no doubt try and persuade her to do the spell, and he'd be angry, perhaps even manipulative.

If she was honest with herself, she didn't want to cast the spell. She wanted to see the end of it. She couldn't see how there was a future for the Malancy, it had caused so many issues. And whether Simon loved her or not, she most definitely loved him, and Mr Taylor had been right. Looking at the pros and cons, she could think of very few reasons for extending the power. The Malancy had had its day, and Beth knew in her heart it was over.

'Are you okay?' Simon's voice suddenly cut through

Beth's thoughts. She turned to him with relief.

'You're awake?'

'How long have I been out of it? I'm so sorry.'

'Like a day. Are you okay?'

'A bit groggy, but I'm all right. I'm so sorry.'

Beth's heart stopped and a sickening feeling wrenched in her stomach. This was it. The pretence was over. He was awake and now they had to talk. Suddenly it was the last thing in the world she wanted to do.

'You must have had such an awful time,' Simon muttered, gently cupping Beth's face with his hand before wiping away a tear with his thumb, just as he had done on their first date. 'What happened? We'll figure it out, don't worry. You must have been so scared.' Beth looked into his sincere eyes but she couldn't speak. 'Do you want to talk about it?' Again, Beth couldn't find any words. Where did she begin? Simon scanned her face and then a comforting smile warmed his lips. What was he doing to her? She hadn't expected him to be so nice. 'I tell you what, let's pretend, just for tonight, that none of it happened. I've missed you so much. Let's celebrate being back together and put everything out of our minds, just for one night. What do you say?'

Beth still couldn't find any words. She was so scared that once she spoke, it would start the end of their life together. Instead all she could do was nod.

'Great,' Simon smiled, then he kissed her forehead. He got up and stripped himself of the clothes that he'd been wearing for days. He neatly placed them on the back of a chair and then reached for a fluffy dressing gown in the wardrobe before looking back at Beth. 'There must have been a reason why you brought us to one of the most romantic cities in the world,' he said with a glint in his eye. 'Let's at least enjoy it.'

A tear rolled down Beth's cheek as the real reason why she'd brought them here made her gag, but Simon was already heading to the living room so he didn't notice.

He picked up the phone and Beth heard him call for room service. 'Could we have a bottle of champagne, please? That sounds perfect... yes, two glasses. Thank you... Yes, that would be great. Whatever you think is best.' He placed down the receiver and returned to the bedroom.

He sat down next to her on the bed and looked into her glistening eyes. He kissed her gently on the cheek. 'If you want to talk, I'm all ears, any time. I'm always here for you. I just want you to be happy.' He studied her face, trying to read her, but she was just too frightened to speak. 'Come on, we're back together. And it's our two week anniversary. If that's not a reason to celebrate!' he grinned.

Beth felt her lip quiver. 'Our anniversary was yesterday,' she whispered.

'It's Saturday? Oh of course. Sorry, I'm so confused. Teleporting is not good.'

Beth shook her head, thinking how magic was not good full stop, but she bit her lip. Then it occurred to her that this might be the final milestone in their marriage.

'I just have to go to the bathroom,' she said, trying so hard to control herself. She raced to the en suite and closed the door tightly behind her. The tears poured down her face as she silently sobbed.

What was he playing at? Was this a kind gesture or a cruel trick? Did it matter? Either way, she had to acknowledge that this could be the last night that they'd ever spend together. This could be it. Maybe it was his way of saying goodbye? She might never know. But whatever it was, she knew that if she did anything to ruin her last chance of loving him, she'd regret it forever. She had to see tonight as a gift, before everything was gone tomorrow. She'd been given the chance to make it last one more day, and she knew she had to take it.

She took a deep breath and looked at her smudged face in the mirror. She was in such a state. She filled the sink with water and washed all her make-up away, along with the pretence of the day, and she composed herself. She slipped out of her dress and wrapped herself in the safety of her big dressing gown. Then she stood tall.

She heard the knock at the door from room service and she knew it was time to face Simon again. She opened the bathroom door, let a smile crack through her sadness and she made her way to the living room.

The night had been truly lovely. After a few glasses of exquisite champagne accompanied by strawberries, smoked salmon, olives and bread, Beth had managed to push the darkness to the back of her mind and she relaxed into the mood of the evening. It was nothing more than husband and wife enjoying each other's company in a luxurious suite.

They'd shared stories of their childhood, exchanged silly secrets and admitted to bad habits, all with great humour. Then they'd moved their fun to the bedroom, where they'd made love. It had been amazing, the connection between them fusing their bodies as one as they moved so naturally together. At that moment Beth couldn't have been more sure of his love for her.

However, by the early hours of the morning, reality hit home. Simon had been asleep for quite a while; his strength was still quavering and their lovemaking had taken its toll. Now, with him fast asleep next to her and the alcohol wearing off, Beth was left to face her situation once again.

That had been one of the best nights that they'd ever spent together. Their intercourse had literally taken her breath away and the love that she felt from him seemed so credible. But rather than it convincing Beth that Simon was sincere, it in fact had the opposite effect.

Beth was so deeply sure of Simon's dishonesty and so swayed by Damien's words, she made herself believe that all of the night's many wonderful moments had merely been Simon's way of saying goodbye.

He was far from a heartless man, Beth knew that. She could almost understand why he was using her like this. He didn't mean it maliciously, he just wanted to secure his future. Who could blame him? But it left Beth feeling utterly distraught, and she sobbed quietly into her pillow.

She tried so hard to stay awake, too afraid of what heartbreak the next day might bring. She prayed that it might never actually come but her tiredness eventually got the better of her and sleep finally took its hold.

TWENTY

Just like the day before, Beth woke up with cold sweats. She'd once again had those vivid dreams of her and Simon and they'd left her shuddering.

'Morning,' Simon smiled next to her, forcing her back to the real world. He was already wide awake and checking his emails on his phone.

'Hi,' she whispered back. The prospect of the day ahead suddenly flashed in her mind and her stomach knotted.

'What do you fancy doing today? I was thinking, we're in this incredible city, I haven't even left the hotel yet, why don't we stay here for another couple of days?'

'Why?' Beth asked with deep suspicion. She sat up straight so she'd be better prepared for whatever was coming her way.

'I thought it might be nice for us to have some time to ourselves.' Beth didn't know how to respond. 'And we have to make the most of this beautiful suite.'

'I want to go home today,' she announced, fearful that she was being led into some sort of trap.

He studied her for a moment and then a smile burst onto his face. 'We'll get you back for Wednesday, don't

159

worry about that. I wouldn't ruin such a special day.'

Beth felt sick. She hadn't expected him to blurt it out quite so casually. Now they had to talk about it. Now there was no going back.

She hesitated with bated breath, so afraid of the next thing that she needed to say, but she knew there was nowhere else to hide. 'What if I don't want it to be a special day?'

Simon regarded her with absolute confusion and Beth's heart started to throb. 'Why wouldn't you want it to be a special day?'

The arrogance of Simon's reply enraged her. 'I can't believe you've just assumed that I'd want everything you want.'

'I was doing it for you,' he justified.

'That's so controlling, Simon. Look, I'm really sorry, but it's not happening. I know this is really hard for you, but I can't do it.' Beth got out of bed and hid herself in her dressing gown. Then she quickly escaped to the balcony. She needed some space. She couldn't look at him.

She was so mixed up. He'd obviously just assumed that, whatever happened, she'd be going ahead with the spell. But then, in all honesty, why on earth would he think any differently? Why would she question it? He was the Malant, not her. Doesn't it make her selfish to deny him his future?

But no, Mr Taylor was right. She was doing this for him. No matter what happened to their relationship after this, this was absolutely the best thing for Simon. But just saying it to him had been so hard. She felt awful.

'So tell me what you do want then,' Simon said, now robed himself and joining her on the balcony.

'It's not about what I want, it's about what's best for everyone.'

Simon took a second to compute what she was telling him. 'So you know my plans?'

'I know everything, Simon.'

'Okay.' Simon took a moment and Beth could see that he was struggling with acceptance. 'How about instead-'

'No.'

'I was just going to say-'

'No, it's not happening.'

'What are you saying, you just want to cancel the whole day?'

'You had a whole day planned?'

'I thought you knew?'

'Whatever, Simon, just cancel everything. It's not happening.'

Simon stared at her, completely perplexed. 'What's brought this on, Beth?' She glared at him sternly and his face softened. 'I'm sorry, I suppose I know the answer to that. I know the last few days have been awful for you, I can't imagine what you've been through. As soon as you're ready to talk about it, you'll know I'll be there for you. Don't let them ruin it, though. If you do this, you're letting them win.'

'Letting them win?' Beth gasped, shocked. 'They were so right about you. You really are manipulative.'

'Excuse me?' Simon was genuinely taken aback by this.

'I want what's best for both of us. You're only looking after yourself.'

'What does that mean?'

'Damien's told me everything.'

'Damien?' Simon asked with confusion. Then, as if a lightning bolt had struck him, his eyes widened. 'Oh my God! You were in bed with him! What was he doing there? I thought he was locked up?'

'Well, yes, that was a surprise to me too. Like lots of things this week. Unlike you, though, Damien's thinking more with an open mind these days. We see things in the same way.'

'What did he say to you? What happened?'

'The truth.'

'Oh my God, he was kissing you! It's all coming back

to me. I just had to get you out of there. I didn't-'

'So what if he was!'

'What has he done to you? I'm really worried about you, Beth. Why were you letting him kiss you?'

She couldn't take this anymore. She needed this conversation to be over with. 'I just want Wednesday to go by unnoticed,' she shouted. 'Let's just get past it and then we can move on. Can you deal with that?'

Beth could see Simon was broken by this. She knew that he'd be upset, that was no shock, but it hurt her so much to see him so beaten. He didn't say a word, he just nodded his head, the impact of it all seeming to have silenced him.

Then it occurred to Beth that it was all a little too easy. She'd been ready for a fight, this couldn't be it. He had to have more tricks up his sleeve. 'You're just giving in?' she asked, dubiously.

'For God's sake, Beth!' Simon barked, his hurt turning into anger. 'What do you want from me? What is this, one of those reverse-psychology things? If you don't want to do anything, then fine, it's your choice. All I want to know is why were you kissing him?'

'I'm not trying to manipulate you Simon, I would never do that. I'm just telling you the truth.'

'Then why do I get the feeling you're hiding things from me?' Simon glared at her fiercely and then he turned and left. He went back into the bedroom and she heard him make a phone call. She assumed that he was calling Paul, breaking the bad news. No doubt soon enough Paul would be on his way over to talk her into it. He was so predictable. Damien had been so right.

She took a few deep breaths and looked over the sunlit city. The orange hue dominated the skyline and she so wanted to relax and enjoy it, but she was now shaking she was so angry.

Eventually, Simon reappeared. 'I've just sorted our flights out. The car will be here to pick us up at midday. Be ready.' He then disappeared again.

Beth chased after him. 'Have you got nothing else to say to me?' she snapped.

'What do you want me to say, Beth?'

'So you're just going to let it pass by like that without a fight?'

'Are you serious? And you say that I'm the manipulative one. What are you doing? If you don't want to mark the occasion, then whatever, neither do I.' Simon shook his head, so clearly upset and confused. 'What the hell did Damien do to you? You know, I've always tried to be there for you, but I don't deserve this. If you're mad at me because it took me so long to find you... well, they blocked the magic. I tried really hard, Beth.'

'I know you tried hard. I know how much this means to you. I just don't know whether it was me you really wanted. Can't you see?'

'What are you talking about? What did Damien say to you? You need to tell me. You have to talk to me, Beth. Why was he kissing you?'

'You know exactly what he said to me. The hard truth. The truth about us.'

Simon shook his head again. 'Beth, I can't do this. You need to tell me what he said to you. Tell me what happened.'

'Why? So you can talk me out of it? It's not going to happen, Simon. They haven't just filled my head with loads of crap, they've given me information and I've made up my own mind.'

'Information?'

'The facts.'

Simon rubbed his head. This was clearly straining him. 'Look, Malants and non-Malants-' he started.

'Just because you're a Malant and I'm not does not give you extra rights. We're in this together.'

Simon took a deep breath. 'I thought we were too.' He turned to walk away. Then, not a second later, he snapped back around and glared at her. 'You know what, Beth, this isn't good enough. I was going out of my mind with worry about you. I did everything in my power to get you back, but then, when I finally reach you, you're in the bed with that sick bastard kissing him. You need to tell me, why the fuck were you kissing him? I think I have a right to know.'

Beth saw red. She couldn't believe his nerve. He'd lied to her for so long and now he had the audacity to put himself on the moral high ground. No chance. 'Because I was furious with you! That's why! At least he was there for me, and least he tells me things as they are.'

'I tried everything to get to you! Ask Paul, ask Jim. I would have turned the earth over to find you. I couldn't stand being away from you.'

'And now I know why.'

'What did Damien say to you? Why won't you tell me what happened?'

'You know what happened. Let's cut the crap, you know exactly what happened. The problem is, Simon, you just don't want to hear it. I'm never going to agree with you. It's my life and my decision and you're just going to have to live with it!'

Simon opened his mouth to say something, but he stopped. Instead he just shook his head with deep frustration and then walked away from her.

He headed into the bathroom, slamming the door behind him. Beth stood for a few seconds, hating herself for their argument, hating herself even more for having kissed Damien, but most of all hating that she was causing Simon so much hurt. She knew he'd come to understand one day, it was just too raw at the moment. She needed to give him time.

She heard the shower turn on and she moved back out onto the balcony, trying very hard not to cry.

As soon as Simon had come out of the shower, he'd quickly dressed himself and then he'd disappeared, only returning just in time for the car. The friction between them was blistering as they made their way to the airport, and by the time they'd arrived, they'd barely acknowledged each other's existence.

They both silently read books in the departure lounge, they were like complete strangers on the flight, and when they finally landed at Heathrow, the atmosphere couldn't have been more suffocating.

Jim was waiting for them at arrivals and he greeted them with a smile, but it was not returned. Although clearly concerned, he chose not to react, he just led them to the car, not saying a single word.

It was only when they reached the Lexus that Beth finally broke the silence. 'Jim, please can you take me back to my flat?'

'What do you need from there?' Simon queried. He was still seething.

'I think it's best that I stay there tonight, don't you?'

'No. Your home is with me.'

Jim just drove on silently.

'I want to go back to my flat tonight. You don't own me.'

'I never said I owned you. Where is this coming from?'

'I just think it's best that we keep clear of temptation, don't you? It's not going to be easy.'

'We're only just back together. This is ridiculous, you're my wife. You need to talk to me.'

'Let's just get to Thursday. I'll come and see you on Thursday. Then we can talk about the future.'

'The future?' Simon asked. His anger had now evaporated into pure desperation.

'That is what you want, isn't it?' She asked it, but she didn't know if she wanted the answer.

'I want there to be a now.'

Her moment of weakness quickly vanished as she translated Simon's plea. 'That's the problem, Simon, isn't it? That's all you can think about. Jim, take me back to my flat.' Beth then turned to Simon. 'Or is it better that I just disappear for a few days?'

'Why are you doing this?'

'Are you going to leave me alone? Are you going to respect my decision?'

Simon sighed, his face completely broken. 'If that's what you want.' He then looked out the car window and didn't face her again.

'Where to then?' Jim asked for clarification.

'To my flat, please.' Beth could see Jim open his mouth to argue, but then he stopped.

It was one of the most uncomfortable, stifling car journeys that any of them had ever experienced. After what seemed like hours, Jim finally pulled up into the car park next to Beth's flat and she got out. Simon still couldn't face her. She wanted to say goodbye, but it seemed like such a waste of breath.

She walked to her front door, hating that things were going to end this way, when she suddenly heard a car door open. 'Beth,' Simon called, racing to her side. They looked at each other silently, neither of them knowing what to say next.

'I'll come and see you on Thursday,' Beth finally uttered.

'Thursday?'

'I promise, I'll be there on Thursday. We just have to get through Wednesday.'

'There must be something I can do to change your mind?'

'I'm so sorry, Simon. I really am sorry. This is for the best, though, you'll see. In time to come, you'll see that this is the best for everyone.' Beth paused for breath. 'Take care. I love you.'

'I love you, too.' As soon as he'd said these words, all Beth could do was pray that he really meant them.

'Bye.' Beth turned to her front door, but before she took another step, she stopped. 'I don't have my key.' This was the final straw and she suddenly sobbed. 'What am I doing? What am I going to do?'

Simon looked at her with sorrow. He curled her hair behind her ears and then touched the door with his palm. It clicked open. 'You can do the door to your flat. You know what you're doing now.'

'How ironic,' Beth whispered. 'Thank you.' Then she disappeared into her flat leaving Simon all alone on the doorstep.

* * *

Back in London, in Malancy HQ, in George Malant's very own office, Damien, Mr Taylor and George himself all sat around his desk.

'You assured me two hundred and fifty Malants would be enough,' George snapped.

'It was. Well it was for a bit. He couldn't have had his powers, we don't understand,' Mr Taylor explained.

'We can't let them do this spell, it's getting too close for comfort now. What took your team so bloody long to get to Florence?'

'Teleporting is exhausting them. They can't keep doing it.'

'Where are the Birds now then?'

'They're heading back home now.'

'Oh come on, they're not that stupid. That's the first place we're going to look.'

'With all due respect, Mr Malant, that's probably the safest place for them to be. I don't think we'd be able to slip in again unnoticed. Simon is clearly far more powerful than we've given him credit for.'

'You need to find a way!'

'I think we're all worrying for nothing,' Damien suddenly chipped in with, quite casually.

'The future of the Malancy hangs in the balance; I'd call that worrying for a reason,' George argued.

'We got to Beth. I can't see her going ahead with it. And anyway, even if she does, I got her to sign the contract. We've backed ourselves up.'

'You play such dirty little games. It's despicable,' Mr Taylor spat, shaking his head. 'I thought this was all going to be above board?'

'Your way wasn't working. You said that it would take Simon weeks to find us, he was there in a couple of days,' Damien countered.

'And that's a lesson learnt. He's incredibly strong,' Mr Taylor said. 'Nothing is a certainty with him.'

'We need certainties!' George declared. 'We need to keep them apart. It's the only way to make sure that this spell is not cast.'

'Maybe not,' Damien shrugged. 'I've had an idea. It's a bit of a worst case scenario, but I guess we're there.'

'I don't want to be part of any more unscrupulous activity,' Mr Taylor stated. 'It makes us just as bad as the Malants.'

'We have to fight fire with fire,' George said. 'Go on, Damien.'

'Let's just say, there's a way that we can control things from afar and still be sure that they won't be casting that spell.'

TWENTY-ONE

It took Simon a few minutes to find his composure and walk back to the car. He gestured for Jim to wind down his window. 'I'll meet you at the pub down the road. I just need a few minutes. I need to clear my head.'

'Certainly sir,' Jim confirmed, then he drove off to The Rose, where Beth used to work.

Simon walked through the car park to the back of the building, out of sight. It was only about six o'clock and the sky was very bright, but he needed to be alone. He checked that no one else was around and then touched the outside of Beth's block of flats. He closed his eyes slowly and summoned his power.

Using both of his hands, he pushed his strength against the brickwork. Within seconds, a slight golden tinge, barely visible to the naked eye, wrapped itself around the building. When it was complete, Simon stepped back. It was now shielded.

He hadn't blocked magic completely. He wanted Beth to still have her skills. He'd just made sure that no other Malant could now enter the flat; whether through vision, like with a location spell, or physically, like Damien turning up.

If Beth wouldn't go home with him, the least he could do was still try and keep her safe. It's the best he could do for now, but it was something.

He headed on to The Rose where Jim was waiting in the car park. 'Do you want to go in for a drink, sir?' he asked.

Simon shook his head. 'I just want to get home.'

'Very well.' Simon then got in the back and Jim pulled away.

It was a sombre journey and Simon tried not to think of Beth, but it was an impossible task. He couldn't make any sense of what had happened. He'd rescued her from what must have been an awful few days, yet she was mad with him.

Was she really mad because it had taken him so long to get there? If only she knew what he'd been through. It seemed more than that, though. Something had happened that she wasn't telling him. He didn't even know why they'd taken her. Damien had got to her somehow. He had an angle somewhere, he always had an angle. Simon dreaded to think what they'd done to her; he couldn't even start to imagine what she must have been through. What on earth would make her want to kiss Damien?

They finally reached Simon's gate where they found Paul already waiting for it to open.

'Where's he been?' Simon asked.

'He went to the office, sir. He was trying to clear some of your backlog, to give you a bit of a break. We must have been just behind him all this way.'

Jim parked the Lexus next to the Jaguar that Paul had borrowed and they all got out.

'Hi mate!' Paul grinned. 'Where is she then?'

Simon just shook his head and marched into the house. He headed straight for the drinks cabinet and poured himself a whiskey.

'Si?' Paul asked, following closely behind him. 'What's going on?'

'I wish I knew.' Simon flopped on the sofa, defeated.

'When you emailed me this morning you seemed really happy. You said everything was okay.'

'Everything was. Until a few minutes later. They've done something to her.'

'Where did you find her? What happened?'

'She was with Damien!'

'Damien? As in Damien Rock?'

'That little fucker.'

'I thought Jane had taken care of him?'

'He was in bed with her when I found them. They were kissing.'

'Kissing? Are you sure?'

'She had no problem admitting it. She was saying all sorts of weird stuff.'

'Like what?'

'She called me manipulative. She said that Damien had told her the truth.'

'The truth about what?'

'It was as if she thought I knew. Maybe that's where this manipulative things comes from. Damien's clearly been filling her head with loads of crap, but she refused to tell me anything. And now she's decided that she wants to completely cancel Wednesday.'

'Wednesday?'

'Her birthday. She's been so excited. Then suddenly, out of the blue, she said she wants the day to go by unnoticed and she'll come and see me on Thursday. I mean... what have they done to her?'

Paul thought for a second and then he sat down next to Simon. 'Where is she now?'

'At her flat.'

'On her own?'

Simon looked around to check that Jim wasn't in earshot, but he was nowhere to be seen. 'Don't worry, I've shielded the building. No one will find her. She refused to come home with me, what could I do?'

'She refused to come home?' Simon just shrugged, he had no words to explain it. 'Damien knows where her flat is, don't forget,' Paul added.

'No other Malant can enter, just me and Beth. Even if she wants him to.'

'I'm so sorry mate. I don't know what to say. Do you have any clue as to why they took her?'

'Why would she be kissing Damien?' Simon asked. It was all he could think about.

'I can't explain it, mate. She hated him. We all do. Do you think he's cast some sort of spell on her?'

'He couldn't have done. All magic was blocked. She said she did it because she was mad at me for taking so long to find her. It's just not Beth, though. It doesn't make any sense. She said something about how he'd given her the facts.'

'Facts about what?'

'You tell me. Whatever it is, it's probably a load of bullshit. No doubt something about how Malants and non-Malants can't really be together.'

'How would that work? He's a Malant.'

'Oh, I don't know. He's such a slimy fucker, who knows what he's doing. He's just... I can't... why? We're supposed to be newlyweds...'

'Look mate, Beth's been through quite a lot of late, maybe letting her have a bit of time on her own is a good thing. She's no fool. Whatever Damien has said to her, she's going to see through him eventually. You know how smart she is. Just give her the time to see it for herself.'

'See what, though? Why did they take her? What have they done to her? That's the bit that bothers me. I haven't got a clue. Beth never hides anything. She's about as open as a person can possibly be, but suddenly today she just wasn't telling me something. I know it.' Simon sighed and rubbed his forehead. 'Do you think I've lost her?'

'Are you kidding me? I've seen the way she looks at you. She couldn't be more in love with you if she tried.

No, this is something deeper, and we're going to get to the bottom of it. There's one person that we still haven't spoken to, and I bet that person will give us all the answers we need.'

'You mean Jane? You think we should go and see Jane? But she let Damien out of jail.'

'We don't know that. We don't know anything. I think we have to trust her. We'll go and see her first thing tomorrow morning.'

'Tomorrow? I can't wait that long.' Simon felt sickened at the prospect of waiting again for answers.

'It's Sunday night, Si. She won't be in the office.'

'You've got her phone number.'

'I can't call her now.'

'Please Paul. Please. Beth's family. Something's wrong with a member of our family. I need to know. If there's any chance she can help, we have to know.'

Paul considered Simon's plea and then he nodded. 'All right mate. You're right.' He pulled his mobile phone out of his pocket and dialled Jane's number. Simon waited anxiously, but after a few seconds, Paul hung up. He looked quite pale. 'It went straight to voicemail.'

'Leave a message. Ask her to call us straight back.'

'It never goes straight to voicemail.'

'She's probably on the tube.'

'You don't understand. As she's in charge of security, they tweaked her phone so that she can always be contacted. Okay, she might not always answer it, but it never fails to ring.'

Simon and Paul stared at each other. Nothing seemed to make any sense. 'You have her home number don't you?' Simon nudged.

'I'm not calling that!' Paul snapped back.

'Why not?'

Paul shifted awkwardly in his seat. 'It's her personal number.'

'I think under the circumstances she'd be okay with it.

Why do you have it if it's not okay for you to call?'

'What if her husband answers?'

'That's better than no answer at all.'

Paul swallowed hard. 'Yeah, of course mate. Of course. Let's dial her home.'

Paul did just that and waited while it rang. 'Hi. Hi there. It's... err... Paul... Paul Bird. Sorry to bother you on a Sunday, this is kind of urgent, though. It's work related. Is Jane around?'

Simon watched Paul's face turn from anxious to surprised to desperately worried, all in the space of ten seconds.

'What do you mean?' Paul asked the person on the other end of the phone. 'What happened? But that was when... Right. Of course. You know I will. I'm so sorry.' Paul hung up.

Simon's breathing stopped as he awaited dreadful news. 'What is it?'

'That was her husband. He doesn't know where Jane is. No one does. Apparently no one has seen or heard from her since Tuesday.'

'Tuesday?'

'The same day that Beth disappeared.'

'Oh my God. They've got Jane too?'

'I don't know, but this is too much to be a coincidence. I tell you what, Si, we need to get down to Malancy HQ and we need to get answers now. Enough is enough.'

'Who's going to be there on a Sunday night?'

'There's always someone there. Even if it's just security, we're getting some answers.'

Simon knocked back the remainder of his whiskey and then he stood up. He felt back in control for the first time that day. They were doing something proactive and it's what he needed more than anything.

'Jim!' he shouted. 'We need to go into London.' Simon waited for Jim to appear, just as he always did, but nothing happened. 'Jim!' he called again, and then he walked to the hallway. 'Jim?'

In all the years that Jim had worked for him, whenever Simon had called out his name, he'd always immediately responded. Jim was always there, indeed like magic. This was very out of character.

'Jim's gone now?' Paul asked.

Simon walked back into the living room and looked out the window. 'The Lexus has gone. He's taken the car.'

'At least it's explainable this time. I suppose it has been a bit tense of late.'

'Do you think Jim's left me, too?'

'Oh Simon, stop being so soppy. He's probably just giving us some space. I think he did a good thing.'

'But we need him.'

'I'll drive us into London. You've had a drink.'

'Where are we going to park?'

'Oh for fuck's sake, Simon, we're Malants, we'll park wherever the hell we want to. Get a grip.'

Simon sighed and followed Paul out.

'Don't think you're taking the Aston,' Simon warned, not a pinch of humour in his tone.

'As if!' Paul remarked, grabbing the keys to the Jaguar. Then they both left the house, pinning all their hopes on this journey.

TWENTY-TWO

Beth had curled herself up in bed. She was snuggly wrapped up in a woolly cardigan that she'd found in her wardrobe, one of the few remaining garments left in her flat. It wasn't a cold evening, but Beth needed the comfort and security that her trusty cardigan gave her.

She was so depressed. No matter how much she prayed that she was wrong, she couldn't see a future for them now. Her head was like a tornado of negativity and she couldn't see any goodness at all. It pulled at her heart like an anchor.

Suddenly her buzzer went off. Someone was at the front door.

Her heart pounded and she wrapped the duvet around her, determined not to answer the intercom.

It buzzed again and she remained stock still, as if the mystery caller one floor down might hear her breathing and know she was there. They buzzed again.

Suddenly her fear metamorphosed into anger as she twigged it must be Simon. She didn't know anyone else in the area and surely the anti-Malants would be happy that she was far away from the other chosen one, why would they rock the boat? No, it was Simon. He couldn't keep his word and he couldn't keep away. She didn't know what she was going to do.

Making her jump, the buzzer went off for a fourth time. She quickly leapt out of bed and picked up the intercom receiver.

'What?' she snapped.

'Mrs Bird?' This was not Simon. But her anger didn't fade as she deduced that Simon was now simply sending other people to emotionally blackmail her on his behalf. And she knew exactly who this was. 'It's Jim. Can we talk?'

She couldn't turn him away. He was surely harmless, after all. Whatever Simon had told him, it couldn't be the truth, and at least she might be able to find out something about Simon's current state of mind.

'I'm buzzing you up, Jim.' Beth did just that and she waited by the door, but nothing happened. She went to pick up the receiver again. 'Are you coming up?'

There was a slight hesitation in Jim's response. 'No, Mrs Bird. It doesn't feel right me being up there with you. Can we go for a drink?'

'Oh Jim, I'm really not up for it.'

'Please.'

'I'm shattered.'

'Look Beth, I need to speak to you. It's about Simon.'

Beth fell silent. Since when did he call them Beth and Simon?

'If you trust me at all, Beth, please join me for a drink.'

She paused. This Jim sounded different. He'd lost his formality, both in words and tone. She was fearful and intrigued, and she suddenly felt that she had far more to gain by going out with him than staying put. 'I'm on my way down.'

Beth grabbed her little bag, but she stopped in her tracks when she realised that she only had Euros on her. Virtually everything in the world that she owned was at Simon's house. She really was completely stuck. She definitely hadn't thought this through. She had no money, no phone, no food, barely any clothes, nothing. Maybe Jim's arrival had been more convenient than she'd thought.

She left her flat, still snuggled up in her comfortable cardigan, feeling highly grateful that at least her magic meant she could get in and out without a key. For now, anyway. Although what she was going to do after six o'clock on Wednesday, she did not know. She'd have to ask Jim to bring her over some stuff.

She reached the bottom of the stairs and opened the door to the warm spring evening where Jim was waiting patiently for her just outside.

'I take it you're happy to go to The Rose?' he asked.

'Yes, it will be nice to be on the other side of the bar for a change.'

They started the short journey with an awkward silence that Beth couldn't stand. She hated it when people didn't speak and she'd had quite enough of that for one day. 'What's all this about, Jim?' she nudged.

'Let's get you a drink first, then we can talk.'

'I have to be honest with you, all I have is Euros. I've been a bit of an idiot.'

'Please don't worry, it's my round anyway.'

'You shouldn't be buying me a drink.'

'Oh yes I should.'

Despite Beth's best efforts, Jim would tell her no more until they reached the pub just a few minutes later.

'Hi Beth!' the girl behind the bar said. This girl was Katy. Beth had done a couple of shifts with her in the few weeks that she'd actually worked there. She was a bit younger than Beth but they'd got on very well.

'Hi Katy. How's things?'

'Same as always.' Katy then pointed slyly to Jim and silently queried if this was the new husband.

'No. This is Jim.' Beth felt ridiculous describing him as their butler. It was too Downton Abbey and she hated it. 'He's a family friend.'

'Nice to meet you,' Jim nodded, not a flinch to his face

from Beth's description. 'What are you drinking?' he then asked Beth.

'Would you judge me if I had a pint?'

'Don't be silly. We'll have two pints of lager, please Katy,' Jim requested.

The drinks were poured and Beth followed Jim to a quiet corner. The pub was reasonably busy, but just enough so they could talk without anyone really hearing.

'How is he?' Beth asked.

'If you mean Simon, not good. Not good at all.'

'Since when have you started calling him Simon?' Beth had to know now, it felt so weird.

'Beth, take a sip of your drink.'

She did as she was told, her adrenaline running high as she anticipated bad news coming her way. 'Why are you here, Jim?'

'I can't let you do this.'

Beth shook her head. 'Things are more complicated-'

'I know what the complications are.'

'I seriously doubt you do.'

'No Beth, I seriously doubt you do.'

Beth hadn't expected this. She looked at him, not quite sure what else to say.

'First things first,' Jim continued. 'You need to know my real name.' Beth's stomach knotted. 'Simon and Paul know me as Jim Smith.'

'But that's not who you are?' Beth clarified with a dread as to what was to come.

'No Beth. I was born James Malant.'

Beth's mouth fell unintentionally open. This was the last thing in the world she'd expected. 'Malant? You're are...?'

'I'm not just a Malant, Beth. I'm a direct descendant from the original Malant family.'

'Like George?'

'You've met George?' Jim was shocked by this.

'No. Mr Taylor told me about him.'

'So I was right. They've told you about being a chosen one, then?'

'You know about that? Mr Taylor told me everything. Are you related to George?'

'He's my twin brother.'

'You have a twin brother? How come he ended up in charge of the Malancy and you're a butler?'

'I'm not a butler.' This properly confused Beth. 'I'm sure Mr Taylor told you a lot, but I bet not everything. Here's the stuff that you need to know. I'm guessing he told you about Samuel and Elizabeth?' Beth just nodded. 'Well, their son documented what they did and how they changed the capabilities of all future Malants. To keep it as controlled as possible, he passed the information on to only his first born. Then his first child passed it on to their first born, who passed it on to their first born, and the tradition went on and on, and was always destined to continue until the next generation - that is you and Simon - were ready.'

'Next generation?'

'It was all going very well but then things changed quite significantly for the Malancy when my great grandfather founded Malancy HQ.'

'Your government.'

'There had been some loosely based control prior to this, but it needed formalising as the Malant population was growing massively, far bigger than I imagine Samuel or Elizabeth could ever have envisioned. After he died, the ruling and the knowledge got passed on to his daughter - my grandmother - and then she passed it on to my father when she retired. Then, more recently, myself and George were handed the baton. As twins, they decided to treat us both equally, but, let's just say, things haven't gone quite as planned.'

'You can say that again.'

'What you need to know is that my father was a bit of a control freak,' Jim continued.

'Was?' Beth asked hesitantly.

'He died over a decade ago. It really doesn't matter. He was a control freak who wanted absolute power and he thrived on being in charge of our little government. However, knowing that the five hundredth anniversary of the spell was fast approaching and seeing that his family's reign was in threat, he started to petition the end of the Malancy.'

'That's so selfish.'

'I completely disagreed with it, but George supported him. That being the case, our father gave George ultimate control of the Malancy government and I was left with just an advisory role.'

'You still work for the government, then?'

'I'm on the payroll, as is all the family, but they never seem to request my advice. Funny that.'

'So how come you ended up going into... butlering?'

'I'm not a butler. Look, what I'm about to tell you, nobody knows. It has to stay between us; you have to swear. I'm only telling you as I think you need to know all the facts to make a truly informed decision. I don't want Simon or Paul to ever know this.'

'I promise. I won't say anything.'

'I'm deeply ashamed of this, and you have to know that I had nothing to do with it and I've made my feelings on the matter very clear to all involved.'

'What is it?'

Jim took a deep breath. 'My father killed Simon's parents.'

'What?!' Beth gasped.

'About fifty years ago, my family starting preparing for the chosen ones. They knew those who were either going to continue or end the Malancy could be born at any time, so they kept their ears to the ground. Then, when Simon was born, my family instantly knew who he was. He caused such a commotion, he was so different.'

'Oh my God! Is that why his parents took him away?

To protect him from your family?'

'Exactly.'

'That makes so much sense. But why kill them?'

'Because they were very good at hiding him. From my perspective, I agree, we needed to keep an eye on Simon. We needed to find out who the other chosen one was and we needed to make sure you both fulfilled your fate. However, my father didn't want to just observe, he wanted full control.'

'Full control?'

'I'm mortified to admit it, but my family has been manipulating Simon's life ever since the day he went to live with Paul.'

'Manipulating?' then everything clicked with Beth. 'You mean your family has been wiping him off the internet and making people scared of him?'

'It's all George, I have had nothing to do with it. You have to believe me. He's spread dreadful rumours about Simon killing people and all sorts of horrific rubbish. The logic was that if everyone either feared Simon or knew nothing about him, then it would be harder for the chosen female to make contact.'

Beth smiled. 'They didn't count on how much I was going to fall in love with him.'

'How much you were going to fall in love with each other,' Jim corrected. Beth just shook her head. 'Anyway, they couldn't take the risk of killing Simon just in case it secured the future of the Malancy somehow. A chosen one's death was never factored in and that scared them. So, instead, they got his parents away for the night and then... it wasn't so much a freak gas explosion, more my father's magical intervention.'

'At the French restaurant?' Beth whispered.

'Simon told you? Anyway, it was put down to a pure accident. No one suspected a thing. Why would they?'

Beth felt a deep sadness weigh down inside of her. 'You couldn't have stopped it?'

'I was barely seventeen. It was only afterwards that I learnt my father was involved and that's when I started to pull back a bit from my family. I'm utterly ashamed of them.'

'Simon has to know this.'

'No!'

'But Jim-'

'No Beth.'

'But he's been so mad with his parents. He thinks they let him down.'

'Simon is very powerful, Beth. I can't take the risk of what he'd do if he ever found out the truth. We have to protect him.'

'All these secrets! Don't you see, you're controlling him as much as your brother!'

'How dare you! Simon needs to focus on the future and he needs to do it objectively. If he finds out the truth about his parents it will skew his perspective. I've seen what his anger can do to him. You have to trust me, Beth. I want the best for him, that's all I've ever wanted.'

Beth glared at Jim. She hated the fact that she'd promised to keep this awful truth a secret. Then she remembered witnessing Simon's anger literally pulsate through him. Maybe this wasn't the right time for Simon to find out. 'Okay, I'll keep it to myself for now. But I don't agree with the lies.'

A moment of tension passed between the pair as Beth cogitated all that she'd been told to date. Then a hole in Jim's story revealed itself. 'If they wanted to control Simon so much, where does Paul fit into this? Why did they let him off the hook?'

'Off the hook? What do you mean?'

'Surely he's a threat to them?'

'Not at all. Why would he be?'

'He's going to help keep the Malancy alive.'

'How?'

'Working with Simon. Why can't you see that?'

Jim studied Beth for a moment. 'Do you think that Paul knows? No, only Simon's parents knew. And we have no clue how they ever found out.'

'But Simon's clearly told Paul since. It's obvious.'

'Simon? What are you talking about? Simon doesn't know anything about this.'

'Of course he does. Don't be stupid.'

Jim looked Beth directly in the eyes. 'You think that Simon knows about this?'

'He must do.'

'He absolutely does not. One of my family's only advantages has been that Simon doesn't know a thing. The same with Paul. They know about as much as you did a week ago.'

'But Damien said that-'

'Damien? Why on earth would you believe Damien?'

'He said that Simon would have sensed it.'

'You both can sense it. That would be the warm feeling you share when you're together. But did you know why you were feeling that? Of course you didn't. So why would Simon? Did you really think that his parents would tell their teenage son that he was a chosen Malant, destined to control the future of the Malancy forever?'

'What about since then, though?'

'Who would tell him?'

'Well why kidnap me then? Surely if neither of us knew anything, the day would have just gone by unnoticed and the Malancy would have ended anyway? Why all the fuss?'

'Two reasons. Firstly, because you're destined to find out. We don't know how, or at least I don't, but when the day comes, you are both meant to know. Then there's factor number two, and that's me. They know that one way or another I'll make sure that you both find out. That's why I manoeuvred my way in as Simon's butler. I needed to keep an eye on him, and who else outside the family is closer?'

'Oh! That makes sense. So why haven't you told Simon

the truth yet? What are you waiting for?'

'I've been trying to protect him. Protect both of you. The less you knew, the better. I didn't know how you were going to find each other, but I didn't want to put any pressure on it. The less you knew, the more natural I thought your meeting would be. I thought it best to let fate take charge. And I was right.'

'Don't they want to kill you now, though? You're getting in the way, aren't you?'

Jim smirked. 'George is manipulative, cruel even, but he's not a murderer. That was just my father. George would rather out manoeuvre me, and he must definitely believe he's winning. And besides, even if he did ever get desperate, I've made sure the truth will always get out. They know I've been scheming but they don't know any more. They can't take the risk.'

'No, hang on, Simon must know.' Another hole in the plot struck Beth. 'He told me earlier that he wanted us to be back for Wednesday. He knew all about the importance of Wednesday.'

Jim rolled his eyes. 'Beth, what else is happening on Wednesday?' Beth just looked at Jim. She had no clue what he was talking about. 'You've made sure it's a day that Simon is never to forget.' Beth thought hard, but she couldn't see past the idea that Simon had been lying to her. 'Does the thirty-first of May ring any bells?'

'Oh shit, it's my birthday!'

'He's been making so many plans for you. He wanted the day to be extra special. And you basically told him to forget it all, didn't you?'

'Oh no. I feel awful. I can't believe that I forgot all about it. Everything makes so much sense now. I was such a bitch to him.'

'You've upset him quite a lot. Doesn't that show you how much he loves you?'

'So he really does love me?'

'How could you think anything else?'

'I feel dreadful. I can't believe that I doubted him. What have I been thinking? What did Damien do to me? We have to tell him. I have to explain.'

'I think it's probably time he knew. I wanted to tell you both after your night at Piccadilly Circus. You both seemed so happy, it seemed the perfect time. But then those feathers ruined everything.'

'You knew he turned into a bird? You weren't even there.'

'I know everything that happens with Simon. That's what makes me the perfect butler.'

'So you knew that Damien cast the bird spell?'

'Only afterwards. Not at the time.'

'It was the anti-Malants-'

'The anti-Malants?' Jim queried.

'Yes. That's what they are. They gave Damien the bicantomene. They were behind it all, weren't they?'

'What?' Jim seemed properly confused by this. 'Did Damien tell you that?' Beth nodded. 'It seems to me that Damien has fed you a lot of rubbish. Why did you trust him?'

'But what he said made so much sense. How did he get away with it, then?'

'When my grandmother took charge of Malancy HQ, she set about ridding our country of all dark materials. They're completely banned substances and they were all exiled years ago. That being the case they only get detected now if they enter into the country. Damien must have had it for a very long time. God knows from where and how he hid it, but it was already in his possession, I know that for sure. I'm still part of the government you know, and believe me that whole episode caused quite a stir.'

'Why is he not in jail then?'

'Because it caused a stir in a good way. Damien is just the sort of person that my brother takes a shine to. It must have been Damien's lucky day. He must have been recruited as one of the new... what do you call them?'

'Anti-Malants?'

'Anti-Malants. I like that.'

'So he doesn't really want the Malancy to end?'

'Damien? I doubt it. But it's better than life in prison.'

'I don't know how I feel about it.'

'Feel about what?'

'The Malancy. Damien might be a complete bastard, but Mr Taylor made a lot of sense. The Malancy has been abused.'

'Abused? How can you say that? Why are you listening to those awful people? Look me in the eye, Beth.' She did as requested. 'Now tell me, from your gut, who do you trust more? Me or Mr Taylor?'

Beth knew there was no competition. 'You, of course.'

'Then listen to this. Did Mr Taylor tell you about the wars that the Malancy has stopped? Did he mention the lives that we've saved through our charity work? What about the good deeds that many Malants do? Take your husband. Why do you think he's been gifted with a talent such as his?'

'He's a chosen one.'

'Not his powers, his mind. He's so clever, but he also has a deeply caring soul, and he uses his powers for good. The impact of some of his magic has been truly incredible. He's changed lives, and stopped lawsuits and bankruptcy, and that, in turn, has prevented the inevitable downturn that always derives from such events. It may seem like tiny actions to you and I, but to the person he does it for, it means the world.'

'He does it for financial gain, though. He's a millionaire off the back of it.'

'Why not? It's small compensation for the good he's done, and for the suffering that he's had to go through himself. Maybe that's justice.'

'Okay, I admit, maybe there's more to what the Malancy has done for our world than I know, but answer me this: if George, as an original Malant, brings the

Malancy to an end, what happens to him? Surely he loses everything? If he was so selfish, why would he deliberately set about bringing down his own power? It makes no sense.'

'Beth, whatever happens in three days' time, he loses everything anyway. As soon as you and Simon cast the spell, you start the new line. My family has stronger powers than any other Malant except for you and Simon, yet they will become worthless against the both of you when you cast that spell. That's the thing. It's all about control to them. If they can't have it, then why should anyone else.'

'They'll become like normal people?'

'No, they'll still have some powers as far as magic goes. But it will be nothing compared to what you will have. And you'll see everything in a different light. It's a new era for the Malancy, it's inevitable.'

'I don't want to be running a government. We're business people.'

Jim chuckled at this. 'You won't have to run the country, but you'll have ultimate power, and George's less than ethical ways will get called into question. There's no way you'll allow him to continue to be in charge. Trust me, it'll all become clear. And he knows it.'

Beth sighed. She took a second to mull it all over in her head and then she turned back to Jim. 'You definitely think the Malancy should continue?'

'There's no question. Just as Simon's parents knew. Don't let their death be in vain. That's why I wanted you to know everything. This is fifty percent your decision, but out of the two of you, you're the stronger one to make the choice. You needed all the facts.'

'It's such a responsibility.'

Jim paused for thought. Then he asked her, 'You're excited by the powers you've gained, aren't you?'

'I was.'

'Okay, so you might play around a little and enjoy them, but won't you ultimately use them for good?'

'Always.'

'And that's why you and Simon are the chosen ones. That's why the decision is nothing to do with George or anyone else in the world. Your ethics are solid, so just go with your heart.'

All of a sudden, Beth realised that she was the most relaxed she'd been in days. Her brain had calmed down immensely, and for the first time, in what seemed like forever, she knew what she had to do. She wasn't confused anymore, everything had just slotted right into place. 'Jim, would you please take me home? I think we need to speak to my husband.'

TWENTY-THREE

Paul pulled Simon's Jaguar up right outside the front door of Malancy HQ. It was technically illegal to park there, but, stepping out, Simon brushed his hand against the car and it disappeared from view.

The door was always open to Malants, and they walked straight in.

'Mr Bird!' the security guard greeted as they both reached the reception desk, but he was clearly talking to Simon over Paul. A stocky man in his forties, he was the only person around. 'You're just the man we've been waiting for.'

Simon had not been expecting this, and he remained silent for a second as he assessed the situation. Paul, on other hand, didn't falter. 'You've been expecting us?'

'More like hoping. You'd better go on up. Ralph's on four.'

The pair hesitated before moving. They'd been preparing themselves to beg for information, not to have it thrust upon them in such a way. With a pinch of suspicion but a greater need for answers, they made their way to Ralph's laboratory on the fourth floor.

Ralph, a highly skilled Malant, who'd approached his

ability from a more academic viewpoint, was sitting at a desk in the corner of his lab, pouring through pages of notes.

It was a large, very tidy space, and the majority of the room was crowded with shelves. Half of the shelves were filled with Ralph's important "elements", but the other half were strangely empty. "Elements" was the Malancy term for any third party device that allowed them to cast spells. The very things that Simon rarely needed, but were pivotal for any other Malant to harness their power.

'It's been a while,' Paul said, catching Ralph by surprise. The petite man stood up, nearly a whole foot shorter than Simon, and in every way inferior.

'Mr and Mr Bird!' Ralph beamed, clearly very happy to see them. 'Please, take a seat.'

They pulled up a couple of chairs from the corner of the room and sat with Ralph.

'What's been going on?' Simon asked, making immediately sure that he stayed in control of the conversation. He wasn't going to tell Ralph anything that he didn't already know, unless he deemed it vital for Beth's welfare. Trust was now a thing deeply in question.

'Weird things,' Ralph replied. 'But I'm guessing you must already know that to be here.'

Paul went to reply, but Simon cut him off. He was sure that Paul would automatically trust Ralph, they'd known each other for such a long time, but Simon knew that they had to be objective. 'We were hoping to see Jane,' he simply said.

'It's all so peculiar.'

'Tell us what happened,' Simon virtually ordered.

'Jane went out for lunch on Tuesday and never came back. After a few hours, her team started to get quite worried. That's when they found it on her desk. Her resignation letter.'

'Jane resigned? I don't think so,' Paul stated, shaking his head.

'Neither do we,' Ralph agreed. 'She's been thriving of late, really getting a handle on things. It doesn't add up.'

'Have you tried to contact her?' Simon asked.

'In every way. No one's seen or heard from her since she left here. Not even her husband.'

Simon flashed Paul a look that told him to be quiet. He wanted to hear Ralph's version of events and keep it to that.

'My immediate thought was to do a location spell,' Ralph continued. 'But this is where it gets even more curious. They've taken all the potent elements off me. Security came in and said there was to be a review of some reported power abuse and all the strongest elements were to be confiscated until further notice. Without them, I'm useless; I can't do the spell. And it's not like I can easily put my hands on anything that powerful.'

Simon knew he was talking about more precious items that wielded the greatest power to Malants; and for someone like Ralph to cast a location spell, he'd have to have several of them just for starters.

Simon suddenly felt Paul's gaze burning into him. They both knew that Simon could perform such a spell very easily, but Paul was now keeping very quiet.

Ralph, on the other hand, although well aware of Simon's greater power, had no idea just how powerful Simon was. Simon had been careful to rarely use his magic in public, and very few Malants had ever witnessed the extent of his true ability. There was no way Ralph could know that Simon had the power to perform such a spell with ease. Simon had thoroughly protected himself, and had made sure that his true strength had been downplayed, even to a Malant as wise as Ralph. But maybe now was not the time for caution. Simon was the only one who could give them the answers they needed, and, weighing it up, he saw no harm in taking charge.

Simon stood up and walked to Ralph's shelves. He searched through the occupied ones, the ones that still had the weaker elements. He came across a stone; just an ordinary stone. It was a good size, enough to fill Simon's hand.

He walked back over towards Paul and Ralph and once again took his seat. 'In a minute, you might want to close your eyes,' he simply said. Then he did just that himself.

He held the stone out squarely in his hands and he thought of Jane. He built up the vision in his head and the spell started to work. As always, the stone burned vibrantly in his hands before slowly consuming his body, and then beams of light swallowed up the entire room leaving nothing untouched. The spell was complete.

Simon dropped the stone to his lap. He had his answer.

Ralph removed his hands from his face and squinted. He sat staring at Simon in awe, completely lost for words.

'Fuck me,' Paul said.

Their astonishment at his ability was the break that Simon needed as it gave him time to think. The spell had failed to show him anything, just as it had done with Beth a few days earlier. He knew he'd done it right, he was certainly well practised, but she too was being blocked in some way. This ran deeper than he cared to admit. Now he had to decide what to do with this information.

'You are remarkable,' Ralph finally uttered. 'How on earth did you do that?'

'It's just who I am,' Simon replied, quite to the point.

'I'd love to learn more,' Ralph virtually begged.

'I'm not an experiment.' Simon's response was again clipped.

'It would be my honour to work with you sometime, Mr Bird. You are a man to be respected.'

'Where is she then?' Paul asked, rubbing his eyes.

Simon breathed hard. What was he going to do? He wanted to tell Paul, but he felt the information would be far safer with them than with Ralph. He also didn't want to say anything within the walls of the building. Everyone and everything was suspect.

'We need to leave.' Simon stood up, taking the stone with him. He placed in back exactly where he'd found it, then he made his way to the door.

'Mr Bird, please. What did you see? Was it bad? I need to know.' Ralph was obviously desperate.

'Don't worry, Ralph,' Simon replied. 'Sometimes it's better not to know, and trust me, this is one of those occasions. Are you coming, Paul?'

Paul smiled to Ralph, clearly a little awkward with Simon's reaction, but he followed Simon out nevertheless.

'Well?' Paul asked when they stepped inside the lift. 'Where is she?'

Simon looked to the floor. He was desperately trying to find the will to continue, but just at that very moment something broke inside of him, and that was it. Enough was enough.

All he wanted, all he'd ever wanted, was to be at home with his wife. But it seemed right from their very first date, the world had been conspiring against them; and now it had got so bad she wouldn't even see him. He didn't even know why.

After a lifetime of dejection, he'd now hit the lowest he'd ever felt. His heart hurt and his head closed down. None of this other stuff mattered to him, all he wanted was to be with Beth.

He was sick of being a Malant and having to deal with so much endless crap. All he wanted was a normal life. Why was that so difficult for them?

'Si?' Paul nudged as they reached the ground floor.

'I've had enough.' Simon paced through the reception and headed straight outside, ignoring the security guard's pleasantries. He tapped the car and it reappeared, as if from nowhere, and then he jumped straight in the driver's seat. Paul wasn't far behind. 'I can't take this anymore!' Simon roared. 'What have I done to deserve all this shit all the time? Why won't they just leave us alone?'

'Where is she?' Paul asked, settling into the passenger's

seat.

'Nowhere! The same bloody place that Beth was in: nowhere. They're playing with us. I don't know what to do, but I've had enough. I'm so fed up. All I want is Beth.'

'We can figure this out, Si. We can. They won't win.'

'But win what? What do they want? What have Beth and I done to them?' Simon started the engine and headed off with speed. He'd made up his mind. 'I can't face going home tonight. I'm sorry Paul. If she's not there, I don't want to be there either.'

'That's fine by me.'

'Instead, we're going to spend an extortionate about of money and we're going to get utterly shitfaced.'

'Sounds like a good plan to me, Si. I think it's long overdue. You need to let it all out. Let's have a boy's night and let's put all this crap behind us. We can worry about Jane tomorrow.'

'We're already on our way.'

'I've been dying to try the Shangri-La,' Paul suggested.

'Not tonight. Tonight it's going to be like the old days.'

'Park Lane?'

'We'll be there in fifteen minutes.'

That night, for the first time in a very long time, Simon splashed his cash. They checked in to the best suite available at the hotel and they immediately ordered champagne.

After freshening up a bit, Simon summoned up some suitable attire for them and they headed into the West End.

Feeling in an exceptionally anti-Malant mood, Simon refused to go to any Malant venue, and they instead visited places that they'd never been to before. They had a pint or two in a few pubs to begin with, and then they moved on for shorts and cocktails afterwards in some more sophisticated bars, all the time refusing to acknowledge the strange looks of their fellow drinkers who were, as expected, reacting to Simon's chilly aura.

As many establishments slowly started to close on the badly timed Sunday night, they decided to head to Paul's favourite Casino. It was another place that Simon had never been to, but it was the sort of venue that he was just in the mood for. Tonight was all about letting it go, and if that meant relinquishing some of his hard earned money, then so be it.

It was the most freeing experience that Simon had had in years. He let himself go in a way that he hadn't dared to in over a decade, and it felt amazing. Win or lose, he didn't care, he was surrendering his control and refusing to give a crap about anything. Nothing mattered that night and it was just the tonic he'd needed.

Well into the early hours of Monday, the taxi dropped them off back at their hotel, but they were still not ready for bed. They knocked back one more bottle of champagne, listened to music, and reminisced about their lads' nights of the past.

At about four am, though, the alcohol finally took its toll. Collapsed on a sofa, Simon suddenly felt undeniably sad. He'd allowed himself to put on hold all of his woes; not just from recent times, but from pretty much his whole life, but nothing was buried deep. As the excitement of the night dissipated, so did Simon's free spirit, and a tear crept down his cheek.

'Oh mate,' Paul said, sympathetically.

'I let myself think I could be happy. How stupid was that.'

'This isn't your fault.'

'It's got to be. If things keep happening to you, at some point you have to stop blaming everyone else. This is all me.'

'And how do you figure that exactly? You didn't give yourself powers, you didn't turn yourself into a bird, you didn't kidnap Beth. Blaming yourself is ridiculous, and hugely counter-productive.'

'All I can see is that I'm destined to a life of misery. It's inevitable.'

'I thought we'd got past this, Si. Come on, we were having such a good time.'

'We did. Thanks Paul. I needed it. But the second I wake up tomorrow, it's back to reality. My wife won't speak to me, the only woman we trust at Malancy HQ has vanished, and Damien has yet again got the better of me.'

'And we'll deal with all that tomorrow. But not now, Si. Don't dwell on it now.'

'I'm going to bed.' Simon wobbled to his feet and stumbled to the main bedroom. He lay straight on the bed, not even undressing, and within seconds he was fast asleep.

TWENTY-FOUR

When Beth woke up the next morning, her heart was pounding. She was back in her marital bed, back in her proper home, but she was completely alone.

It had been about half past ten the night before when Beth and Jim had got back to the mansion. They'd walked in expecting to see Simon straight away, expecting questions and smiles, and expecting that everything could be laid out on the table and sorted. It came as a great surprise when they found both the Bird men out.

Assuming they'd be back soon, they'd waited with anticipation. Jim had made them a cuppa and they'd sat quietly in the living room, hoping that they wouldn't be long.

But as the hours had drifted away so had Beth and Jim's patience. They'd tried phoning them many times, completely unsuccessfully, and as the sun had started to dawn on Monday, the ambience had slipped from anticipation to just plain irritation.

Finally giving in and going to bed, Beth had found it virtually impossible to sleep. It was yet another night away from her new husband, but this time it was all her fault. She was plagued with guilt. She wanted so desperately to understand how she could have doubted the one man that she trusted more than anybody, and how she could have been so easily fooled by Damien's web of lies.

She couldn't remember what time it had been when she eventually drifted off, all she could remember were the vivid dreams that had once again lit up her mind. Just like the previous nights, she'd dreamt that she was with Simon and they'd been blessed with ultimate power. They could control everything and all they had to do was cast a simple spell. The world was theirs for the taking.

Now sitting up in bed, her heart was still pounding, but this time it wasn't met with cold sweats. This time she was stirred with a deep sense of love, and all she could think about was being with Simon. Forget about their destiny, forget about the Malancy, all Beth wanted at that moment was to be in Simon's arms again and to feel the safety of his touch.

She turned to the bedside clock. It was just before eleven and she knew she should get up. But with Simon still gone and her guilt still bearing down on her, she buried herself under the covers and she willed the world away once more.

It was nearly one o'clock by the time Simon eventually clicked the key in the door and returned home. He looked so bright, far better than he should; polar opposite to Paul's droopy eyed, major hangover.

That was another part of Simon's gift: self-healing; even in the case of a hangover. But today, he cursed it. Rather than being able to dwell in the misery of his own self-inflicted ailment, he now had to face life as if everything was the same as it always was. He was growing to hate his powers more and more with every passing minute.

'Where have you been?' Jim asked, running to the door. He looked very tired himself.

'Never mind where we've been, where were you?'

Simon asked in reply, his sour mood evident in his tone.

'I think we need to talk.'

'You're damn right we do. I needed you last night. We had to go into London and you'd just vanished without a word.'

'That's what we need to talk about.'

'You know I have no issues with you running personal errands, I never have, but the least you could do is come and talk to me. Don't I deserve that much?'

'You don't understand-' Jim was clearly getting exasperated.

'Paul had to drive me in the end. You'd even taken my car. That was pushing your luck just a bit, don't you think? In fact, you know what, from now on you're only permitted to use the car-'

'Will you shut up!' Jim suddenly shouted.

This shocked Simon into silence.

He'd barely had chance to contemplate Jim's uncharacteristic behaviour, though, when a shriek came from upstairs.

'What was that?' Paul asked with horror, but Simon knew. He'd know that shriek anywhere.

'She's back. That's what I've been trying to tell you!' Jim declared, but Simon was already darting up the stairs. He had to see it to believe it. It's all that he wanted. He hadn't even properly absorbed that she'd shrieked and what that could mean, he was just so relieved to know that Beth was home.

'Beth!' Simon yelled, racing into the bedroom. He couldn't wait to hug her tightly and wipe the past few days out of existence, but he was halted in the middle of the room when he saw her.

She was sitting on the side of the bed and her face was emblazoned with terror. Then he followed her wide eyes down.

Her cardigan sleeve was pulled up and resting, quite comfortably, in the middle of her arm, was a bright red feather.

TWENTY-FIVE

Beth was shaking it hurt so much. It was like a raw, burning sensation that enflamed all the skin around it.

She wanted to pull the feather out, but it was too deeply set in her body. It made her feel sick. Beth turned to Simon desperately, but all he could do was look back at her helplessly.

'What is it?' Paul asked, running in behind Simon. Then Jim came in just after.

'I've got a feather! I'm turning into a bird!' Beth cried. 'Why didn't you tell me how much it hurt?' she yelled at Simon. 'It's so painful. It's so itchy! Make it stop!'

'Calm down. The first thing you have to do is calm down,' Simon soothed. 'Remember your stress rash theory?' He moved forward to comfort Beth but he was stopped in his tracks when he heard Jim's voice.

'Oh my God!'

Simon glared at Jim. Then he glared at Paul. 'Jim! This isn't what it looks like. Beth has... err...'

'Oh bloody hell, he knows!' Beth spat out. All three men looked to Beth with surprise. 'Jim knows. He knows everything. He's a Malant.'

Then all eyes turned to Jim. He stood still. This

obviously wasn't the way that he'd expected Simon to find out. 'We need to talk,' he muttered.

'You're a Malant?' Simon asked, utterly gobsmacked.

'More than that,' Beth added. Her irritation levels had soared, such was the extraordinary discomfort on her arm. She needed them to get to the point, especially before she turned into a bird. 'Tell them Jim.'

'Let's go downstairs,' Jim said. 'We can talk more easily down there.' He quickly led the way, turning around just to add, 'I'm going to make us some tea and I'll see you in the living room.'

Beth rolled her eyes. Why was he procrastinating? Couldn't he just get on with it?

'Roll your sleeves down Beth, stop looking at it,' Simon gently instructed. She did just that, grateful that she could hide it from view, but it didn't stop her knowing it was there. It made her shudder.

They all headed downstairs and waited silently in the living room for Jim to join them with the tea. He placed four mugs on the coffee table and took a seat. He waited for everyone else to sit down as well and then he looked to Simon in particular.

'I'm not who you think I am,' Jim started.

'You're not a Malant?' Simon asked, a little confused.

'He's not a butler,' Beth butted in.

'Please Beth,' Jim hushed. 'I need to tell this.' She nodded her understanding and sat back.

'Beth is correct, I'm not a butler. My real name is James Malant and I'm a direct descendant from the original Malant family.' This rendered Simon and Paul completely speechless. 'It's a long story and we don't have time for all the details now, but basically the Malant legend isn't quite as you've been led to believe.'

'We're just like the original Malants,' Beth butted in again.

'What?' Simon asked, even more confused.

'Beth is referring to Samuel and Elizabeth Malant, my

ancestors, and the first two powerful beings. They didn't just come across their powers, as you've always been led to believe, they were actually both born with them. Powers exactly like you and Beth have.' Jim was now looking directly at Simon again. 'To cut a long story short, they struggled to control their magic and it led to many unfortunate consequences, including the death of their children. To help make things more manageable moving on, they cast a spell that meant their new offspring had a more limited power that would be easier to use, exactly like the majority of Malants today. That limited power has been passed on through generations for five hundred years. Five hundred years to the day this Wednesday.'

'Wednesday?' Simon queried, the cogs in his brain clearly kicking in to life.

'It's too huge for me to explain it all right now, but the original Malants didn't want to determine the future of the Malancy forever, so in their spell they left a loophole. On the five hundredth anniversary of when they cast the spell, two chosen ones would come together to decide the new future for Malants.'

'Chosen ones?' Simon queried.

'Us!' Beth confirmed.

'Yes,' Jim agreed, getting slightly agitated. 'You and Beth. You've been gifted with unlimited powers, just like the original Malants, so that you can cast the spell.'

'But if we don't cast it by six o'clock on Wednesday, Malancy will vanish forever,' Beth added.

'It will what?' Paul asked with shock.

Jim sighed, now visibly irritated by Beth's constant interruptions. 'The choice is yours. You either cast the spell by six o'clock on Wednesday and nothing will change, the Malancy will continue just as it always has been, or you can let the date pass by and Malancy will end forever.'

Simon took a moment to let the news sink in. It was clearly a little overwhelming for him. The whole room fell quiet, no one really knowing what to say next. Then Simon finally broke the silence when he turned to Jim with a stern face and asked, 'Why is it now, just two days before the deadline, that it's the first time I'm hearing about this? Why didn't I know before?'

'I was waiting for the second chosen one,' Jim simply replied.

'You didn't think I needed to know that my destiny is to either continue or end the Malancy? You didn't think that I needed to know the reason why I'm so different, the reason that people keep away from me; the reason why I've been so lonely all my life?'

Simon looked down and shook his head. Beth felt so sorry for him. She hated secrets, they always caused problems. Then the secret that she'd promised to Jim that she'd keep popped into her head.

Beth suddenly felt very passionately that Simon needed to know about his parents' death. He was right, he should have been told earlier. It was his destiny, no one had more right to know than him, and he needed to know the full truth about how it had shaped his life. She looked to Jim and willed him to tell Simon everything. But Jim just glanced back with cautious eyes.

Beth hated that she'd promised to keep it to herself. She felt like she was betraying her husband, and it wasn't right. She toyed with the idea of spitting it out. What could Jim do once it was out there? What's the worst that could happen?

Then she looked to Simon again. He was bent over with confusion and she could see the pulse of his anger surging through his arms. She backed down in her mind and decided to keep it to herself for now. She again gave Jim the benefit of the doubt. One step at a time.

'I was the only one who was ever willing to tell you,' Jim explained, 'but I didn't know when the right time was. I thought if you knew there was another person out there, just like yourself... I didn't know how you'd react. It might have made you crazy waiting for them. I'm sorry if what I did was wrong, but I had to go with my gut, and that told me to keep quiet until you'd met your partner. Then you could both deal with it together.'

Simon turned his attention to Beth. 'Why have you only just gained your powers?'

'I don't know,' Beth replied. 'I suppose I didn't need them until now. I really don't know.'

His glare then hardened. 'This is what you were talking about in Florence.' His eyes were so filled with confusion and anger, all Beth could do was nod in response. 'You want it to end?'

'Not anymore.'

'That's why they kidnapped her,' Jim explained. 'My twin brother-'.

'George Malant,' Beth chipped in.

Jim's sigh was far weightier this time, but Beth barely noticed, she was far too edgy with her new affliction. 'My twin brother, George, is head of Malancy HQ and, for a long list of reasons, he wants it to end. He kidnapped Beth to keep her away from you so you couldn't do the spell. Don't blame her. They played a lot of tricks on her to get her to believe that ending it would be for the best.'

'You knew where she was?' Simon accused.

'No. I had my suspicions that it was related to my brother, but that's about it. I tried to help as best I could.'

It was then as if a lightbulb had pinged in Simon's head and he once again focussed all of his attention on Beth. 'You thought I knew about this.'

His glare was so intimidating. Beth felt her guilt at the way she'd behaved throb once again in her stomach and it took her a moment to find her words. 'Damien told me you did. He made it all so convincing.'

Simon's eyes tinged with green at the mention of Damien's name and Beth felt her guilt magnify. 'I didn't,' was all he said, but his glower didn't move from Beth's face.

'I know that now. Jim explained everything.' Beth

found herself a little breathless as the tension in the room became suffocating. 'I didn't mean to kiss him,' she suddenly said. She could see in Simon's eyes that he was fixating on that sickening blunder and she had to try and extinguish its relevance. 'He filled my head with so much nonsense. I thought you'd been using me. I didn't think you even loved me.'

'How could you think that?' Simon was almost shaking.

'They'd been planning this for a long time, Simon,' Jim tried to explain. 'Beth was in a losing battle, you have to forgive her.'

'Okay, so they filled your head with crap. They made you doubt me. They successfully duped you into believing that I'd been keeping this from you, no matter how well I thought we knew each other. Say that I can accept all that. But how could you kiss him? After everything he did to us.'

'I don't know. You don't know what it was like.'

'Because you won't tell me.'

'I thought you knew! I thought you were the one holding back. I felt so cheated and used.'

'So next time we have a fight, you're just going to go and kiss the first man that comes along? Or worse, a man that tried to...' Simon couldn't finish his sentence.

'You weren't there! He wore me down. He told me that he loved me and that I'd broken his heart.'

'He did what?' The green tinge in Simon's eyes was now flaming.

'I feel like such an idiot, but he was so convincing. Then I could hear his heart. He said that it was some magical bond. I was so confused, so tired, so upset. They wouldn't let me sleep, and then suddenly... I don't know what it was that he'd given me, but they weren't normal sleeping pills.'

'He drugged you?' Simon stood up as his anger rose.

Beth didn't say a word. She felt it better not to admit that she'd actually been drugged twice.

'For fuck's sake, Beth, what were you thinking?'

The patronising tone in Simon's question shot rage throughout Beth's body. She'd had about enough of his accusations. 'How dare you! Have you any idea of what I've been through of late?' Beth stood up to better meet Simon's towering scowl, then she let it all go. 'Let me see. Well, after surviving seeing my boyfriend turn into a bird and nearly being forced into a horrendous marriage, I still suddenly get married. I'm happy, don't get me wrong, but I don't know if we were ready for it.

'I'm then just handed the job that I've always wanted but I can't handle a second of it. I feel like a complete fraud, and I know that's what everyone else is thinking. Then, at about the same time that I'm dealing with this, I develop new magical powers, out of nowhere. A few weeks ago I didn't even know that people could have magical powers. That takes some getting your head around.

'Then, if that's not enough, I'm kidnapped, locked up and told that I'm a chosen one destined to continue the future of some magical community; again something that I was quite happily ignorant to not a couple of months ago. So you'll have to excuse the fact that when someone, who is very convincing, comes up to me and tells me that a man I barely know – yes, that's you. Despite the fact that you might be my husband, we actually don't know each other very well. So when someone who has quite easily chipped away at my already vulnerable state tells me that a man I've only known for a few months has been lying to me and manipulating me ever since the first time that I met him, I don't think it makes me the worst person in the world to, under the circumstances, question it, do you?'

Beth paused for a second to calm herself before continuing. 'Everything he said to me made perfect sense. You could have known about this, it wasn't that big a stretch. Everything I thought I knew about this world has been turned upside down, and I've had to deal with it all in a matter of weeks. I'm sorry I kissed him. I hate the fact that I did, you have no idea. I had a momentary lapse of sanity, but can you really blame me for feeling absolutely, utterly, fucking messed up with everything?'

Simon's face had softened throughout Beth's rant. His whole body had relaxed a little and his stance wasn't quite so threatening anymore. He took a deep breath. 'It was my heartbeat you could hear. Not Damien's. It's us that has the bond.'

'I didn't even know that you were near. How could I understand that?'

'I know.'

The whole room fell momentarily silent as everyone absorbed the impact of recent events.

'They've tried everything in their power to keep you apart,' Jim said, breaking the tension, 'but your love for each other is just too strong. You have to both understand that and take solace from it. When you cast the spell, the Malant family will lose the power they have. All you've been through of late will be a thing of the past and you will find the happiness that you've been dreaming of. Nothing like this will ever be able to happen again as soon as you cast that spell.'

Simon was still looking at Beth. 'If the Malancy ends, my powers will vanish. My creepy aura will vanish. I'll be a normal man.'

'Simon, your powers are your life,' Beth said, shaking her head. 'Mr Taylor tried to-'

'Who?'

'He's one of the anti-Malants.'

'The what?'

'It's what she calls them,' Jim explained.

'He told me you'd be better off without your powers,' Beth continued. 'He convinced me that you losing them would be the better choice for you. For a while I believed him, you know how they got inside my head, but now I see your power is truly a great gift. You've helped so many people and done so many amazing things. Just like countless other Malants. If we end the Malancy then we'll be taking away something so important in this world. Something so many people take for granted. It's something we've been born to continue, and we must do that. I don't want to be the one to end such a wonderful gift, and neither should you.'

Simon remained motionless. He processed Beth's words carefully. 'At least I now know why I'm so different.'

'And it explains our incredible connection,' Beth added.

'That won't go, will it, once we cast the spell?' Simon asked Jim with concern, for the first time moving his eyes away from Beth.

'Of course not. You've literally been born to be together. It might be a little contrived, granted, but it's probably the most genuine a love can be. I'd embrace it if I were you.'

Simon sighed, and then he moved towards Beth. 'I'm so sorry. I love you.' Beth felt such relief at hearing those words.

'I love you too.' She grabbed him tight, so in need of his warm hold, but the second he touched her, it burnt her skin. She screamed with agony and backed away.

'What was that?' Simon asked, taking a step back himself.

'I don't know.' She tried again to touch him, but her skin enflamed once more, like a raw sensation scraping away at her.

Simon rolled up her sleeves to reveal dozens of feathers now spread across her arms.

'Help me!' Beth shouted, flapping her body, willing the feathers to disappear, to fall off, to go away in any form possible. 'Why is this happening to me?' Simon touched her arm once more, and where his skin had touched hers, a new feather shot up with searing agony.

'It's me,' he uttered.

'It can't be. You weren't even with me before.'

Simon fell quiet and Beth could see him thinking hard.

'Jim?' he said, turning to face his former butler. They were sharing a thought but Beth couldn't work out what it was. And then she realised she didn't want to know.

'Okay,' Jim nodded, as if he'd understood Simon's secret message. 'Can I please borrow your car?'

TWENTY-SIX

Jim walked purposefully into the Malancy HQ reception. He was greeted with surprised eyes by the receptionist. 'Good afternoon, Mr Malant,' she said as he made his way straight to the lifts.

'Afternoon,' he replied very politely before stepping in and heading to the top floor.

He didn't bother knocking on the door when he reached his brother's office, he'd had about enough.

'James!' George greeted with genuine shock as Jim took a seat opposite him at his desk. George was virtually the spitting image of Jim, the only difference was in weight. Jim was visibly the fitter of the two.

'What are you playing at? You've gone too far this time.' Jim came straight out with it.

This immediately broke a knowing smile onto George's face. 'Damien's spell's working is it?'

'Damien?'

'I really haven't given him enough credit. He's far more than the devious little git I first thought of him as. It was a stroke of genius, his idea, you have to admit.'

'So Beth can't touch Simon without sprouting feathers?'

'The essence of the spell, I believe, is that if they show love, emotion or connection towards each other in any way, they grow feathers. Then they'll eventually, well actually quite quickly, both turn into birds.'

'Both?' Jim queried.

George paused, surprised by Jim's question. 'Has he not told her?' Jim refused to respond. 'He's such a gallant one. Everything aside, you can't not like him.'

Jim just shook his head, so disappointed to call this man his twin.

'It's such a great spell, isn't it?' George enthused. 'What do they do? Do they think of themselves, not cast the spell and remain human? Or do they sacrifice their lives and save the Malancy? Because, if I understand my Malancy lessons correctly, they have be fairly close to do it, don't they? So although they would, for the time being, have saved our lovely magic, they will be birds. Horrible, useless, little birds.'

'You bastard. Even if they do cast the spell, they'll never be able to finish it.'

'You haven't told them about that bit yet, have you? How to add more pressure, eh? If you do let them go ahead, imagine how furious they're going to be with you when they find out the whole truth.'

'It'll be fine. Simon will find a way around this. You know how strong he is.'

'I'm sure he'll give it a go.' George smirked. 'But I think you must have figured out by now that it's not like last time. For the two of them to turn back into humans, even for a few days, they'd have to effectively fall out of love. I'm quietly confident about that one, being that they're destined to be together.'

George's growing arrogance was irking Jim greatly. 'Why not just let it carry on, George? Why all these games? Surely you don't really want the Malancy end? Forget about dad, he had his own reasons, but you... You love your magic. You'll miss it.'

'I like your use of dad as a tactic.'

'You'll have nothing if the Malancy ends, don't you see?'

This made George properly laugh. 'No, you don't see. I don't think you've thought this through. There are thousands and thousands of Malants out there who have no clue that any of this is just about to happen. Suddenly, just after six o'clock on Wednesday, all the little spells they've been doing, they'll all just stop. All the spell workers at Bird Consultants, all the people cheating at DIY or mending that broken toe, it'll all just end. Just like that. No reason, no rhyme. Who do you think they're going to turn to for answers? Me! Malancy HQ! That's who. We're set up for quite a while as a support network for all those out there suffering. It's going to be quite a shock for some people.'

'You want to start a Malancy support business?'

'I'll have all the answers, James. It's our next logical step.'

'And what after that? As the new generations are born with no powers and the Malant family is forgotten about along with everyone else?'

'It'll be forgotten anyway! You know that. We were only given a short run. This at least means we get the glory a little longer.'

'Five hundred years is not short.'

'The Malancy is rightfully ours. It's the Malancy, for goodness sake, not the Birdsy. It's not theirs to take.'

'By the very fact that they've been chosen means it is theirs to take. Our ancestors would have wanted the decision to be theirs. It's not yours anymore. It's time to hand over the baton and it's time for a new era to start. It's what they wanted.'

'They had no clue what they wanted. They couldn't have imagined a world like this. They couldn't have imagined so many Malants. It's beyond their scope.'

'I always gave you some benefit when dad died as I

knew how close you were to him, but now I see that you're just as crazy as he was. Your selfish power struggle is going to cost us all. Can't you see that?'

'Selfish power struggle?' George chuckled. 'Hundreds of people agree with me. I have a massive following. You're the one on a solo mission.'

'You're only followed because you've given people a skewed version of the truth. And you've only done that because you know if they have the facts, they will never follow you.'

'Whatever James. I'm getting bored now.' George looked back to his laptop dismissively.

'You're going to ruin everything. You're going to end one of the most significant things to ever happen in our world.'

'Oh stop being so dramatic, James,' George spat back, his humour now all gone. 'Now you're skewing the facts. Yes, the Malancy has done good, but it's also come at a cost, and you know it. For every good deed, a bad deed is also done. Someone cheats the system and someone else suffers. You're so righteous, but the truth is, there's always a balance. Where there's good, there's evil, and doing this will rid the world of as much darkness as it will light.'

'That's vastly exaggerated. There has been far more good done-'

'How do you know? You silly little man making silly little cups of tea for the all-powerful Simon. You know nothing.'

'I know as much as you.'

'I want you to leave now. I've heard enough.'

'George, don't do this.'

'You know if I call security, they'll come and take you. Leave with your dignity, James. Don't be stupid.'

'George, listen!'

'Do I need to make that call?'

Jim sighed with frustration. He could see that his efforts were getting him nowhere. George was so deep set in his twisted world, nothing could be done. He stood up, flashed one last dirty look at his brother, and left.

The Bird family sat at home eagerly awaiting Jim's return. He was their only hope.

Simon was very quiet, sitting alone in the kitchen, staring out at the garden. He was still trying to consume the vast amount of information that had been thrown his way earlier that day. He was starting to sympathise with the amount that Beth had taken on of late.

At first his thoughts were positive. He was a chosen one. A special Malant. As much as he'd been shocked to hear this, it had also not really come as a surprise. Something about it all made sense, like he'd always known on some level.

They'd been given the power to cast a spell that meant Malancy could live on. That was quite a responsibility. He actually felt quite honoured to be chosen. And he'd been chosen to do it with the woman he loved. Or maybe it was that he loved the woman he'd been chosen to do it with. Either way, it made him feel complete.

Then he thought to the day before. It had felt as if he'd hit rock bottom when leaving Malancy HQ. Beth wouldn't talk to him, all matter of strange things were going on, and he couldn't work out why so much seemed to happen to him. He hadn't been able to find a reason as to why his life was so eventful. At last he knew.

Despite this new knowledge, though, things were no less dramatic, and now the threat of being a bird again was casting its dark shadow; and this time not only just over him. He couldn't let Beth go through that. He couldn't see how she'd cope with it. It was horrific; such a painful, agonising experience.

He touched his arm. The feathers were safely hidden under his jumper, and despite the warmth of the spring day, the jumper was most definitely staying on. He knew Beth would look to him for the solution. If she believed he could save her, then he knew she'd have the strength to cope for a while. He really wanted to save her, but the reality was, this could be impossible.

'Simon?' Beth's voice snapped him out of his deep thoughts. He turned to find her standing in the kitchen doorway and he smiled.

She didn't say anything, she just moved to sit next to him at the breakfast bar. She went to touch his hand but backed away, clearly thinking better of it. For a moment they just looked at each other, the realisation of their relationship, of their significance in the world, at last setting in.

Now it was finally just the two of them, Simon knew he had to take the opportunity to talk to her. He had something very important that he needed to say. 'You were right earlier. I want you to know that I took on board what you said.'

'Right about what?'

'The only people that I've ever been close to in this world are my parents and Paul. Then you came into my life. Your acceptance of me and the way that we've worked together, I feel like I've known you forever. You seem to know me so well. I took it for granted, though. You were right, we haven't really known each other that long. There's still so much that we need to learn about each other. Maybe after all of this is over with, we do need a sort of honeymoon. I think we need some us time. God knows, we've had very little of that.'

'I'm so sorry I doubted you. We might not know each other that well, but I know how much I love you. And I love your idea of a holiday.' A smile edged up on Beth's lips. 'I can't think of anything better than having you all to myself for a few days.'

'I'm thinking two weeks,' Simon grinned.

'Can we afford the time off work?' Beth asked, more seriously.

Simon chortled. 'Your boss insists upon it.'

Paul suddenly breezed in to the kitchen and Beth and Simon fell quiet. Paul looked at them, seeing that he'd interrupted something. 'Everything all right?' he asked.

'As well as can be expected,' Simon shrugged.

'Shall I make us a cuppa?' Paul suggested. 'Actually, how about I teach you?' he aimed at Simon with a smirk. 'You're going to have to be more self-sufficient now.'

'Of course! Your butlerless now aren't you!' Beth commented.

'Butlerless?' Simon chuckled. 'To be honest, I haven't even thought about it. I actually feel quite guilty now for bossing him around so much. It's such a shame, he was a brilliant butler.'

'Are you going to get another one?' Beth asked.

'It's what we're going to do now, isn't it. What do you think?' Simon felt a warmth in his soul as he reminded himself that he had a wife, a companion for life, a true love. He still hadn't quite got used to it. Just as the thought spread, though, the strike of a new feather ripped at his skin. He fought hard not to react.

'If I'm perfectly honest, I think it would be nice if it could just be the two of us. We can run around naked then without worrying about it,' Beth added with a giggle.

'I don't want to know!' Paul chipped in, taking three mugs out of the dishwasher.

'But seriously, why do we need anyone else?' she asked. 'Wouldn't it be better if just the two of us could live here on our own? We could cook together of an evening and clean the house together on a Saturday morning. You could be doing the gardening whilst I hung the washing out. It'd be our little life. Why do we need help? Normal people don't have help.'

Simon studied Beth. He so admired her. She always looked at life with such an idealistic viewpoint. He knew that she'd now be imagining them running across a field, hand in hand, the wind in their hair and not a care in the world. Then reality would set in. Beth was no domestic goddess and he'd seen that first hand.

He loved her innocent dream, but he couldn't help but tease her a little. 'If that's what you want, then that's what we'll do. I just want to make sure, though, that you've properly considered the size of this house. And the garden. There's the best part of an acre of land out there. Maybe our Saturday morning cleaning might turn into whole weekends being wiped out. But if that's what you want. Then, what if you have to work late? We need to spend two weeks in New York? You don't get up until midday? Still, your wish is my command.'

'Err...' Beth screwed up her face and Simon wanted to laugh, he adored her so much.

'You're right, normal people don't have help, but we are certainly not normal people. You're a millionaire director of a major international company now. And married to the millionaire CEO of said company. It does change things. But even if we weren't in that position - and you know I love you when I say this - you are not a natural with a scrubbing brush.' He couldn't hide the chuckle.

Beth looked to the garden and for a moment she considered her response. A second went by where Simon thought she was actually going to still insist that they do it all on their own, and he couldn't help but momentarily panic. He couldn't remember the last time he'd done housework. But then a smile spread across her face and he was pleasantly relieved. 'Maybe just a cleaner and a gardener then?' she laughed. 'But I'm doing this for you, you know. I may not be a natural with a scrubbing brush, but at least I know where to find it.'

'Touché!' Paul laughed, pouring hot water into the mugs.

'I know exactly where to find it!' Simon claimed. Beth and Paul both stared at him expectantly. 'It's... in the kitchen!'

'I rest my case.'

'So a butler's really off the table?' Simon nudged.

'You know he hates the tube, Beth,' Paul sniggered.

'Okay, let's compromise. We'll get a gardener, a cleaner and a chauffeur,' Beth smirked.

'But who's going to make me tea and collect my dry cleaning?' Simon asked with feigned aggravation.

'You can do it yourself you lazy git!' Beth spat back with a smile.

'No, now I remember! That's why I got a wife.'

Really laughing now, Beth slapped Simon's arm playfully before pulling back quickly. It burnt him. It was like she was fire to the touch. The amusement quickly broke and all three of them fell silent again.

Paul handed out the tea and they sat quietly. Simon hoped Jim would be home soon. Then his wish was granted.

'In the kitchen, Jim,' Paul shouted as they heard the front door shut.

Any hope they had of Jim's success was immediately eradicated when they saw the look on Jim's face. He stood at the breakfast bar and shook his head. 'George can't help.'

Beth immediately turned to Simon. She had that familiar desperate hope all over her face. He normally relished being her knight. Her ideal balance of independence and reliance was yet another thing that he loved about her, and it made them work together so perfectly. This time, though, it quite literally pained him that he couldn't help. Another feather tore away at his flesh as if to punish his loving thoughts, but he refused to react. He wasn't ready to tell her yet, there was still time for hope.

'I'm not stupid,' Beth suddenly announced. 'I've worked out that we have to touch to do the spell. I'm not a coward, I can put up with a bit of pain. The spell's got to come first, surely.'

'We have plenty of time for the spell yet,' Jim said.

'I'm not having you in pain unnecessarily,' Simon

agreed.

'Maybe we need to go to the other person who's really behind all this?' Beth suggested. Simon looked at her inquisitively. 'Jane Parker.'

'Jane?' Jim asked, a little startled.

'We've already tried that,' Simon replied. 'She's disappeared. Just in the way that you did.'

'Jane's disappeared?' Jim asked Simon. Then he turned to Beth. 'Why do you think she's involved?'

'Damien told me.' As soon as the words left her mouth, Beth shook her head and Simon could see her berating herself for her naivety. As much as he'd hated how much Damien had influenced her, he didn't want her to lose her beautiful, pure soul. It was such a rare thing. He didn't want their dark world to be her undoing.

'Jane is not involved in any of this,' Paul stated.

'It's all irrelevant anyway,' Simon added. 'The fact of the matter is that Jane is not around and we don't know where she is, so she can't help us. We're running out of time.' Simon stood up, he knew what he needed to do.

'Where are you going, Si?' Paul asked.

'To do what I should have done earlier. To stop Mr Malant's heart.'

'That won't work!' Jim argued, following Simon out of the kitchen.

'Of course it will. Who's going to stop me?'

'He's not the one who cast the spell!' Jim announced. Simon stopped in his tracks. Beth and Paul were now standing behind Jim and all eyes were on him, waiting for the answer. 'It was Damien.'

'Damien?' Simon felt his blood boil at the mention of that name again.

'Damien did this?' Beth said, clearly hurt.

'He'll be properly hiding this time, mate,' Paul warned.

Simon thought. Where could Damien be? Would he be hiding? That wasn't really Damien's style, he liked the attention too much. He'd hate it more if Simon didn't come to find him. There was no way that Damien would hide himself. He'd protect himself, sure, but Simon would cross that bridge when he came to it. The first step was to find him.

Simon headed towards the garden. Then he stopped. For the first time in his entire life he realised that he wasn't alone. It was as if a massive weight lifted off him as the truth of their situation sunk in. And Beth had literally just told him that she wanted them to do everything together. How he loved that idea.

A new feather suddenly scratched its way through his skin and he clenched against the pain. But this only made him even more determined. There was no way Damien was getting the better of him. Damien had played that game too much of late and it had to end.

'Beth,' he said. 'Fancy doing your first location spell?' Her eyes lit up and Simon had his answer.

He led Beth out into their garden. It truly was huge, and very well looked after. Simon had a gardener with incredible pride. The grass was never an inch longer than it needed to be, and the open space was uncluttered and beautiful.

The early evening sun was blinding and they squinted as they made a beeline for the solitary tree that stood tall towards the back of the garden. Underneath it were dozens of stones, Simon's very own collection.

'First thing, you need to find a stone,' he instructed as they stood beneath the tree.

'A stone?' Beth mocked.

'Even us special Malants need a little help for some of the more demanding spells. And believe me, this is a demanding spell.'

'Okay,' Beth said, taking it suddenly more seriously. She looked around and picked up a tiny round pebble.

'That's too small. But we don't want anything too big either.' Simon looked to Beth's hands. They were quite large for a woman. In fact, he'd never quite noticed before how dominant Beth really was. Her slim figure hid it well, but she was in fact quite intimidating in stature. In every way, Simon's perfect match. 'You want something that will fit quite nicely in your hand. Not overcrowding it, but not leaving much room to spare either.'

'That's quite a precise size,' Beth nodded, searching again. She scoured through Simon's rather large collection and then she picked up the perfect article. It was a little jagged around the edges, but it fitted nicely into her hand, just as described.

'Excellent,' Simon said, being very careful not to touch her. It was so difficult. 'Now hold it in both hands squarely before you.'

'Like this?' Beth asked, standing tall and placing the stone out in front of her.

'You're a natural,' he grinned. 'Now close your eyes.' She did just that and Simon took the moment to admire her beauty. It was so hard to resist. A new rawness taunted his shoulder and he knew he had to stop thinking loving thoughts. He had to be strong. 'This is where it's all over to you. You need to do exactly as you have before, channelling all your emotion into that ball in your chest, but this time draw the emotion out of the stone as well.'

'Emotion out of the stone?' Beth asked dubiously, flopping out of her perfect stance and staring at him.

'Feel it once, Beth, and you won't be able to stop. To Malants, every element has a potency. Paul tells me he can only feel it when he touches the item, but to me I feel it around me all the time.'

'Are you serious?'

'Seeing is believing. Hold the stone up and connect yourself to it. Find its power and then channel it with your own. Give in to it. Don't hold back.'

Beth eyed Simon suspiciously, but then she did as he asked. She stood tall once more and held the stone out in front of her. She then closed her eyes.

Simon could see the transition in front of him. At first

she looked nonchalant, but then she relaxed into it. He could see her focus and then he could feel the stone's energy growing before him. She was doing it. And as she took the force from the stone, he could see a little smile edge up on her lips. She understood.

'Now picture Damien in your head. Not where he is, just who he is. Think of everything you know about it. What does he look like, what mannerisms does he have, how does he speak, how does he hold himself? Think hard Beth, and don't stop thinking about him until the image takes on a life of its own. You'll know when.'

Simon watched as Beth's eyes tightened with her concentration. He could almost see her mind churning through Damien's life. Then the stone came to life.

It sparked a bright, golden glow and then quickly flamed to red. As Beth thought harder and harder, the stone's vibrancy intensified and Simon knew she was doing it. He was so proud of her. She was such a remarkable person. As tender thoughts of Beth seeped into his mind, the singe of feathers teased at his skin again. He tried to shake it off but it was getting worse. They needed to find Damien quickly.

The stone was now burning brilliantly. As it reached its peak, it soaked up Beth's whole body. She was now a scarlet blaze herself, adrift in the magic. It was really working.

Simon had never seen anyone else perform a spell like this before and he was surprised by just how bright it was. He then realised how shocking it must have been for Ralph and Paul back at Malancy HQ. More than just the blinding beams that Simon knew were to come, the whole spell was quite a spectacle.

Beth started shaking as the heat increased. The stone was burning hot. He knew it wouldn't be burning her, but the intensity was undeniable, and he remembered that it was a little scary the first time.

'You're doing a perfect job. It's working. Just keep

doing what you're doing, don't stop,' he encouraged.

Then the silent, dazzling beams that Simon had been waiting for eclipsed the garden and he knew that whatever was in her head right then was the answer.

'What do you see?' he asked, no longer able to see Beth herself against the blast.

'I see him! I see him!!' she gasped, still in the depths of the spell. 'I don't know where he is, though.'

'That's fine. Explain it to me. Tell me what you see.'

'He's on a settee. He's watching television. He's just sitting there watching television, like he's not got a care in the world.'

'Is it a bluish room?'

'Yes. Blue and black. It's quite horrible.'

'I know where he is, Beth. You did it! Just drop the stone and you've completed the spell.'

As Beth let the stone fall from her fingers, the incredible light instantly vanished, as if it had never been there at all.

'That was amazing!' she said, her face delighted with her achievement.

'How do you feel?'

'Great! Well a little overwhelmed, I suppose. It was a bit draining, but I'm so excited that I managed to do it. All this spell stuff is bloody fantastic!' she cheered, before the reality of their situation set in. Then both their faces dropped. 'Where is he, then? Where was that?'

Simon looked to her. It was the most obvious place in the world but it was the last place he would have thought to look. It was so Damien. 'He's at home.'

TWENTY-SEVEN

'He's at home,' Simon announced as he darted through the kitchen.

'You saw him?' Paul asked, following Simon and Beth as they headed straight for the hallway.

'I did!' Beth beamed. She was thrilled. That spell had given her such a rush and it had helped to temporarily calm the irritation that taunted her arms.

'Ready?' Simon asked Beth as he picked up his car keys from the hook near the door.

'You're damn right I am.'

'You know you don't have to go,' Simon checked.

'Try and stop me,' Beth replied, her determination to seek revenge on Damien thrusting her forward.

'What do you need me to do?' Paul asked.

'Wish us luck,' Simon responded.

'You got it, mate.' Paul opened the door for them and Simon and Beth promptly exited.

They hopped in the Aston Martin and waited for the gates to open, ready to start the ten mile journey to Damien's house.

'When you stop his heart,' Beth asked, imagining Damien in great pain, 'can I help?'

This made Simon smirk. 'What do you want to do?'

'I don't know. You kind of had it all in hand last time, I know, but I'd like to help pin him down or something. I want to do something.'

'Pinning him down is your task then.'

'You can start it. I just want to give your power a little extra oomph. Not that you need it.'

'When it comes to Damien, extra oomph is always needed.'

It took them nearly half an hour to make their way to Damien's. Their conversation had been light, with both of them just focussing on the task in hand.

When they arrived, Simon didn't hesitate in parking on Damien's drive, right next to his car. Then they swiftly got out.

Beth's heart was pounding at the prospect of what was to come, although her head was deeply optimistic. Damien's powers were worthless against Simon's - against both of theirs. This could finally be the end.

'Are we going to knock the door down or something?' she asked as they approached the front door.

'No,' Simon replied.

'Why not?' she urged.

'Believe me, there's nothing more that I'd love to do than kick his door down and wrap my fingers around his scrawny neck, but we need to stay focussed. He has neighbours, nosey neighbours, and it's not really in our best interests to encourage any unnecessary attention. The non-Malant police turning up is the last thing we want.'

'I suppose so.' Beth suddenly imagined how she'd explain an arm full of feathers. Then her mind flitted to a scene of her being tied down by scientists who were experimenting on her. The creepy thought made her momentarily doubt whether being magic really was that good after all. Then a new question paused her thoughts. 'We're just going to knock?'

'One step at a time, Beth. Let's do the right thing first.

Then we'll look at our other options.'

'You're the boss.'

'Do you want to do the honours?' Simon asked. Beth nodded eagerly, and then with a rush of adrenaline she banged on the door with her fist, despite the fact that Damien had a bell. It felt more dramatic.

They waited patiently, allowing him just a few seconds before they moved to phase two. Then suddenly, much to their surprise, he opened the door.

'The Birds!' he greeted with a smile. 'Looking more bird like every second.' Seeing his face again made Beth instantly nauseous. She didn't know what to do next and she told herself to just follow Simon's lead. She turned to her husband. He was standing silently, intently studying Damien.

'I'm all yours,' Damien grinned, but Simon still refused to move. Beth knew that look of his and it wasn't good.

'What is it?' she whispered to him, but he still didn't move. Beth could almost hear his brain scanning the possibilities. Then Simon placed his hand on the wall next to the door. He left it there for a few seconds, then he removed it slowly.

'What is it?' Beth asked, utterly confused as to why Simon wasn't leaping on Damien and killing him. So much was at stake.

Damien was now rolling his eyes. 'You're so boring!'

'What's going on?' Beth pushed to know.

'Don't worry, love, we can't all be as smart as super Simon,' Damien sneered.

'The house has been shielded,' Simon explained. 'We can't get in. We can't touch him.'

'What? We'll override it!'

'We can't. I'm guessing your Malant friends are behind this?' Simon asked Damien.

Damien shrugged, now clearly disappointed. 'They wanted to hide me, but I thought it would be far more fun for you to try and stop my heart and fail miserably. You have to ruin everything.'

'You said we're really strong together,' Beth argued. 'We can do this!'

Simon looked at her. His face was completely void of emotion, she couldn't tell what he was thinking. He was far too good at that. 'It's a live spell. It's at its most potent and they could change it around us. They know what they're doing. They learn fast.'

'Can't we get him to step outside, then? Like start a fire in his kitchen?' Beth suggested. 'Come on, Simon.'

'He's completely sealed, and I'm guessing it's a two-way seal as well, just in case he's stupid enough to leave by accident.'

'You've trapped yourself inside your own house?' Beth asked Damien, incredulously.

'Not because I'm stupid, it's to make it fool proof.'

'Fool, like an idiot,' Simon confirmed.

'Shut up. The thinking was, no way in, no way out, no loop hole for the all-powerful Simon Bird,' Damien justified.

'You're just going to stay trapped in there forever?' Beth asked, bewildered by how silly Damien's plan seemed.

'No. Just till a minute past six on Wednesday,' Damien grinned with satisfaction.

'Nice try, but we're going ahead with the spell. Your mind games didn't work,' Beth retorted.

'You're going ahead with it? Even though you'll be trapped as birds for life?' Damien asked with disbelief.

Beth's stomach churned at this horrifying prospect, but she knew it was just more nasty games. 'I'm not going to be bird. You know Simon will find a way around it. He always does.' Beth turned to Simon with pride. He was so strong, he'd not failed her yet. But as she thought of him with praise, the sting on her arm enflamed and she knew another feather was growing as a result of her passion. She grabbed her arm in agony. It made no sense. She hadn't even touched him.

'I imagine it gets far more painful,' Damien threw in Simon's direction. Then the tension suddenly upped a gear.

Simon's glare increased in intensity, so much so that it almost ate away at Damien through the shield. Damien was brought to silence, so powerful was the imaginary hold that Simon had over him. No one moved for what seemed like ages and Beth couldn't understand why Simon wasn't reacting more. Why wasn't he trying to find a way around this? Surely there was a way. There was always a way.

Then, out of the blue, Simon said, 'You need to tell her the truth.' Beth's heart stopped.

'What?' Damien asked, also not expecting this.

'Tell her what spell you cast,' Simon stated, his voice growing in power.

'What?' Damien repeated, clearly confused.

'Tell her.'

'I don't know-'

'Tell her what the spell was.' This time Simon's words yielded such power, Beth inched back against the force.

'Don't you know?' Damien asked.

'Tell her.' Simon's voice was now eerily strong and Damien instantly complied.

'It's not your anger that makes you bird-like, this time it's your love. The more you love, the more feathers you grow, and eventually you'll turn into a bird.'

'Tell her the rest,' Simon hissed.

'Like what?'

'Tell her!'

Damien was visibly uncomfortable. Any humour was now all gone. 'You have to touch each other and share your love to keep the Malancy alive. The spell you have to do is all based on companionship. That's the emotion you have to use.'

'What are you saying?' Beth gasped. 'If we do the spell, I turn into a bird?'

'Not just you,' Damien corrected, looking to Simon for clarification.

Beth joined his gaze, desperately needing clarification herself. For a second, Simon didn't move his stare away from Damien, then he slowly turned to face her. He hesitated for a moment and Beth felt her breathing extinguish as she anticipated even more bad news. Then he gently rolled up the sleeves of his jumper. Underneath she saw dozens of feathers, the same red plumage that was currently stinging her own arms.

She couldn't believe the horror in front of her. 'Why didn't you tell me?'

'I didn't want to make it worse.'

'You lied to me?' Her horror was now turning into anger.

'I omitted the truth.'

'Same difference!'

'Trouble in paradise?' Damien taunted, this new event having perked him up again.

'What's it got to do with you?' Beth snapped.

'You're on my property,' Damien stated, 'therefore it's my business.'

'You're such a vile person!' Beth shouted at him. 'Why are you doing this? What have we done to you? I mean, what have we ever done to you? Simon gave you a job. He looked after you, paid you well, gave you everything you have right now. And as for me. Well you told me that you loved me. You made me believe all sorts of rubbish about how sorry you were and how seeing the fear in me made you look at everything differently. But you're not different. You're just a nasty piece of work. I feel sick thinking about how much you tricked me. I'm ashamed to know you. I can't believe for one second that I ever considered anything even remotely decent about you. What an idiot I must have been.'

Damien stood up tall, hidden in the safety of his hallway. 'I do love you, Beth.' This caught Simon's attention, but Beth was on a roll. She was too deep in her fiery zone to notice the green tinge that once again flickered in Simon's eyes.

'Love me? You don't know the meaning of the word. You have no idea what compassion is or how it feels to put someone else's needs before your own. You wouldn't know love if it slapped you in the face. You'd just spit it out the way!' Beth was fired up with such anger, and it felt good. On the one hand she'd needed to get this off her chest, but her fury was also really helping to calm the inflammation stinging her arms.

'You don't know how I feel,' Damien said defensively.

'I don't need to. It's obvious. You don't cast a spell on someone you love that will put them through sheer agony, especially when it's for your own gain. That is not love.'

'I do love you. But sometimes things are bigger than two people.'

'What utter rubbish!' Beth spat at him.

'Enough!' Simon yelled. He had such power to his voice that it shook the shield of magic around Damien's house and Beth saw the wall of protection flicker a tiny red glow. It had sheathed his whole house, like a giant safety blanket.

Simon was really mad. His feathers physically rustled as the intensity of his rage pushed against his skin, and Beth unintentionally edged back against the force she felt coming.

'Damien,' he bellowed, glaring at him, his eyes now an inferno. 'I made it clear to you that if you ever messed with me, my family or my business again, I would come for you. If I was mad before, that is nothing in comparison to now. You ever so much as think about my wife again, let alone touch her, or have the audacity to tell her that you love her, and I will burn you. You are now marked.'

'What are you going to do?' Damien asked, pretending not to care, but Beth could sense his fear. Simon was very scary, she had to admit. She was so glad that he was on her side. 'You're either going to be a bird or your powers will have gone. You're no threat to me.'

'You think I need powers to make your life a misery?'

Damien swallowed hard at this. Beth could see him physically shrink a little. 'What's done is done,' he threw back. 'The choice is yours. But before you make that decision, Simon, I'd tell her exactly what being a bird is like. She needs to know what's coming her way.' Damien then turned around and slammed the door in their faces.

TWENTY-EIGHT

Simon wasted no time in getting Beth back to the car. They were now spurting away from Damien's house and Beth was sitting tall in the passenger seat not allowing herself to deal with the situation at hand. She was too scared to believe that things were as black and white as Damien had painted.

'What's next then?' she asked, but her voice gave her lack of confidence away.

Simon didn't respond. Beth thought better than to probe, as desperate as she felt. However, as his silence stretched out, panic started to set in. Minutes went by and nothing was said. Beth knew that if Simon had no answers, no answers were to be had. Then she realised that everything really might be lost.

'What's the plan?' she pushed, anxiety rising in her voice. 'Don't give up on me now.' Palpitations pounded in her chest as she saw her future. She couldn't be a bird. It wasn't even a bird, she'd become that horrible bird-like creature thing. What sort of life was that?

It was so bad a prospect that marrying Damien was actually a better option. She couldn't go through that. It was mind-numbingly terrifying.

Simon still hadn't spoken. His face was deadly serious. This panicked Beth even more. Tears started forming in her eyes and she became disorientated as her brain started to contemplate the reality ahead of her.

'We can't let him win!' she cried. 'You must have a plan. There's got to be something we can do. This can't be it, Simon. I can't do this. It hurts so much.' Tears were now streaming down her face and she felt unbearably dizzy.

Before she knew what was happening, Simon was staring at her. He'd stopped the car. They'd pulled in somewhere. They were in the middle of nowhere.

'I'm not going to let you suffer, Beth. Nothing in this world is as important as your well-being.' She heard the words, but she couldn't quite grasp them. 'Beth, listen to me.' She took a few deep breaths and turned to face Simon. She so wanted him to hug her, to make her feel better. This hex was cruel beyond all reason. In every way she felt vulnerable.

She wiped her tears away before looking into Simon's eyes. 'It's all going to be okay,' he said in such a soothing tone it really helped to calm her. He wielded such power over her, his words were truly magic in themselves.

'How?' she asked, choking on the remains of her tears.

'In two days this will all be gone.'

'What are you going to do?' she asked with a welcomed pinch of hope.

'Absolutely nothing.'

'What?' Beth asked, hitting rock bottom again.

'Screw the Malancy, screw everything. No one deserves to suffer like this, not least you. You're an amazing woman.' As he said it, Beth could see him wince at the pain it caused him. 'You've suffered at the hand of the Malancy for so long, and you're not even a Malant. Chosen or not, the burden is too much for you to have to bear.'

'You have the same burden, if not more so.'

'I've reaped the benefits of Malancy for many years.

I've enjoyed it.'

'No you haven't. But you're about to. Casting this spell would make your dreams come true.'

'No they wouldn't.'

'But-'

'What is it that you think I want?'

'Power. Money. Success.'

'You,' Simon simply replied. 'All I want is you. The rest of it can go to hell. And if we cast this spell now, that's exactly what I'll lose.'

'We have a responsibility.'

'To whom? The Malant family? We owe them nothing. We had a choice and it was taken from us by the direct descendants of the people who wanted us to have that choice in the first place. Walking away is the only option. They're not winning if we agree.'

'You'll lose everything.'

'If I only want you, and that's what I get, then how is that losing?'

'That's very sweet, but it's not real. You'll lose your business, your power, everything you've ever known.'

'Everything that's caused me so much misery. All the stuff that's stood between you and me. The source of everything bad that's ever happened to me. And to my parents. Malancy may not have directly caused their death, but if I hadn't been so different, they never would have taken me away. They never would have been in that restaurant and got caught up in that explosion.'

Beth felt sick at this. The truth was so different to what he believed. She wanted to tell him, but she bit her lip. All it would do at that moment in time was confuse an already tricky situation. No good could come of it.

'So that's it? We end the Malancy?' Beth asked, now far calmer.

'We're not choosing to the end the Malancy, we're choosing not to suffer. Who could ask us to spend the rest of our lives as birds in order to keep alive something that most people don't know about anyway? It's not worth it.'

'But Jim said-'

'Jim's not giving up his life for this.'

'He sort of did,' Beth reasoned, she couldn't help it. 'He infiltrated himself into your home to wait on you hand and foot, and gave up his life in so many ways.'

'Did it hurt him, though? He got financial reward, a roof over his head. I wasn't there most of the time, it was hardly the same as what we'd have to go through.'

'So that's it? The end of the Malancy is upon us?' Beth suddenly felt so guilty. After days of believing it to be the best decision, she was now heavy with the burden. She was going to actively end an important gift to the human race.

'You're not doing this, Beth,' Simon asserted, grasping her attention. 'You're reacting quite sanely to a position that you've been put in. This is all on them.'

'The anti-Malants?'

'The anti-Malants. They've forced our hand and we've been left with no realistic choice. We can't feel bad.'

Beth nodded, but she couldn't help the tears that escaped. She didn't want to change the decision, she was quite relieved on some levels, but it didn't stop it being so difficult.

'I love you, Beth,' Simon whispered, despite the clear pain that it put him in.

She hesitated in her response, knowing the words would cost her. But they were worth it. 'I love you, too,' Beth finally uttered before the blaze of her skin tearing yet again silenced her. Another feather had reared its head and she took a few deep breaths as she braved the agony. As the worst of the stinging dissipated, she added, 'Promise me one thing.'

'Anything.'

'No matter what happens, we'll always have each other. We're a team now, aren't we?'

'Beth, nothing is ever going to come between us. Look at what we've already been through. We've faced more in a few weeks than most couples face in a lifetime, and it's only made us stronger. We're in it for the long haul. If nothing else, we know for a fact that we're each other's destiny.'

Beth could tell that Simon's declaration caused him more pain, so she decided to leave it there. The decision had been made and it was time to go home and wait for the Malancy to end.

The first thing they had to do when they arrived back home was break the news to Jim.

'I appreciate your fears,' Jim reasoned, sitting in the living room with all the Birds, 'but this is far bigger than the two of you. You have to see that.'

Beth had barely said a word. Her guilt at letting Jim down weighed heavy on her shoulders, although it didn't compare to her fear of becoming that bird-like creature. The decision was made, but this conversation was not easy. She was quite happy to let Simon do the talking.

'It may be far bigger, but it's Beth and I who will have to suffer. Whether you like it or not, this does all boil down to the two of us. More than just ending our lives as we know them, casting the spell would subject us to an infinite cycle of horrific agony where death may in fact be a much better option. You can in no way ask us to go through that. Believe me, if you were to experience such terror, you would not be arguing with us right now.' This was the first time that Simon had described his time as a bird so graphically and Beth's fear multiplied.

'It doesn't have to be that way,' Jim replied. 'We'll find a way to sever the spell. We'll do anything to stop Damien's heart, you have to trust us. It won't be forever. It can't be.'

'Don't you think I've already thought of that?' Simon argued. 'How are you going to do it? Kill Damien? Your family will make sure that he's kept safe forever. They'll never let Beth and me free, they can't afford to. And even if a miracle happens and you do manage to end his life, how are you going to live with that? That's more pain and suffering that one of us will have to go through. It's just not worth it.'

'How can you say that!' Jim snapped, standing up. 'This is the Malancy we're talking about. It's all worth it. I will take Damien down with my own bare hands if I have to, you need to trust me.'

'You're not thinking straight.'

'No, you're not thinking straight. How are you going to be able to look at yourself on Wednesday night when the Malancy has ended forever, and it's all your fault?'

'That's not right,' Beth suddenly added. 'In five hundred years' time, two new chosen ones will be born and things could change again, or at least that's what Mr Taylor led me to believe. So in that case we're only looking at ending it for five hundred years.'

Jim just stared at her with bewilderment. 'To us, Beth, that is forever. And if we let them win now, they'll just win forever anyway. You have to see that.'

'The decision has been made, Jim,' Simon said, standing up himself. 'I'm sorry. I know how hard this is for you to digest. The only two people in the world that should be able to make this decision are Beth and I, but we've been cruelly manipulated into a situation where we've been left with no choice. I will never see Beth go through the nightmare of becoming that creature, and I don't really relish in the idea of ever going through it again myself.'

'But-'

'I'm sorry Jim, this conversation is over. Unless in two days you can find a way of severing this spell, then Beth and I will not be casting the spell to continue the Malancy. Come on Beth, let's go to bed.'

Simon walked out the room but Beth was momentarily stiff with tension. She looked to Paul and Jim, but neither of them said a word. Simon had been so firm, what could they say? She knew that Jim wouldn't give up, and she really hoped that he'd find some incredible way for them to continue with the spell without the threat of them turning into... that thing. She knew it was an impossible task, though. She knew Simon would have considered every possibility before making the decision himself. She was quickly learning that if Simon couldn't figure out a way, it meant there was no way at all.

She took a deep breath and left the room, not making eye contact with anyone. She followed Simon up to their bedroom. She needed a hug so badly, it pained her that she couldn't touch her husband. This was such a cruel curse. It resulted in pain whatever she did.

She found Simon in the en suite, brushing his teeth. 'I'll sleep in the back room tonight,' he said.

'No!' Beth argued.

'Being together is too risky at the minute. We need to limit the effects of the spell. It's only for a couple of nights and then we'll be free. The end is in sight now.'

'I don't want that! Since we've been married we've had more nights apart than together, it's ridiculous.'

'Two nights, Beth, then we have the rest of our lives together. This is the safest choice, you must know that.'

'It's not fair, though.'

'None of this is fair! Not to anyone. The only people in the whole world to gain are the likes of Mr Malant and Damien. They truly are evil.'

Beth headed back into the bedroom and slumped down on the bed. Simon finished his teeth and then joined her, not sitting too closely. 'At this point it seems hard to believe it's only two more nights,' she whimpered. 'We keep believing it's the end and then life throws more crap our way.'

'Not life; the Malancy. In particular the bad side of the Malant family. This isn't a twist of fate, this is down to the hands of a few sick people. At least we know that now. But once the Malancy has gone, they'll have no use for us anymore. We'll just be two ordinary individuals and for the first time ever we'll be truly free.'

'I hope so.'

They looked at each other for a moment, breathing each other in. 'I better go, you offer far too much temptation,' Simon smiled. 'Although I think a kiss is worth the pain.'

Simon kissed her gently on the lips, but just as he touched her she felt the sear across her shoulder as another feather forced itself through her skin. The tension to Simon's mouth told her he too experienced the sting, but he was right, it had been worth it. That one kiss was all she had to get her through the night.

Simon left and Beth curled herself up under the duvet. She took a moment to wallow in self-pity. She turned her sorrowful head to the clock and saw it was just after eleven. She quickly did the maths, calculating that she had forty three hours of this torture left. That also meant that there were only forty three hours of the Malancy left. All they could do now was wait.

TWENTY-NINE

By seven thirty on Tuesday morning, the Bird men were already fully suited and starting breakfast. Paul was putting bread in the toaster and Simon was sitting at the breakfast bar sipping his coffee.

He'd needed the caffeine that morning. A huge day lay ahead and he'd barely slept at all. He'd been through some tough times in his life, but this was one of the most difficult he'd ever had to deal with.

'Morning,' Beth mumbled from behind, suddenly appearing in her pyjamas.

'Morning,' Simon said. Without thinking about it, he placed a kiss gently on her head as she sat down next to him. The rip in his skin as a consequence was brutal, but he refused to let the pain stop him loving his wife. He just hoped it didn't hurt her too much. She only seemed to wince a little.

'So Jim's butler duties are well and truly finished?' she asked, marvelling at the sight of Paul tackling the toaster.

'He's gone out already. He's looking for a new place to live. I guess he's got a lot to sort out,' Simon explained. 'He's not happy. Who knows, maybe he's gone to speak with Damien too. I'm sure he's not giving up.'

'I think even after six pm tomorrow, he won't be giving up.'

'I feel for him, I really do, but he can't expect us to give up our lives. No one can ask that of us. It was hell on earth, I'm never going to let you go through that. I love you too much to ever see you suffer in that way.' As the words came out of his mouth, Simon grabbed his arm in pain.

'Is it getting worse?' Paul asked, coming over to check on his nephew.

'About the same,' Simon replied.

'Me too,' Beth nodded. 'We just need to get through the next day and a half. We can do it.' There was a moment of awkward silence as they all let the reality of the future sink in. Then Beth quickly said, 'Enough of that. Let's not think about it. How come you're both so smartly dressed?'

Paul looked to Simon. 'We need to start preparations,' Simon replied. He tried not to react.

'Preparations?'

'As of Thursday, we're out of business.'

Beth exhaled sharply. 'What are we going to do?'

'We're survivors, Beth, don't worry,' Paul grinned. 'We're all in it together and we'll find a way to start again.'

'Should I ask for my job back at the bar?' she asked with all sincerity.

This broke a large smile out on to Simon's face. 'Beth, if we're sensible, we'd probably never have to work again. Business was very lucrative while it lasted. I don't think there's any need for panic.'

'I don't want to live off your wealth, though. That's not why I moved to London.'

'I wasn't saying that,' Simon responded defensively. 'If you know me at all, you'll know that I have to work, I know no other way. We're completely the same in that respect. I just meant that there's no need for us to rush in to anything. We're lucky enough to be in a position where we can take some time to figure out our next step. We can start afresh, together.'

Beth's expression grew more serious and Simon detected a flash of doubt in her eyes. 'Would we be equal partners?'

'What?'

'Could you do that?'

'Why would you think anything else?'

'It's up to you two now, I'm too old to be starting over,' Paul interjected. 'The brand new Bird Consultants will have a husband and wife team.' Paul then thought for a second. 'Okay, maybe I could be a silent partner.'

Simon smirked. 'I was wondering where my uncle Paul had gone.'

'So we're going to move on together? All of us equally together?' Beth checked.

'Of course. What makes you think otherwise?' Simon asked, very confused by her concern.

'No reason. Just being silly I guess.' Then a huge smile broke out on her face. 'We'll be like the three musketeers. The three Bird-a-teers!'

'Bird-a-teers?' Simon chuckled. 'Where do you get this stuff from?'

'Can I come to the office with you?'

'Why would we go without you? You have to stop feeling so left out. I wouldn't have just left you in bed, you know.'

'Sorry. With everything that happened last week, I guess I'm just...'

'Forget the past, it's all irrelevant. Everything we've ever known is about to change forever. It's all about the future now. Our future. Together.'

'Okay. Good. I'll just go and get ready. I won't be long.'

'Do you want breakfast?' Paul asked.

Beth stopped and thought for a second. 'Could I have a slice of toast, please?'

'Chef Paul is on the case!' he grinned, grabbing another piece of bread.

Beth headed upstairs and Simon carried on sipping his coffee. The idea of shutting up the business was heart-wrenching. Yes they could start a new Bird Consultants of some description, but it wouldn't be the same. An era of his life was over and he felt undeniable grief.

'I know you've got a lot on your plate, mate,' Paul suddenly said, 'but can I ask you a question?'

'Of course,' Simon replied, putting his negative thoughts aside.

'Any thoughts about Jane?'

'Jane? As in Jane Parker?'

'Yeah. You know, with her missing and all.'

'It hasn't crossed my mind.'

'I thought it could be related, you know, to everything else that's been going on.'

'It's undoubtedly related, but it doesn't change a thing. The only way that any of this could change is if Damien dies. Other than that, Beth and I won't be casting that spell.'

'But where do you think she could be? What do you think's happened to her?'

'I really don't know.'

'No idea at all? Nothing lingering in the back of that brilliant brain of yours?'

'No. Why?'

Paul turned back to check on the toaster. Simon watched him fiddle with the buttons, he was clearly troubled. This was something new, something that Simon hadn't noticed until that moment, but before he'd had chance to properly consider his uncle's behaviour, Paul turned around again and shrugged his shoulders. 'Clinging to hope, I guess.'

Simon took a moment to choose his response carefully. 'If she's involved, I'm sure in time we'll find out.'

'She's not involved! She can't be!'

Paul's outburst threw Simon a little. 'I know you trusted her...'

'I've known her for years. She's a good woman. She would never want to see the Malancy end.'

Simon was now deeply suspicious. 'What aren't you telling me?'

'Nothing.' Paul turned around again to check on the toast.

'Paul.'

'It's just messed up, that's all. She's a piece of the puzzle that we've not figured out yet. And you can't say it isn't seriously weird that she's just effectively vanished from the face of the planet.' Paul took the toast out and started to butter it, taking a few seconds to calm down. Then he sighed. 'Just false hope, I guess. You're right. We can't dwell on what we can't change.'

Simon didn't know how to respond.

'Do me a favour, mate?' Paul asked, looking across at his nephew. Simon had never seen such vulnerability in his eyes.

'Anything.'

'I know you need to get through today and tomorrow, I know your head is filled with all that for now, but if she doesn't show up again soon, will you help me find her? I just need to know she's safe. Malancy HQ won't be the same without her.'

'Of course. No problem.'

'Cheers mate. I just need to know she's okay. She'd do the same for us.'

'Sure.'

Paul left the kitchen, taking Beth's toast up to her, and Simon sipped at the last of his coffee.

All thoughts of the Malancy ending were now put aside as Simon contemplated, not only his uncle's uncharacteristic distress, but also the truth of Jane's disappearance. Ever since he'd done that location spell, he'd not had chance to give Jane a second thought. He needed to change that now. There was something going on, something that he was clearly missing.

* * *

By ten o'clock that morning, all three members of the Bird family were in the office. The eight directors of Bird Consultants UK were called into an emergency meeting in the boardroom and Paul was on a conference call with New York at the same time in Simon's office, breaking the news simultaneously. This was highly unusual and Beth could sense the tension. It really was the end.

Simon stood at the front and Beth sat with her peers. 'I don't want lots of questions on this,' he started. 'What I'm about to say is just how it is. I need you just to get on with it.' Simon looked across the room and Beth could see him trying to hide his forlornness. 'As of today, no contracts are to be discussed, agreed or negotiated until further notice.'

'What?' Eric spat. 'What's going on?'

'You don't need to know any more now.'

'We've got seven major jobs in the pipeline,' another man argued.

'What about those on pro-forma?' Nathan asked.

'Did I not make myself clear?' Simon stated. 'All work on contracts is to cease. Anything currently live can be dealt with today, but by close of play, everything must be finalised one way or another.'

'So are we putting jobs on hold or just cutting them off completely?' Eric queried.

Simon considered this. 'On hold for now.'

'What do we tell customers?' the spell director asked.

'Nothing.'

'We can't just tell them nothing.'

'I'm asking you to do as you're told until further notice.'

'What if a customer phones up?'

'Tell them we're having a contract review and you'll be back in touch soon.'

'This is ridiculous. What aren't you telling us?' Rumbles from all of the directors then started. They were throwing questions back and forth, at each other and towards Simon. The tension in the room escalated and Beth looked to her peers with sympathy.

Then something in her peripheral vision made her stop. One director, sitting very quietly in the corner of the room, away from everyone else, didn't seem confused at all. Quite the opposite in fact. He almost seemed to be enjoying the spectacle in front of him. It was Brian, the new Sales Director.

She knew that she needed to bring this to Simon's attention. He was far too caught up in repeating himself against the barrage of questions to notice how quiet Brian was, but he had to find out. This all seemed terribly suspicious and she knew that Simon would read the situation far better than she ever could.

She knew that she couldn't just shout it out or stand up and tell him, it was important that Simon viewed Brian's behaviour surreptitiously. Being subtle was her only option.

Suddenly remembering that she had powers, she quickly flicked through options in her head as to how she could magically tell him. She hadn't developed telepathy, so that was off the table. Maybe she could write him a note and float it towards him? But that was far from furtive. Her mind went through countless possibilities, but all of them were either ridiculous, unfeasible or just way too obvious. Knowing that she hadn't got much time, she rubbed her head with frustration, and then it came to her. Sitting in her hands was her phone. It was so simple yet so effective. And it came as a relief that magic wasn't always the answer.

She quickly typed out a text. She knew that Simon had his phone in his pocket, and although, as he was so conscientious, she believed it to be highly unlikely that the ringer would have volume, she was confident that he'd feel the vibration. She sent the message and waited.

She waited and waited, but he just ignored it.

Not sure if he hadn't got it or if he just didn't believe a message warranted his attention right now, she decided it was best to phone him. She pressed his name and it started to dial.

She looked to him standing tall against the torrent of questions from his team and she knew that his phone was now actually ringing in his pocket, but he didn't acknowledge it at all.

Refusing to give up, she tried again, and then again, and then, thankfully, he finally rolled his eyes and yanked his phone from his trouser pocket. He stopped before answering and looked slyly towards Beth.

She hung up, making it clear to him that she had her phone in her hand. Then she watched him read the text.

Look at Brian. He's acting oddly.

She saw Simon's eyes casually move over to Brian at the back of the room who was still silently watching the arguments play out in front of him. She then viewed Simon's brilliant mind at work.

After just a few seconds, he suddenly bellowed, 'That's enough!' The room fell silent at his command.

'You need to tell us what's going on,' Nathan urged.

'The contracts end today and that is final. Further news will come your way when I decide you need to know. If that is not acceptable, I'll be happy to receive your resignation, otherwise do as you're told.' The power in Simon's unforgiving tone ended the discussion. With nothing else to be said, each of the directors slowly stood up and, silently, one by one, they made their way out of the room.

Everyone, that was, except Brian. Beth could see him trying to stand up, but he was pinned down. The other directors walked past him, not seeming to notice, but he couldn't get up.

When everyone had gone, except the two Birds and Brian, the door slammed shut. Simon was now very much in charge.

Brian's eyes grew wide with fear as Simon approached him. 'Are you going to tell me?'

Brian's enjoyment had now expired. Beth watched in awe as Simon bore down on him, leaving him a little trembled.

'I don't know what you mean,' he spluttered.

'You didn't seem too alarmed by this morning's announcement. I want to know why.'

'I was. I was in shock.'

'Do I look like a man that tolerates being lied to?'

'You can't hurt me.'

'I beg to differ.'

'It's all irrelevant anyway. No matter what you to do me, it doesn't change your options.'

Simon stood silently for a second, then he asked, 'Does Jane know?'

Brian eyed Simon cautiously. 'Jane knows exactly who I am.'

'Was it her choice?'

'Jane phoned me up and offered me the job herself.' Simon stood silently again, his eyes almost burning a hole in Brian's head, so intense was his stare. 'This is my first job for Mr Malant. Jane said she knew I was the best man for it.'

'So Jane really is behind all this?' Beth asked, standing up.

'You don't know what you're messing with,' Brian warned. 'You think because you have your chosen one powers, you have it all. The Malant family has the true power, you're nothing.'

'Why are you here?' Simon asked.

Brian sat back in his chair. 'To keep an eye on you.'

'It was you!' Beth gasped. 'That's how Mr Taylor knew

so much, it was you.'

Simon then suddenly said, 'Beth, pull the phone out.'
Beth took a second to absorb his out of the blue request,
then she walked to the front of the room and disconnected
the meeting room's landline from the wall. She placed it on
the desk near Simon. Simon then reached into Brian's
pocket and removed his mobile. He then turned to her
with softer eyes. 'This is going to hurt, Beth, but I need
your help.'

'Anything.'

'Hold my hand.'

'What?'

'Hold my hand. Please.'

Despite fearing the pain that was to come, Beth
hesitantly did as Simon asked. The second their flesh
touched, the agony shot through her arm and she glared at
Simon with desperation. He closed his eyes.

As she battled with the flaming rawness that electrified
her body, a gust of wind blew through the room, sweeping
chairs across the floor, such was its strength. Simon then
quickly let go of her hand and she gasped at the relief.
'What did you do?'

'I absorbed all the power. This room is now useless to a
mere Malant like yourself,' he said to Brian. He then
turned to Beth. 'Are you okay?'

Beth just nodded, although her whole body throbbed.
Simon picked up the landline and headed to the door,
gesturing for Beth to follow.

Once the door was shut behind them, Simon placed his
hand on the glass panel and closed his eyes again. All the
windows went black and the room instantly sealed itself
off.

'That should keep him secure for now,' Simon said.

'You're going to leave him in there?'

'He'll be free by tomorrow night. That's inevitable. At
least it keeps him in place for now. I want to give those
anti-Malants as little ammo as possible. I think they've had

enough.' Simon's face then softened again. 'Are you sure you're okay? I didn't mean to hurt you, I just want to keep us as safe as I can.'

'What's a few more feathers?' Beth shrugged, happy that the burning was slowly starting to fade. She was surprised, really, by how much she'd been able to cope with the pain. She'd never imagined that she could handle as much as life had thrown at her recently. In that moment, she felt very proud of herself.

'The end is in sight,' Simon assured her before making his way to the lifts, but Beth stopped him.

'Do you think Jane is behind all this?'

Simon considered her question for a moment. 'I don't know. It's hard to believe, but things aren't looking good for her. We need to find out more.' Simon then regarded her more seriously. 'Let's not mention this to Paul.'

'Why not?'

'He's too close to Jane. He can't see things objectively. I don't want to worry him unnecessarily.'

'So what do we do now?'

'Nothing.' Beth couldn't hide her surprise by his answer. 'Even if we had time to start another search or another battle, I don't have the energy anymore. I'm sick of all this. I just want to go to bed with my wife and wake up free from it all. I want to finally start our life together.'

Beth knew this honesty would come at a cost to Simon, but she was glad that he'd said it. They'd struggled so much and it had got them nowhere. It was time to just let it all happen now. There was just over a day to go and it would finally all be over.

THIRTY

The rest of Tuesday was downbeat and eventless. They'd left the flurry of the office behind them to sit in a sombre home, watching the time tick by, waiting for the inevitable to happen.

There was still no sign of Jim, and they'd opted for a take-away for dinner instead of tackling the oven. Not only were none of them quite sure how it worked, they were far from in the mood for cooking.

When the pizza was finished and they'd polished off the last of the wine, they all headed to bed at an unusually early hour. With nothing to hope for other than the arrival of Wednesday and for the hell that they were going through to end, they decided there was little else to stay up for.

After spending yet another night on her own, and knowing they'd decided not to go into the office again until after the Malancy had ended, Beth had no urge to get out of bed on Wednesday morning at all. In fact, it was only when Simon called her from downstairs, insisting that she get up, that she found any strength to move.

She sat on the edge of the bed and sighed. Her whole

body was enflamed and she was sick of the pain. She'd cried most of the night and the tears still hadn't properly cleared. She couldn't understand why time seemed to be moving so slowly.

'Beth!' Simon called again. 'Will you get out of bed! We need you!'

She flopped down the stairs, well aware that lunchtime was approaching, but she had no desire to get dressed at all. She looked in the living room, but no one was in there. Then she moved to the kitchen.

'Happy birthday!' Simon and Paul beamed as she entered the room. They were standing in front of a massive iced cake that had two candles stuck in it.

Beth's heart sank. She tried to keep her composure, but all she could do was cry.

'Beth!' Simon said, running to her side, but being careful not to touch her. 'Don't cry.'

'This is the worst birthday ever.'

'We can make it good.'

'Why? What's the point? It's better that we just forget it. I guess what I said in Florence was right after all. This needs to be the official day in our lives where we do absolutely nothing and we let it all pass by.'

'You can't let them win like this, babe,' Paul soothed.

'They have won! They're controlling us and we have nowhere to go. Look at Simon. They've controlled your whole life for years. It seems inevitable that it was always going to end this way.'

Jim suddenly appeared in the kitchen doorway. 'I'm so glad you can celebrate,' he mumbled sarcastically, looking at the cake.

'Oh for God's sake, Jim,' Beth cried. 'What would you have us do? You're not the only one with something to lose here. This isn't just about you, you know. I'm know you're upset but Simon and I are being tortured beyond anything you could possibly comprehend. Believe me, this feels way worse than it looks!' Beth yanked up her sleeves to display her feathers for everyone to see.

Just at that moment her mother and father appeared in the doorway behind Jim. They looked straight at her feathers and gasped.

Completely flustered, Beth quickly rolled her sleeves back down. 'What are you doing here?' she demanded to know. The shock on her parents' faces was palpable.

'What on earth was that?' Alice asked.

'Nothing. Why are you here?'

'Well if you'd bothered to answer our calls or even take a minute to call us yourself, you might know.'

'We've had a lot on,' Beth bit back. The last thing she needed right now was a lecture from her parents.

'Sorry, I saw them at the gate,' Jim explained. 'They said they were here for your birthday.'

'Your loving husband invited us,' Alice added.

Beth turned to Simon. He went to speak but nothing came out.

'We're here for your party tonight, but as we haven't heard from either of you in a week, we thought we should come early to check that everything was still okay,' Alice clarified.

'Party?'

'It's a long story,' Simon explained.

'Is anyone else coming? I don't want to be celebrating today. I don't want this!'

'Our Bethany not celebrating her birthday?' Frank questioned. 'And what was that on your arm? I want to know what's going on! What have you done to her?' He turned his attention fully to Simon.

'It's not his fault!' Beth screeched back at her dad.

'Whose fault is it then?' Frank asked.

'Tell us what's going on, Beth,' Alice pleaded. 'We're worried about you.'

'I can't.'

'You've hurt her, I know you have,' Frank said, squaring up to Simon, or at least trying to against the height difference.

'He's done nothing.'

'What was that on your arm? I want to see,' Alice insisted, moving forward to get a better look, but Beth backed away. 'Tell me, Bethany.'

'No. It's nothing to do with you.'

'I knew you were no good for her,' Frank hissed at Simon. Simon just stood tall, refusing to respond.

'Show me your arm,' Alice said, trying to reach for her daughter, but Beth backed away again. 'Tell me what's on her arm,' she then said to Simon, now approaching him. Both of them glared up into Simon's eyes, his intimidating stature no threat to them at all.

Simon remained stock still but Beth could see the defeat in his eyes. She knew that he'd be blaming himself, but that was ridiculous. It was far from his fault. She moved to his side. 'Simon has done nothing but love me. That's all he's ever done.'

'Then why doesn't he just tell us what's going on?' Frank challenged.

'Because it's none of your business.'

'Our daughter is clearly in distress, I think that's most definitely our business.'

'It's not!' Beth insisted, her temper now starting to flare. And it felt good. As her anger towards her parents grew, her burning skin soothed.

'What has he done to you?' Alice pushed.

'Nothing! In fact Simon's just as much a victim here as I am.'

'A victim of what?' Alice demanded to know.

'What have you done to our girl?' Frank spat. 'We never should have let her come down here.'

'You don't control me!' Beth spat back.

'You let him control you,' Frank retorted.

'He does nothing of the sort.'

'What is on your arm?' Alice asked.

'Leave it alone!' Beth's anger was really firing now. Her

already state of heightened irritation was quickly moving to a massive explosion of rage.

'Beth, get dressed. You're coming home with us,' Alice ordered.

'No!'

'You're not safe here!'

'I'm not going anywhere.'

'Get your things. Now!'

'No!'

'I'm just glad we came when we did.'

'Why don't you go away and come back at six?' Beth hissed.

This stumped her parents. 'What's happening at six?' Alice asked.

'It'll all be over with then. You'll have nothing to worry about then. You'll see.'

'What will? What are you going to do with her?' Alice hissed at Simon.

'Beth,' Simon warned.

'The Malancy. What? Confused are we? Now do you see it's nothing to do with you?' Beth glared at her parents, but rather than shouting back at her, they instead fell very silent.

Suddenly Beth felt very let down by them. When she needed help the most in her life, they just couldn't be there for her. They were so different to her. They didn't understand anything. As usual, they were just making everything far more difficult than it already was. 'I'm going through hell at the minute, but you can't see, can you?' Beth cried. 'You always think your stupid little life up in Stonheath is the be all and end all. Why didn't you know? Why didn't you warn me? Simon's parents knew! How come they knew and you didn't?'

Simon glared at her. 'What do you mean my parents knew?' Beth instantly stopped breathing as she realised what she'd said. She looked straight at Jim not knowing what to do next. 'What do you mean my parents knew?' he repeated more sternly. Simon followed her gaze to Jim.

'So you know?' Frank suddenly asked Beth in a calm and steady tone. This silenced everything and all eyes turned to him. 'You know you're a Malant?'

THIRTY-ONE

'What?' Beth asked, staring at Frank in disbelief.

Frank turned to Alice and they shared a silent exchange. 'Can we sit down somewhere?' Alice then said. 'I think we need to talk.'

'Let's go through to the living room,' Paul suggested. They all looked at each other for a second and then, one by one, they piled into the living room.

They all sat down anxiously, no one really knowing where to start. Beth sat away from Simon, the pain of being near him too much to bear. She turned to her parents next to her, desperate to get some answers. 'You know about the Malancy?'

Their hesitation was drawn out and Beth started to fidget with anticipation. 'You tell her, Ally,' Frank said, looking away.

Alice sighed. 'What do you know about the Malancy?'

Beth shrugged her shoulders. 'Simon's a Malant. He's told me all about it.'

'Do you know about your parents?'

This confused Beth. 'What about you?'

Alice turned to Frank and he nodded. Then she continued. 'We're so sorry.'

'Sorry for what?'

'We're not your real parents.'

Beth sat back. Of all the things that she'd expected to be told, this was the last thing on the list. Simon edged forward on his seat, he now seemed very interested.

'They died when you were seven. But years before that they gave you to us.'

'What? Why? I'm adopted?'

'No. Sort of. Do you remember your uncle Elliot and auntie Gemma?'

'Yes,' Beth whispered.

'They're your parents.'

'No! They were your friends.'

'No, Gemma is... was my sister,' Alice explained. 'One day out of the blue when you were very little they gave you to us. We had no choice. They said they couldn't look after you anymore, that something huge had happened that they couldn't talk about. It was awful; such a very worrying time. We felt so sorry for you. We didn't know where they were or how to get in touch with them. As you know, they popped up every now and then to see you, we knew they still loved you, but other than that... We hadn't seen them for a while and then... one day we got news of their death.'

'Oh my God!'

'That's when the letter arrived,' Frank chipped in.

'What letter?'

'It came one week after their death. It was in Elliot's handwriting addressed to us.'

'What did it say?'

'I'm so sorry, Beth.' Alice muttered. 'It said that Elliot was a Malant. It said Malancy was a power that he'd been born with. They told us not to be afraid if you ever showed signs of having magical powers; that it was your destiny. Then it said that if anything was ever to happen to them, we had to look after you. We had to keep you away from danger. And, more importantly, we had to never tell you about any of it.'

Beth stared at them, lost for words.

'You just accepted what the letter said?' Jim asked, curiously.

'We kind of had to.' Frank looked to Alice and she nodded for him to go on. 'It made everything fit.' He then addressed Beth directly. 'A few months before they died, you were sitting one day at the table with your crayons. You were colouring in without touching them. It was the scariest thing that I'd ever seen. When you saw us watching, you quickly stopped. We were terrified. As the weeks went on, you did a few similar things - such impossible tricks – and then we got the letter. Then we knew. Everything just made so much sense.'

'But then it stopped,' Alice continued. 'Once we found out, we never saw you do any sort of magic again.'

'We waited. We kept an eye on you. For years we thought you might be hiding it from us. But actually it was like the magic died with your parents.'

'Jim?' Beth asked, hoping he could enlighten her. Her head was spinning with all this news.

'How did her parents die?' he simply asked, ghostly pale.

'They were in Kent of all places,' Alice started as the whole room seemed to hold its breath. 'They were in some French restaurant one night and there was a freak gas explosion. It was the most shocking thing.'

'Oh my God!' Beth gasped, standing up. She glared at Jim. 'Your father killed my parents!'

'What?' Simon asked, standing up himself.

Beth turned around to face Simon head on. 'Our parents died together! It wasn't a freak gas explosion, Jim's dad killed them.'

'I swear, I had nothing to do with it,' Jim virtually pleaded.

Simon took a second to process the sudden whirlwind of information. 'You said earlier they knew. What did they know?'

'They knew you were a chosen one,' Beth stated.

Simon looked to Jim for clarification. 'I don't know how,' Jim started, 'but they knew about your true destiny. They moved to Kent to hide you away, to keep you away from my power crazy father. It seems, Beth, your parents knew too.'

'Why didn't you tell me?' Simon asked, clearly hurt.

'They couldn't have done,' Paul muttered.

'They knew,' Jim nodded. 'I haven't got all the answers, but that I know to be true. I'm so ashamed to be part of the Malant family, I didn't know how I could ever tell you. This is why I wanted the Malancy to continue. You have the chance to start over. You're good people, not like my family.'

'I'm a Malant,' Beth whispered, taking it all in properly.

Simon walked to the window and looked out. Beth was surprised by how calm he seemed. He wasn't angry, just hurt. And now he was clearly contemplating something, she could almost hear his brain churning over.

For what seemed like ages, everything remained completely silent. It was as if the room was processing the enormous amount of information that it had just been given. Simon then turned to Jim and broke the tension. 'What has your brother got planned?'

'He's going to keep Malancy HQ open and use it as a support base for Malants in need. He's going to milk it until every last drop has been sucked out.'

'Of course. And we'll be the scapegoats,' Simon uttered.

'I don't know,' Jim responded.

'He'll use our childhood against us. He'll use our parents' actions against us,' Simon stated. 'This has been a lifetime of planning. If the Malancy ends then we'll be blamed. This will go on for the rest of our lives. They're going to ruin us.'

'I need this to end,' Beth whimpered, so weary of her flaring skin.

'We're doomed whatever we do. If we cast the spell, we turn into birds, but if we let the Malancy end, we'll be persecuted forever. They need to point at someone if they're going to keep control, to keep some sort of power. They'll need to justify why the Malancy has ended and keep the blame away from themselves. We're the perfect culprits; we're the only ones that are different. And who's going to believe us against the government? They've set it up so everyone is scared of me. I'm the absolute enemy.'

'What are you talking about?' Alice queried.

'Our lives will never be the same again, whichever way we turn,' Simon continued.

'Don't you see? The only way for you to have any sort of future is to go through with the spell,' Jim argued. 'You won't be trapped as birds for life. We can't let that happen.'

'I can't turn into a bird,' Beth cried, the fear of it shaking her.

'What are you talking about birds for?' Alice pleaded to know.

Simon focussed his attention on Beth. She could see the deep determination encircling his eyes and it terrified her. 'Our parents wanted this. Our parents knew each other. They died together, for us; for the future of the Malancy. We have to fight this. I'm so sorry, Beth, but I think it's our only option.'

Beth felt a chill race through her. She hated that Simon was right. Their parents had fought hard to secure this destiny, and the future was bleak whatever choice they made. If only it wasn't all so utterly petrifying.

'Can somebody please tell me what you're going on about?!' Alice demanded. 'Birds? Scapegoats? Spells? What are you talking about?' All eyes turned to her.

'We were born to continue the Malancy,' Beth explained, her voice quivering. 'We were chosen. That's why my parents died. They died with Simon's. It's a very long story, but basically the Malancy is due to end at six o'clock unless we cast a spell to continue it.'

'That's why they were killed?'

'Some people are trying very hard to ensure that the Malancy doesn't continue,' Simon added.

'What has that got to do with birds?' Alice asked.

Beth looked to Simon. She needed his support if she was going to do this. He nodded to her. Then she pulled up her sleeve and revealed her plumage. Her parents gasped.

'The anti-Malants-' Beth started to explain.

'The who?' Frank replied.

'The people who want the Malancy to end! They've cast a spell on us. Basically, if we go through with it, we'll turn into birds.'

'What the...?' Frank asked, rubbing his forehead. 'What sort of world are you living in?'

'This isn't what Malancy is about,' Simon assured them. 'This is the work of some deeply disturbed people.'

'You can say that again! Well, I won't allow it,' Alice declared. 'It's utterly absurd.'

'Alice,' Simon started, turning to face her. 'If we don't do this spell our lives will be ruined. We'll be blamed for everything that happens to any Malant from now on. We'll be persecuted and downtrodden until there's nothing left.'

'That makes no sense!' Frank insisted. 'Surely these anti-Malant people will want to encourage you to end the Malancy, not punish you regardless.'

'Exactly!' Jim agreed. 'That's the point. This has nothing to do with Malancy as a power, it has to do with the power of my family. That's all my brother wants, and he's willing to do anything to keep it. Like you said, Simon, you're the enemy in his eyes. He hates you and always has done.'

Paul stood up. 'I'll kill him.' All eyes turned to him. 'Do the spell and I'll kill him.'

'George?' Beth asked.

'No, Damien.'

'He's protected.'

'For now. But I'll find a way. There's always a way.'

'You'll go to jail. Your life will be over,' Beth reasoned.

'No. Once you're back, you'll be the most powerful people on the planet. You can save me.'

'Don't you see, Beth?' Simon said, turning to face her. 'This is the only way for us to have any sort of life. We'll have more power when it's been cast, we'll find a way to turn back. We'll have to. As sick as it makes me to even consider putting you through this, it's our only option. Once the Malancy is gone, there will be no other options. At least as birds there's a chance of a future.'

'We won't let you stay as birds for long, you have my word,' Jim added.

Beth's brain was now throbbing. There were only a few hours left. She hadn't got time to decide. 'I need some space. Let me just grab a few minutes.' She raced out the living and headed up to the bedroom. She sat on the bed and contemplated her future.

She knew that Simon was right. Their options had got smaller as the day had progressed. The Malant family needed to be stopped. She looked to her feathers. They were grotesque. Being an entire bird would be nightmarish. How could that be a better option than being blamed by the anti-Malants for the end of an era? They could fight back. They could do anything as long as they were still human.

Distant images of her parents then flicked into her mind. She'd only met them a few times, or so she remembered. She'd liked them, they were kind to her. Then she put herself in their shoes. She knew that they'd want her to go ahead. They'd given up their lives to save the Malancy, so wouldn't they want her to do the same?

Then she thought to her husband. He'd already had a lifetime of misery. At least if they were birds, there was still hope. The Malant family's power would be weakened the second that the spell was cast and Paul would find a way.

She had to trust Paul. She knew he'd stop at nothing to turn them back. Could she really subject the man that she loved to a life sentence of more persecution? In that sense, being a bird was their only hope.

She stood tall and went to the bathroom. She looked at her face in the mirror. It wasn't so long ago that she'd stood there with bruises about to marry the worst man that she'd ever met in a bid to save the man that she loved. At that time, she'd had no hope at all. She was convinced that she'd lost Simon forever and she could see no end to the marriage with Damien. She was literally willing to give up everything to save Simon.

She closed her eyes and focussed on the burning torture throughout her body. She'd been surprised by how much she'd tolerated it. It had been awful, but she'd dealt with it. She was sure that she could cope with more. And at least she'd be with Simon. She'd also never have to endure the guilt of letting their parents down.

Was she really going to do this? She suddenly knew that there was only one road she could take; as if there had only ever been one road all along. It was, after all, their destiny, how could she deny it?

She stood tall with a determined spirit.

She took one last look at her face. As weary as it appeared, it would be the last time that she was going to see it for a while, so she took it in, saving it to memory. Then she promised herself to trust in Paul and Jim.

She went back to the bedroom, she threw on some jeans and a jumper, and then she headed back downstairs.

She reached the living room and stood in the doorway. 'Paul, do you really think you can save us?'

'I give you my word.'

Beth paused for breath and then she nodded. 'Then let's get this over with.'

THIRTY-TWO

'Are you sure?' Simon asked, as if to give her a choice.

'No,' she shook. 'But I don't think there's any other option.'

'Beth, don't do this!' Alice pleaded. 'This is crazy.'

'Maybe you should leave.' Beth was close to tears now.

'We're not going anywhere,' Frank stated, standing up. 'Elliot was a good man. He and Gemma gave up their lives to save their girl. Now our Bethany's willing to do the same to stop some power hungry maniacs. She needs our support, Ally.'

'But-'

'This is Beth's destiny,' Simon added. 'This is our destiny. Our choice has been made pretty torturous, but this is the only option we have. Do you really want to give people that are willing to do this the freedom to have power over a whole race? A race so close to your family?'

Alice looked to Paul. 'You better save them.'

'I will.'

Beth sighed heavily. Every part of her body wanted to run. She wanted to hide away and pretend none of this was happening; but it was. There was no escape. No matter what happened by six o'clock, she was going to face a future of pain. The anti-Malants would make sure of it. This was the only way to secure any chance of a positive outcome.

'What do we need to do?' she asked Simon.

'You must know,' he replied, confused by her question.

'No.'

'Have you not been having the dreams?' Simon asked.

'The dreams?' Beth thought to the many dreams she'd had of late about her and Simon and all that power. She'd been so overwhelmed by them, and mostly in a bad way.

'They've been building up each night for a week,' Simon explained. 'At first I was confused but then I realised that they were teaching me a spell. Each night they added more pieces to the puzzle. And then, last night, everything became clear.'

'That's why they wouldn't let me sleep!' Beth suddenly clicked.

'Who?' Jim asked.

'Mr Taylor. Damien. They wouldn't let me sleep.'

'Oh Beth, I'm so sorry,' Simon whispered.

'They knew your dreams would reveal your destiny?' Jim asked.

'Does that mean I can't do the spell?'

'Of course not. I'll teach you. Let's make some space.' Simon picked up one of his settees and moved it to the back of the room. Jim and Paul grabbed another one, and Alice and Frank handled the final one. Simon then shoved the coffee table aside, leaving masses of space, exposing just how enormous the living room really was.

Simon stood quite centrally and Beth moved herself to face him. Everyone else stood back and watched.

'I'm not going to lie Beth, this will hurt,' Simon whispered to her. 'I never wanted you to go through this.'

'I know.'

'I'll always be here for you, whatever happens.'

'I know.' Beth tried to fight back her tears. She knew she had to keep composed if they were to be successful.

'I'll explain everything and then at the very last minute we'll hold hands. Okay?' Beth just nodded in reply. 'Right. You know when you cast spells, you use all your emotion to channel them?'

'Yes.'

'Well, this is more like cross channelling.'

'What does that mean?'

'You have to imagine all the love I feel for you and you have to use that instead. We have to tell each other how much we love each other and then utilise that as the emotion. Everything else will be exactly the same.'

'Why do I have to use your love? Can't I just tap in to the way I feel about you?'

'No, we need to tap in to the way we feel about each other.'

'Why?'

'It's just the way it is. I don't know. It's what my dream told me.'

Beth pursed her lips. She could now see how evil Damien's spell really was. This was far worse than them just having to hold hands, they had to exploit the one emotion that was going to cause them maximum pain. He was so cruel. 'What then?' she asked, her hands now shaking a little. Her heart was pounding with fear.

'Then think to the future. Whatever plans you want to make, wherever you see life taking us, just think to the future. Think of our future.'

'Anything specific?'

'No. Just something about the future.'

'And that's it?'

'That's it.'

'That's all?'

'That's all I understood from my dream.'

'Okay,' Beth exhaled, concentrating. 'So summon your love, think of the future, then... fingers crossed. Got it.'

'Ready?'

'No. But I guess it's now or never.'

Simon lay his eyes directly on to Beth's and she was immediately intoxicated. He had such powerful eyes, they always mesmerised her. 'I love you, Beth,' he muttered, causing himself physical pain in the process, but he continued. 'I love everything about you. I think I loved you the first time I saw you in the kitchen. You've changed my life forever, for the better, and I'd be lost without you.' Simon's eyes were practically watering now, such was the pain that this caused him. 'You are everything I've ever wanted in a companion and I want to spend every day trying to make you happy. No matter what our future may hold, I'm going to always try and make you happy. Thanks for being my wife.' Simon tried to smile against the agony he was clearly in.

Beth knew that it was now her turn. She could barely control her breathing she was so frightened, but she had to persevere. She couldn't let them all down now. 'I love you, too,' she uttered. As she said those four words, her skin singed in so many places. She took a deep breath. 'When you swept into the office that day, I knew my life would never be the same again. You've helped to make all my dreams come true and you've helped me to find who I really am. For that I am eternally grateful. You are the most gorgeous, generous, warm and brilliant man that I've ever met. I'm so proud to call you my husband and whatever happens to us, I'll always be fine if you're by side.' Tears were now streaming down Beth's face as her skin ripped at the words. The feathers were sprouting across every inch of her body and she felt on fire.

Simon reached out and Beth knew it was time for them to hold hands. 'Just close your eyes and focus. Forget about the pain,' Simon said. 'I know it's hard, but we can do this.'

Hesitantly, Beth wrapped her trembling fingers around his. The second their flesh touched, the rawness to her agony doubled in intensity and she wanted to scream.

She snapped her eyes shut, desperately trying to focus,

but all she could think about was the torture. Her skin was now dissolving beneath a torrent of feathers and she felt sick. She knew she had to try and find a way to overcome it.

She turned her mind to Simon's love. She forced herself to remember their first encounter and the email that he'd sent to her soon afterwards. She remembered how he'd thrown away tea bags just so he could speak to her. She recalled how he'd saved her from those awful bouncers on their first date, then how they'd made love and how it had literally taken her breath away.

Thinking of their love drowned her in pain but she refused to let the agony win. She fought on.

As she channelled all his love within her, vehemently thinking of all the ways that he'd shown her his true feelings, she felt the power wrap itself around her heart. It was a warm, satisfying sensation, and it was an iota of relief against the inflammation that plagued her body.

The spell had started. Sensing the power within her meant she was ready to move on to the next step. It was time to think of the future.

She didn't know at first what to think, so she turned her mind to what she hoped it would be. They'd both be running Bird Consultants. They'd be rich and happy and under no more threat from evil anti-Malants. Then her thoughts moved on. She thought way into the future, of how they'd grow old together.

The pain was now increasing and her body convulsed against the force of Damien's spell. The feathers were enveloping her whole frame. She had to focus back on their future. What would they be like when they were old? They'd have a family; a beautiful family. She forced herself to imagine it. They'd have a son and a daughter who would take over the business...

The pain disappeared. She felt nothing. Absolutely nothing. She couldn't even feel the floor beneath her. She was floating. She was completely weightless and she could feel nothing.

Her eyes snapped open. In front of her, still holding her hands, was Simon. He had a warm, happy smile on his face and everything else was completely black around them. 'What's happened?' she asked. 'Have we died?'

'We did it!' Simon beamed.

'Have we killed off the universe?'

'No,' Simon laughed. 'Although we do have the power to do that now. This is us with ultimate power over everything.'

'What?'

'Think of somewhere. Anywhere.'

'Like a place?'

'Anywhere in the world.'

'Think of it, or tell you?'

'Either,' Simon grinned.

'Okay. Florence. One of the most romantic places in the world that we failed to be romantic in.' As she finished her sentence, Beth felt a breeze race through her. Light seemed to spin below them and suddenly they were in Florence.

They were hovering next to the Duomo, looking down on the packed square below them. It was manic but completely silent.

'Are you sure we haven't died?' she asked, trying to make sense of it all.

'No. This is actually Florence, we're really here. We're just separated enough so that we can have control.'

'Control?'

'We have ultimate power.'

'How do you know all this?'

'My dreams have suddenly all made sense. I knew we would have great power, but when I opened my eyes everything just clicked in to place. It was like I'd known it all along but I had to see it to understand it. To believe it. If only they'd let you sleep. I wish you could have had all the dreams.'

'At least one of us knows what's going on.'

Simon looked into her eyes sincerely. 'I'm sorry you had to go through all that.'

'It was a bit painful, wasn't it?'

'That was excruciating. But I mean everything. The past few weeks have been absolute torture for you, without even mentioning what just happened... You are strong beyond all comprehension. Are you okay?'

Beth didn't know how to answer. She'd gone from being in more pain than she'd ever known possible, to having no feeling at all in less than a heartbeat. She'd answer it later, when she could absorb all that was happening.

'Is this our life now?' she instead asked. 'Are we trapped here?'

'Of course not,' Simon smiled. She was relieved that he'd accepted her change of subject. 'This is our decision time. When we return to our bodies, the spell will be complete. This is our chance to make any last minute changes.'

'Changes to what?'

'Anything.'

'What do you mean?'

'I mean literally anything. We can't change people's emotions, that's never going to be possible, but physical things. We can change how the Malancy will move forward.'

'Like give everyone absolute power?'

'We could, I suppose. But is that wise?'

Beth considered this. After spending time with Damien, she thought not. 'What can we do, then?'

'I don't know.' Simon thought for a second. 'How about we remove the chill that always follows us around? Get rid of our unfortunate aura?'

'We can do that?'

'It's a terrible consequence of our great power, but I say let's make it a warmth rather than a chill. What do you say?'

'Let's do it.'

'Great.'

'What do we need to do?'

'It's already done. This is our decision time and we've declared it so.'

'That's it?'

'As easy as that!'

'This is fun!' Beth giggled. She then thought of what else they could do. 'I want to go to that building in Scotland.' Again the world below them whizzed by with a breeze and they found themselves outside the front of the house that Beth had been held captive in.

'Why are we here?' Simon asked.

'Can we knock it down?'

'We could, but do you really want to?'

'Yes!'

'Isn't it better that we know where they are, rather than forcing them to find new premises?'

Beth flashed Simon a dirty look. 'Do you always have to be so right?' she smirked.

Just then Jane and Mr Taylor came out of the house. They headed straight towards a car that was parked right in front of them, appearing to be having quite an intense conversation, although Beth and Simon couldn't hear a word. They got in the car and Mr Taylor drove them away.

'Jane really is involved in all this, then,' Beth said. She turned to Simon when he didn't respond and she saw his eyes simmering with thought. 'Oh my God,' she suddenly announced as an idea popped into her head. 'I've just realised, can we stop ourselves becoming birds?'

'I thought you'd never ask!' Simon beamed, coming out of his contemplative trance.

'Are we going to kill Damien?'

'No! We're not killers.'

'Paul was going to kill him.'

'I would never have allowed that.'

'But you said-'

'There's always another way, I just needed time to think.'

'You had a plan then?'

'Not exactly.'

'You said a minute ago that you didn't know we'd be here like this, with all this power.'

'No, I didn't. Not until we got here.'

'So we really were going to turn into birds then, and you hadn't got a plan? But you thought a solution might pop up out of nowhere? Tell me again how you were going to stop Paul killing him?'

'I had to have faith. Maybe my dreams had given me something more to believe in. I don't know. But I was right, it worked out didn't it?'

'So far so good, I suppose.' Beth couldn't help but smile. If only she could feel something, she knew she'd be enjoying the sensation of relief right at that moment. 'So what are we going to do? Stop his heart like last time?'

Suddenly a cheeky grin spread across Simon's face. 'I have a better idea.'

The world whizzed by again and Beth and Simon found themselves in Damien's living room. It was dark blue and quite a mess. Damien sat on his sofa watching television, as if it was any old day and nothing of importance had been happening.

'How can he just sit there like that?' Beth hissed. 'We're turning into birds in utter agony because of what he did, and he's catching up on his soaps!'

'That's Damien.'

'What are we going to do, then?'

'Watch this.' Simon focussed his attention on Damien. Within a few seconds, Damien's body started to glow red. It was just a tinge, just around his frame, but it was definitely there. Simon then took a deep breath and blew.

In the gust that followed, the redness swept away. It scattered across the room and dissolved into nothing.

Damien shifted, as if he'd felt something, but he couldn't be sure what it was.

'What did you do?' Beth asked.

'I've just removed his magic. He's got as much magic now as a non-Malant. And with no magic, every spell he's currently casting will cease to exist.'

'So we're free? That's amazing! He's not magic anymore? He can't do it again?'

'Never again.'

'Is that going to cause you issues?' Beth suddenly asked, worried that it may have been a bit too hasty.

'What sort of issues?'

'Bird Consultants type issues. Spells he may have cast.'

'Spells? Have you still not learnt? Damien's not so keen on getting his hands dirty, not unless he's getting something out of it. He's never put a contract together in his life, his only skill was to get people to sign them. Although, I will admit, he was very good at that.'

'So it's over?'

'It's over. When we return to our bodies, we'll have absolute power over everything and we'll start a new line of the Malancy. But as far as the rest of the world will know, it's just business as normal. Is that okay with you?'

'It shouldn't be any other way.'

'Is there anything else you want to do before we go back?' Simon asked.

Beth looked around her. She closed her eyes and thought to Florence again. The world flew by once more and they appeared on the balcony of the fancy suite of the hotel they'd stayed at.

'Why are we here?' Simon asked.

'There's one thing that we never got to do.' Beth wrapped her arms around Simon and kissed him. It was the warmest kiss they'd shared in what seemed like forever and it was so nice that they could touch each other without hurting. As they enjoyed a proper moment as man and wife, completely locked in each other's arms, the horror of the week gone by melted away and both of them finally thought to the future. Their future.

'Can we put the others in a hotel for the night?' Beth whispered. 'I want you all to myself. I've waited long enough.'

'Is that your birthday wish?'

'One of them!' Beth smirked. 'Can we celebrate tomorrow for real? Pretend none of this ever happened?'

'There's nothing else I'd rather do. I was thinking of a car as a birthday present?' Simon suggested.

'An Aston Martin?' Beth gasped.

Simon's face dropped. He clearly hadn't been expecting this. 'You want an Aston Martin?' he asked. Then he shrugged. 'I did promise to always make you happy.'

Beth hugged him tightly and kissed him once more. 'I could test drive yours, see what I think.'

'Oi, don't push it!' Simon smirked, then he kissed her again softly. 'So we'll celebrate your birthday tomorrow, and then I'm thinking on Friday we should book up our holiday and finally have some time together. Properly get to know each other.'

'That sounds heavenly,' Beth smiled, moving in for another kiss. 'And then can we start to plan our wedding? Our real one?'

'Definitely. I was thinking September, just to give us enough time to plan it properly.'

'You've been thinking about it?'

'Of course.'

'Okay, but early September. I don't want to wait too long.'

'Deal.' Simon kissed her one more time and then he asked, 'Are you ready to go home?'

'How do we get back?' Beth asked.

'Hold my hands and close your eyes.' Beth did just that and within seconds she felt herself floating back down to her body. Then, with a thud, she hit the floor.

Beth suddenly sat up. She felt very giddy. She looked around, trying to make sense of her surroundings, but she was completely confused. She recognised her parents, although she couldn't think at all why they were there; nothing else was familiar.

Then a man next to her caught her eye. He was lying on the floor, either asleep or unconscious, she couldn't be sure which. She studied him more closely, trying to see if she knew him. Suddenly she realised who it was and she gasped. What on earth was she doing with Mr Bird?

THIRTY-THREE

Beth took a deep breath. She tried to recall what she was doing in this strange house. She was in a huge living room.

All she could remember was being at work and then going home to her flat. There was nothing else she could think of. It made no sense.

'Beth, you did it!' her mother smiled. Beth clambered to her feet. She felt a little sore on her back, but she stood up tall.

'Did what?'

'And you're not birds!' a strange man smiled. 'I mean you were birds, then you suddenly weren't anymore. It was the weirdest thing to watch.'

'Birds?' Beth asked, trying to remember anything about the two strange men that stood in front of her. They seemed to know who she was.

She looked down to Mr Bird. He was still lying on the floor, out cold. He was so scary. He was one of the scariest men she'd ever met. She thought to the stories of how he'd fired people, killed someone even. Everyone in the office feared him and she knew exactly why. She couldn't help but tremble a little. Why was she in his presence and why couldn't she remember? He must have done something to her.

'Are you okay?' her mother asked.

'Why are we here?' Beth whispered, afraid that she'd wake Mr Bird up.

Alice looked to her daughter with confusion.

'Beth, what is it?' the younger of the two men asked. He moved towards her.

'I don't know why I'm here,' she muttered. All the people in the room regarded her with concern.

Suddenly Mr Bird sat up with a gasp. He rubbed his head and took a moment to compose himself. He then looked around the room, as if to take in his surroundings, before stopping his gaze firmly on Beth and her parents. He glared fiercely at them for a second and then turned to the two strange men. 'What's going on?'

'Si, are you okay?' the older man said, moving to help him up.

'Who are these people?'

'I'm terribly sorry, Mr Bird,' Beth mumbled. 'I don't know why we're here. I'm really sorry for any inconvenience.' Beth could barely look at him, so powerful was his stare.

'Have we met?' he asked.

'It's Beth,' the older man responded.

'Your wife!' Frank added.

'Excuse me?' Mr Bird asked with shock. 'And who are you?'

'We're her parents.'

Mr Bird turned to Beth once more, taking her in, his strong eyes bearing down on her. Then his look softened ever so slightly. 'You work in the administration department, don't you?'

'Yes, Mr Bird. Although I don't know where we are now.'

'You're in my living room. Beth, is it?'

'Bethany Lance.'

'This is my house, Miss Lance.'

'She's not Miss Lance!' Frank snapped. 'She's Mrs Bird, your wife. Beth, you have to remember.'

'Don't be stupid, dad,' Beth hushed, shocked at the idea of touching such a scary individual, let alone marrying him.

'Look,' Alice said, grabbing Beth's hand and showing her the wedding ring on her finger.

'Where the hell has that come from?' Beth's eyes widened as she studied the ring, bewildered as to its existence. Then she turned to Mr Bird and they both looked down at his hand. He too was wearing a wedding ring, and, from the look on his face, Beth could see that he also wasn't expecting to find it there.

'Paul, what is this?' Mr Bird asked the older of the men.

'She's your wife, mate. It's true.'

Beth felt sick. What was going on?

'I'm sorry, Miss Lance,' Mr Bird said, turning back to Beth, not a flinch to his face. 'Clearly there's been some mistake. I am not looking for a wife.'

'I didn't ask for this,' Beth retorted. 'I don't want to be married to you either.' Beth could have sworn she saw a flicker of sadness in Mr Bird's eyes at her outburst, but it quickly past. Then she felt very much like she'd overstepped the mark. 'I think it's time we left.'

'Beth-' Alice started.

'It's fine,' the younger of the two men interrupted. 'We're not sure what's happened, we've only just arrived ourselves. All I can conclude is that this is part of some elaborate practical joke, don't you agree Mr Bird? I'm terribly sorry. What an awful mess.'

'There's some trickery involved, that we can be sure of,' Mr Bird agreed, his eyes not leaving Beth.

Beth felt so intimidated, she just wanted to go. 'Here,' she said, removing the ring. She held it out for Mr Bird to take.

'It's not mine,' he stated, not moving an inch.

'Take it, Si,' the older man jumped in. 'Take it off her. We'll deal with it all, if you know what I mean.' Mr Bird hesitated but then moved forward and took the ring from her hand, his fingers just missing her skin by a millimetre as he did.

Up close, she could see how immense a man he really was, with large hands and strong features. He absolutely terrified her.

'Please forgive the intrusion, Mr Bird,' she backed away. 'We'll get on our way now.'

'Where do you want to go?' Alice asked. 'Back home with us?'

'Back to my flat,' Beth stated, as if they were mad.

'Your flat?'

'I think your parents are just slightly confused as you arrived here with all your belongings. They're no longer at your flat,' the younger man explained.

'Why would I do that? I'm so sorry, Mr Bird, I don't know what's going on.' Beth's heart was pounding now as she could sense that Mr Bird was becoming increasingly irritated by the situation.

'Never mind, Miss Lance, we'll sort it out,' the man said. 'I'll go and get everything. Paul would you help me?'

'Paul?' Mr Bird questioned in response to the younger man's words.

'Yes,' the man called Paul replied, although he looked a little flustered. 'I hate Jim calling me Mr Bird, it gets too confusing. So now you're Mr Bird and I'm Paul.' Mr Bird eyed Paul suspiciously.

'Do you need help?' Beth asked.

'It's fine, Miss Lance, it won't take us a second.' The younger man then headed off with the man called Paul.

Beth looked to the floor. How she wanted it to swallow her up. This was all so awkward.

'How long have we been married?' Mr Bird asked, his gaze now firmly back on Beth.

'Nearly three weeks,' Alice answered.

'Three weeks?' Beth gasped. 'How? I don't... We can't... Why don't I remember any of it?'

'It seems we've fallen victim to some sort of dark... force,' Mr Bird responded, his deep eyes almost burning her. 'These things happen. It should be quite easy to get an annulment. It's not like we've consummated the relationship.'

Beth suddenly felt very embarrassed. She shuddered at the thought of having sex with such a scary man. She then noticed her mother grab her father's arm, as if to stop from him doing something.

'How do we get an annulment?' Beth coyly asked.

'Leave it to me. I'll sort it all out and I'll be in touch. You work for Trisha Clock, is that right?'

'Yes,' Beth replied, screwing up her face at the thought of that horrid, waste of space boss of hers.

'I'll let Trisha know should I need your help with anything.'

'Thank you, Mr Bird.'

The two men reappeared at the door. 'Your bags are all in the hallway now, Miss Lance.'

'Thank you. Shall we go?' Beth nodded to her parents, desperate to leave. 'I'm so sorry for any inconvenience, Mr Bird. I hope we can just forget this ever happened. Please.'

'Consider it forgotten.' Mr Bird then made his way towards the door. 'Jim, please see them out.' He then disappeared.

Beth looked to the mounds of stuff piled up in the hallway. Most of her life was there. What would make her bring it all?

The two men helped to pack up her parents' car and then Beth quickly jumped in the back seat. She was in such dire need to get out of the place.

'I'll get the gate,' the man called Paul said. He disappeared for a few seconds and then, as he returned, the gate started to open.

Beth sighed as they slowly drove away. They were now

heading back to her flat, back to her life and back to normality. She was so relieved that it was all over with; whatever it was. She felt sure that Mr Bird would sort it all out and she didn't want to think about it ever again. She wanted nothing to do with him ever again.

She never looked back and she never saw the confusion on the faces of Jim and Paul. They could barely move as the car disappeared, and they could do little more than just stare at each other once Beth had completely gone. They were both left speechless and neither of them knew what to do next.

Things weren't just weird this time, they were bad. Very bad.

ABOUT THE AUTHOR

Lindsay is a British author who lives in Warwickshire with her husband and cat. She's had a lifelong passion for writing, starting off as a child when she used to write stories about the Fraggles of Fraggle Rock.

Knowing there was nothing else she'd rather study, she did her degree in writing and has now turned her favourite hobby into a career.

Her debut novel, Bird, was published in April 2016 and this is Lindsay's second book. You can follow her blog at lindsaythewriter.blogspot.co.uk.

21067535R00169

Printed in Poland
by Amazon Fulfillment
Poland Sp. z o.o., Wrocław